CURSED

CURSED

EDITED BY
MARIE O'REGAN
AND PAUL KANE

TITAN BOOKS

Cursed
Paperback edition ISBN: 9781789091502
Electronic edition ISBN: 9781789091519

Published by Titan Books
A division of Titan Publishing Group Ltd
144 Southwark Street, London SE1 0UP

First edition: March 2020
8 10 9 7

A CIP catalogue record for this title is available from the British Library.

Printed and bound by CPI Group (UK) Ltd. Croydon CR0 4YY

CURSED

TABLE OF CONTENTS

INTRODUCTION

BY MARIE O'REGAN AND PAUL KANE

C urses.

   You've gotta love 'em.

That staple of any fairy tale, the core of the morality stories we've all grown up with – stories that teach us lessons, feed our belief that guilt should be punished, keep us on the straight and narrow path, hopefully... The classic examples draw from folklore across the world, and in this anthology you'll find stories drawing inspiration from the tales of Norway, Denmark, France and more. They include tales by the likes of Perrault, Hans Christian Andersen and the brothers Grimm (the originals written by the latter being much, much darker than a lot of people realise). Sleeping Beauty, for instance, pricking her finger and dropping to sleep for all that time. And look at Little Red Riding Hood, whose family was certainly cursed by that wolf – a curse in itself, if you believe some of the takes on it. Snow White as well, cursed by that witch of a queen and her poison apple. But, without the bad, how would we recognise the good?

Our aim in this book was simple. To use the idea of being cursed as a jumping-off point, offering writers the chance to rework some of the classics – as Jane Yolen and Adam Stemple do in "Little Red", Neil Gaiman does in "Troll Bridge", Lilith Saintcrow in "Haza and Ghani", and Christina Henry in "As Red As Blood, As White As Snow" – making them their own and presenting very different spins on the familiar. At the same time we wanted to include new, modern "cursed" stories – morality tales from the likes of Christopher Fowler ("Hated"), James Brogden ("Skin"), Catriona Ward ("At That Age"), and Margo Lanagan ("The Girl From The Hell"). Not all of these stories fit the traditional fairy tale style, but all of them share the dark heart at such stories' core.

Authors were encouraged to think outside of the box – or even inside it, literally, as you'll see in M.R. Carey's darkly comic "Henry and the Snakewood Box" and Michael Marshall Smith's "Look Inside" – whilst drawing inspiration from sources such as *Peter Pan* (Christopher Golden's "Wendy, Darling") or the Bluebeard legend (Angela Slatter's "New Wine"). Not to mention creating their own mythologies (Jen Williams' "Listen"), drawing inspiration from or blending others (Alison Littlewood's "The Merrie Dancers"), creating curses complete with their own rules (Tim Lebbon's "Again" and Maura McHugh's "Faith & Fred"), or even bringing in horror staples (Charlie Jane Anders' riotous "Fairy Werewolf vs. Vampire Zombie").

By the time you've finished reading all the amazing stories from these outstanding authors, all at the top of their game, you'll realise that curses come in all shapes and sizes and are hidden in the most unlikely of places – as if you needed any more incentive to beware.

Why, they might even come in the form of words in an anthology… You just never know.

Curses.

You've gotta love 'em.

MARIE O'REGAN AND PAUL KANE

Derbyshire, July 2019.

CASTLE CURSED
Jane Yolen

The curse crawled silent as a serpent
Through the roots of the hedge.
Wallflowers wilted, though the garden
Remained as if painted onto the ground.

A hawk in a deep stoop falls
Bill-first onto the loam,
The moat serpent floats.
Horses stop between one whinny and the next.

Three guards, still on duty, draw no pay
For a hundred years, but still keep
Most of the castle safe,
Though not the tower room where the princess sleeps.

She is caught between one sigh and the next,
Lips pursed as if inviting a kiss,
Or tasting the sourness of age,
Or regretting everything except the needle in her palm.

AS RED AS BLOOD, AS WHITE AS SNOW

CHRISTINA HENRY

"It would please me more than anything in the wide world to see this ring upon your finger, for it would mean your consent to be my wife," he said, and knelt before her.

A murmur went around the room – a rush of approval from the courtiers – for what more could their princess want than this prince? He was wealthy and handsome and came from a fair land, or so it was said, for his land was so distant that none among them had ever seen it.

His manners were so delightful that he had immediately been dubbed "Prince Charming", though of course no one would show such disrespect by calling him this within his earshot.

Snow did not find him charming. When she looked into his dark, dark eyes she saw not the fizzy delight of charm but the flicker of a tongue through sharp teeth.

He held the ring before her, his smile white and easy and expectant. Charming had chosen his moment well. She could hardly refuse him before the whole court, however much she wished to throw the ring in his face and flee.

Snow's eyes flickered to the King and Queen. Her stepmother's mouth was flat, the corners of her eyes tight with fear. Snow's father nodded and smiled like an old dotard, like he was enchanted – which he was.

The Prince waited, for he had all the time in the world to wait, and he knew what her answer must be. She saw all of this in his face, in the unworried curve of lips, in his eyes where the snake coiled.

"Of course I will," she said, and she was proud that her voice was clear and ringing and that no one in the court would hear the terror boiling inside her.

She wished she had the courage to run, but a princess is raised to be polite above all else, and if she refused him there would be Consequences – and Consequences always meant war, particularly when a man's pricked honor was involved. Snow loved her country and her people. She did not wish for them to suffer. So she had to take the ring, even though she knew it was a trap.

Snow saw, as if from a distance, her hand moving slowly toward Charming's, saw the fine trembling of her blood underneath her white skin, saw the triumph slither across his fair face as he took her fingers.

Her body quailed as he touched her. The shudder seemed to please him all the more. His grip tightened until it was hard enough to bruise, and she thought he might be testing her, to see how much she would take before she cried out.

I will not, she thought, and her teeth ground together. *I will not give him the pleasure.*

The moment the ring slid over her knuckle and into place, it clamped down cruelly and bound to her skin with small sharp teeth. The ruby shifted in its setting, seeming to watch her like a bloodied eye.

His arm wound through hers, looking for all the world like a lover's clasp, as they turned to face the court. Only Snow knew he held her in place, her butterfly wings flapping uselessly under his pin.

He kept her close for many hours, and she felt her smile straining but it did not falter. Snow would not show him weakness, though she knew he felt her revulsion and seemed to secretly delight in it.

As soon as she was able she slipped out of his arm.

"It is very close in here, my prince," she said. "I must go and take some air."

"Of course, my princess," he said. "But hurry back to me, for I find I cannot abide a single moment without you."

Several of the young ladies (and even some of the older ones, who ought to have known better) clucked happily at this, murmuring about how fortunate their princess was to have received the love of such a devoted prince.

Devoted, Snow thought bitterly as she slipped into the garden and tried not to think of it as running away. She only needed a moment to breathe, a moment apart from the miasma surrounding him.

Snow went deep into the foliage, where none might stumble upon her by accident. She paused near her favorite pond, all covered in thick green lily pads with fat frogs perched upon them. Iridescent dragonflies soared back and forth, alighting here and there, and weeping willows hunched over the water, trailing their leaves.

Snow huddled into the secret shadows under the trees, twisting at the ring on her finger though she knew it was fruitless. The metal looked like silver, though it didn't behave like any ordinary silver she had ever known.

As she twisted it the ring bit harder, its teeth pushing under her skin until blood welled up and Snow cried out.

"It won't come off that way, though I expect you already know that."

"Mother!" Snow said.

She ran to her stepmother, who stood still and weeping at the edge of the pond, her hands twisted together in grief.

The Queen folded Snow in her arms and they cried together, for she loved Snow as if the girl were her own daughter, and she had been the only mother Snow had ever known.

After the storm of weeping passed, they went under the tree again and sat together in silence. The Queen put a finger over her lips to show that Snow should ask no questions. With her other hand she pantomimed Snow dipping the hand bound by the terrible ring into the water.

Snow wondered at it but she obeyed, because her stepmother knew many things that Snow did not. The Queen had been born in an enchanted land – some of the enchantment clung to her still – and she could sometimes make little miracles happen.

The moment Snow put her hand into the pond she felt something shift and quiet. She had a strange sense that the eye inside the ruby had been blinded.

The Queen read the expression on Snow's face, for they were close in heart if not in blood, and nodded.

"Sometimes water can subdue magic, though it is only a temporary reprieve. As soon as you take it from the pond the ruby's eye will open again."

"So it *is* spying on me," Snow said. "I thought it was, though I nearly forgot after it bit me."

The Queen nodded. "This Prince has powers even I have never seen. He cast his spell on your father so quickly and completely that I never had the chance to stop it, or even soften it. But I know that if your father were awake, and himself, he would never consent to this marriage."

"But he is not awake, and not himself. And my three brothers are all away on affairs of the kingdom. There is no one to defend me from this wolf in our midst."

"We shall have to do what we can, for all that we cannot wield a sword against him," the Queen said grimly. "I would not have you harmed. And he does mean you harm. There can be no mistake about that."

Snow nodded. "I can feel it. Though I don't understand why, or why he came here for me in the first place. Or even why his charms don't seem to affect you or me."

"He came for you because of the same reason he cannot affect you," the Queen said, and stroked Snow's hair. "Your mother had a little enchantment in her, too, just a drop, and that drop was passed on to you, her lastborn child. It is not enough for you to weave spells, but enough to defend against them. Enough to keep the net that he casts on all others away from your eyes."

Snow was surprised to hear of the enchantment in her mother, though not as surprised as she ought to be. *I must have known, somewhere deep down. I must have felt it. Besides, it doesn't matter now. The only thing that matters is that the prince wants me for it.*

"If my power is so little then why would it interest him? Surely a man with magic like his would want a true enchantress as his wife, one who could pass the gift into his bloodline."

The Queen tapped her fingers against her knee, as if contemplating if she should tell Snow what was in her mind.

"Whatever it is that troubles you, you should tell me," Snow said. "I may not be married to him yet, but I am well and truly bound to him now."

The Queen sighed. "It is only a rumor, nothing more. When I lived in my own land I heard stories of this prince's father. They said that he had many wives and each one disappeared, never to be seen again. But it cannot be true, for if the princesses of many lands vanished then there would be outcry. Their fathers would march upon the kingdom, demanding to know the fate of their daughters. So this part cannot be true, not really."

12

"Not really" means it might be true. It really might.

"And what is the other part of the story?" Snow asked.

"When this Charming arrived I sent out a messenger in secret to the prince's land. Since he was so unknown to us, I thought it the best thing. The messenger only returned last night, though he rode there and back with all the haste he could manage. He told me that Charming has been married before, and that his first wife died. The prince, of course, has neglected to mention this."

"Did the messenger say of what the wife died?"

"Childbirth," the Queen said.

"But you do not believe this," Snow said.

"There is no child in the prince's household, though I suppose it might have been stillborn. And no one saw his wife after she went into his castle. Not even once."

Snow felt a chill run over her skin. "I can't let him take me."

"I don't think we have any choice about that now. He will marry you and you will go with him, because you cannot refuse without causing a war," the Queen said.

"I wonder if that was what he wanted, really," Snow said thoughtfully. "He did bring a very large army for a prince who claims he came to court a wife."

"My messenger said that Charming's country is not fair, or even close to it, so mayhap you are right. We have many more resources than he. But I don't think he intended to leave without you, in any case, whether he gained you by fair means or foul. It is the way he looks at you."

"Yes," Snow said, and trembled. "I see the way he looks at me."

"But I will try to do what I can. First, we must remove that spy from your finger. It's already swallowed some of your blood, so the charm is well-fixed, but we might be able to poison it into releasing you."

The Queen patted Snow's knee and said, "Wait here."

She went away into the garden and returned with an apple, a beautiful round red one, irresistible in its charms. From a fold of her gown Snow's stepmother took various small vials.

"Did you think you were going to have to free me from an enchantment this evening?" Snow asked, surprised that the Queen had all these items at hand.

"I was hoping to poison the Prince, but I never had the chance. He is very careful with his food, you know."

"Yes," Snow said. "That boy who stands at his elbow tastes everything."

"It was never a very good plan to begin with, I confess, only a desperate one. If he suddenly died of poison in our castle then his troops, who mass outside our gates, would surely have attacked."

"So you'll poison me instead?" Snow asked, watching her stepmother drop various liquids on to the apple.

The queen muttered some words as she did this, words that Snow didn't understand with her mind but with her heart, words that sounded like the hot sun and blowing sand and the cool dark of shadows beneath a pearled moon. They were the words of the Queen's homeland, that enchanted place she had left because she fell in love with a King who lived in a far green country.

"I am tempering the charm so that it will not poison you to sickness. It is just enough to make the ring sick of your blood. But you must only eat one bite of the apple a day, and take care that the ring does not see you doing it, for anything the ring sees so too will the Prince see." The Queen handed the apple to Snow.

Snow took a single bite of the apple before tucking it away in her skirts. That bite was strange on her tongue, spicy instead of sweet, and left a trail of fire in her throat.

"I don't know what else I can do for you," the Queen said, "except that the moment your brothers return I shall send them after you. The prince cannot deny his wife's kin entry into his castle, and he cannot harm you as long as they are near."

Snow did not say aloud what she was thinking, for she saw the same fear on her stepmother's face.

What if I don't survive long enough for my brothers to find me?

"As soon as your hand is free of the ring you can hide from him," the Queen said. "Until then any effort you make would be pointless, for he could track and find you as surely as any falcon. So hold your tongue, and hide your heart, and pretend to be a good and loving wife until that day."

"And then?"

"And then, my daughter," the Queen said, "you must run."

* * *

15

The wedding took place three days later, in the center of court, with the sun shining through the high windows and flower petals strewn upon the stone floor. Everyone smiled and cheered when the prince kissed their princess, and Snow held herself still and did not shrink from him, though she wanted to.

When the prince pulled his head away Snow saw puzzlement there, as if he expected something else.

"What is it, my prince?" she asked in a low tone as streamers and roses were tossed at them.

"It is only that your mouth is like sweet wine touched with spice," he said. "I expected the sweetness, but not the spice."

She knew it was the poison apple that he tasted, and she feared that he might discover her secret, so she said (in an almost flirtatious manner that was very unlike her), "I find that all things sweet taste better with a little bite, don't you?"

He stared very deeply into her eyes, and Snow felt an uncomfortable pricking sensation all over, like he was trying to see into her heart. But she built up a wall of thorns all around it and kept her secrets there, and finally he looked away, a twist of dissatisfaction on his lips.

They were to depart immediately after the wedding, for now the Prince's business was concluded he wanted to return to his own kingdom. He said that this was because he'd been away too long and that he must secure his borders, but Snow knew it was because the sooner he secreted her away then the sooner he could complete his plans for her.

But I have many days of travel, she thought as she climbed inside the carriage. *I have time still.*

The prince had insisted – in a manner both smooth and uncompromising – that Snow had no need of a lady's maid to travel with her.

"I have many servants in my palace, and there is no reason for one of yours to make such a long journey."

The Queen had tried to argue, to speak of the impropriety, but the King had only waved his hand in a vague way.

"Snow will be in the company of her husband. There can be no impropriety," he said, and of course the King's word was the final one.

Oh, Father, Snow thought in despair. *What will you think when you wake up from this enchanted sleep? Will you be horrified at what you have allowed to happen?*

So Snow sat alone in the carriage with the curtains closed while her new husband rode his horse with his men. Every day she took a secret bite of the apple that the Queen had given her and every day the ring seemed to loosen a little, though the gaze of the ruby never darkened.

She tried not to worry about her future, or if she would even have one.

She tried not to worry about what would happen when he demanded his marriage rights.

Thus far her new husband was unfailingly polite and solicitous of her comfort. Each night, when they made camp, he made certain that Snow was comfortable in the grand tent while he went outside to sleep. But she saw the gleam in his eye, the one that said he was anticipating some future pleasure, and that gleam made her shudder and turn away.

At last they arrived in the Prince's country. Snow peered out the window of the carriage and saw only grey – grey rocks and grey tree bark and heavy grey clouds that hunched over the land. There were hardly any crops, and those that she saw were thin and sickly, the same as the people who tended them.

How do the people survive? she wondered, and then thought that this must be a very unhappy kingdom if its ruler neglected his own people so.

The Prince's castle was perched on a high hill with a steep road that rose to meet it. All around the base of the castle was a huge field of boulders that made it impossible to reach the castle by any route except the road.

One way in and one way out, Snow thought, eyeing the rocks. *Unless one is very brave, or very foolhardy.*

As the gates of the castle closed behind her carriage, she thought: *I might be very foolhardy. I may have to be.*

The Prince offered his hand so Snow could climb from the vehicle. As she placed hers in his grasp the ruby ring shifted on her finger. It was only a little, hardly noticeable at all, but the Prince gave her a sharp glance.

Some of the teeth have receded, she thought, and then she smiled at him with her very best princess smile and said, "Where is the chatelaine?"

The Prince narrowed his eyes and said, "My home is very unusual. You will see once we are inside."

Snow was half-sick from anxiety. Had the Prince seen the movement of the ring, or did he think he imagined it? Did he suspect her? She'd hoped that the ring might loosen before they arrived at the castle. She'd had some notion of slipping out in the night and disappearing into the wilderness of the Prince's country. But there was no wilderness here, no easy escape, and though the ring was not as tight as it had been it still would not leave her finger.

I must wait. I must bide my time until he cannot track me, cannot find me.

There was no man at the door of the castle to greet them, nor the chatelaine. There was no servant waiting inside to take Snow's cloak or to lead her to a room where a bath was waiting. There was only the ringing echo of the door slamming shut behind them.

Snow stared around at the empty hall, at the threadbare tapestries, at the rotten straw covering the stone floor.

The Prince's face was no longer charming. There was no need for the mask now that he was away from others.

"Where are all the servants?" Snow asked. Her voice came back to her, a hollow thing in this joyless room.

"Anything you require, this castle will provide," he said. "You need only ask."

More enchantments, Snow thought in despair. *No nosy maids and lads to wonder why the lady of the house is screaming.*

19

She longed to fidget with the ring, to see if she could yet free it, but instead curled her fingers into fists beneath the sleeves of her gown. She would not draw attention to the very thing she wished the Prince to ignore.

The apple was hidden in her skirt. There was only a little of it left now, the seeded core showing on all but one side. Snow could only hope that there was enough poison left to free her.

"When am I to meet your father?" she asked, for of course he was a prince because his father was still king.

"My father has not been feeling well of late," the Prince said. "When he is better, I shall take you to him."

This was patently a lie, but Snow said nothing. She had to stay quiet and submit for as long as necessary. She could not let him suspect that she was planning to escape.

Though where I will go and how I will get there I have no notion.

That was for later. First she had to get out from under his eye. Nothing was possible until then.

"You may go anywhere in the castle except the east wing," the Prince said, waving his hand in the direction of a thin, curving stair to the left. "The castle is very old and it is not safe there. Your room is this way."

He indicated a wider stair and that she should follow him. She did, her heart pounding, wondering what he would do now.

But he only led her to a wooden door with a large red ruby set in it, a ruby like a bloodied eye. It was the twin of the jewel in Snow's ring, and her mood fell further when she entered the room and discovered the jewel was visible on both sides.

Eyes everywhere, she thought. *What am I to do?*

"You may bathe and change and come down to dinner," he said. His lips were curved in that terrible satisfied smile again, as if he'd noted her glance at the ruby.

He knows that I know, and it amuses him. It amuses him because he is certain I can do nothing about it. I am only a rat in a maze to him. No matter how I twist and turn he is certain I cannot get out.

"Thank you," she said, very primly, and showed no sign of the surprise she felt that there was a large tub of water in the corner of the room, steam rising gently from the surface.

Aside from the tub there was only a four-poster bed with a faded red blanket upon it. A white gown was laid over this for Snow to wear after her bath.

As she slid the gown over her head, she wondered how she might bind the laces in the back without a maid. Then she cried out in shock and terror, for the laces tightened without the work of any hand, and the sash was tied behind her waist. A large toothed comb was run through her wet hair which was then bound up in braids and pinned at her crown.

Throughout all of this Snow made no noise except for her initial cry, though inside she trembled and shook. She would not show any weakness to the Prince, who was surely watching and waiting for her to panic.

I will not. I am a princess.

Snow carefully laid her other gown out on the bed and slipped the last bit of apple into her new gown, her body blocking the view from the jeweled eye in the door.

She thought the door might slide open without a touch, but she found she needed to open it the regular way. She also noticed that there was a small, old-fashioned key in the lock. This she took and kept next to the poisoned apple, though she had no illusions that the Prince would not have a key of his own.

The Prince sat opposite her at dinner, making light small talk that she answered without really listening. She noticed his hair was wet and assumed he too had bathed, though he hadn't bothered to shave his face. He had just the beginnings of a beard coming in at his jaw, and the candlelight cast strange shadows that made it appear blue instead of dark as the hair on his head.

When they completed their meal, Snow wondered what would happen next. At home there would be singing or sewing or storytelling after a meal, or sometimes dancing. She did not wish to dance with her husband, nor did she think that music would echo sweetly in this hall. Any song would be fouled by the air.

"You may go up to your room now," he said. "I have some business to attend."

"Of course," Snow said, and climbed the stairs.

Her heart lodged at the bottom of her throat. He would come to her when his business was completed, whatever that might be. There was no army to hear him now, as there had been on the road.

Am I to sit in my bedroom trembling like a little rabbit, waiting for the fox at the door to come and eat me at his pleasure?

She entered the room and shut the door behind her. The red eye blinked at her, and she felt a sudden surge of anger.

Why should I be spied upon like a criminal? Why should he have that satisfaction? At least with the ring I can tuck it in the folds of my skirt.

Snow yanked her traveling gown from the bed and tore the sash from it. She pulled several of the pins from her hair and tacked the sash up on the door, covering the ruby eye. A strange buzzing sound emitted from it as it was covered, like it was an angry bee trying to loose itself.

"See how you like that," Snow said.

Then she took the key out of her pocket. She couldn't fool herself that the Prince would be kept out by such a feeble attempt, but she locked the door anyway. At least she would have a few moments to prepare herself while he unlocked it.

A wisp of smoke curled out of the keyhole.

Another enchantment? Something to stop me from using the key?

Snow bent down to get a closer look. She didn't see anything obvious, but she smelled something sweet and spicy in the air.

The apple, she thought. *The poison from the apple. It must have rubbed off on the key.*

She turned the knob and pulled the door. It held fast. Would it keep the Prince from her bed?

Snow's trunk had appeared in her room while she was downstairs at dinner. She took out her nightdress. She expected the ghostly hands to come and unlace her gown as they had laced it up, but there was nothing.

Is that because I covered the eye on the door? It was an interesting notion, to be sure, one that might have implications for Snow's freedom. But it didn't help her remove a gown that required an extra person to put on in the first place.

After several irritating minutes attempting to wriggle out of the white gown Snow gave up and lay down on the bed in it, removing only the sash that pulled the gown close around her waist.

She thought she would be far too terrified to sleep but she must have dozed, for the next thing she knew it was dark and someone was fumbling at the door.

Snow sat straight up, blood roaring. She slid the ruby-eyed ring beneath the coverlet so that it would not know she was awake. The Prince's voice came through the keyhole, the words indistinct but the meaning of them clear.

He's trying to magic the lock open.

She heard his voice rise in frustration, heard him curse.

But the lock held fast.

"Open the door, my darling," he said.

There had never been less affection in the word "darling" in all the history of the world.

Snow kept still, so very still, more still than the smallest mouse caught in the gaze of a cat.

"Snow White," he called, low and crooning and meant to seduce, to charm, to enchant. "Open the door to your husband."

I will not.

His hand shook the knob. She felt his anger then, his frustration, his *hunger*, and his hunger was a terrible thing, a thing that wanted to consume her. It was like a crashing wave that pushed against the door, seeping through the grain of the wood, pummeling her. Her hands grasped the bedclothes for dear life and she bit hard on her lower lip so she would not whimper.

"Snow White!" he said, and there was no more pretense then. "Open this door, I say. You have no right to refuse me."

Snow wondered how much worse it would be for her later, for she knew in some way that she was only staving off the inevitable. But she could not bring herself to open the door. She could not invite the wolf inside.

After a time the rattling of the doorknob ceased. She heard him laugh, low and dark.

"There's always tomorrow, my darling," he said.

Snow did not sleep again that night.

* * *

The next morning, she took the last bite of the apple. There was hardly any magic left in it at all, for it didn't burn with the same fire when she swallowed it. She knew some of the charm had come off on the key.

Snow parted the curtains and opened her window wide. The outside air was thin and chill but a weak sunlight filtered through the clouds. She turned the ring this way and that in the sun. The silver had a fine dark vein running through it that hadn't been there at the start, and she thought the eye appeared cloudy, but it might have been wishful thinking.

She took a deep breath and unlocked her bedroom door. The Prince was not lurking in the hallway, waiting to punish her as she'd expected. Snow padded softly down the stairs and found breakfast laid out at the table, but there was no plate for the Prince and he was nowhere to be seen.

There was a small piece of parchment on her plate, a note written in a beautiful hand:

My darling wife, I have other duties that I must attend to today, but I will certainly see you this evening.

Snow thrust the note away from her. To anyone else's eyes the note might look like the reassurance of a lover but she recognized it for what it was – a threat. And a promise.

Snow took her place at the table and ate, for she could think better if her stomach was full. She found she was hungrier than expected. She was reaching for another serving of toast when it happened.

The silver ring flew off her left hand and landed in the butter dish.

Snow's heart swelled, for now that the ring was gone she could escape. In fact, she could escape at that very moment. The Prince was not there to stop her, and if any of the soldiers asked she could simply say she was going out for a walk. She was their princess now, and they could not control her.

She rose from the table with an idea of changing into something more suitable – the white gown was like a flag that would draw all eyes to her in the grey landscape *(and perhaps that is what he meant for it to do when he gave it to you).*

That was when she heard the woman crying.

Snow stopped, arrested by the sound. No, the woman wasn't crying. She was half-sobbing, half-screaming, and the sound was coming from the east wing.

Snow only hesitated for a moment. The Prince had said not to go into the east wing, but Snow couldn't ignore a person in pain.

But what if the Prince returns, and catches you? What if you miss your chance to escape?

These were selfish thoughts, and perhaps they would have convinced Snow if the woman's sobbing hadn't grown louder.

"I can't," she said. "I can't leave her, whoever she is."

Snow mounted the stairs to the east wing.

At least all the Prince can see at the moment is the view inside the butter dish, she thought, and wiped her damp hands on her crumpled gown, and tried not to be afraid.

At the top of the stairs there was a long hallway, and at the end of the hallway there was only one door.

The woman's voice was fading, a thin weak stream emitting from the room beyond.

Snow ran to it, and tugged on the handle, but the door held fast.

She took the poisoned key from her pocket and slid it into the keyhole.

The door swung open.

In the first room there were boxes on pedestals, boxes made of shining dark wood covered in jewels of every color. In the corner of the room there was a heavy red curtain that must have led to another room.

There were terrible noises coming from that room, and Snow hesitated, because her stomach and lungs and throat were filled with terror so thick she could hardly breathe. She tiptoed past the boxes until she reached the last one.

This one was open, as if it were waiting for something. And it was covered all over with red jewels just like the one in her ring.

For me, she thought with sudden certainty, and then she had to know what was in the others.

She touched the lid of the box beside the empty one, and it opened.

Inside was a heart, red and lush and beating.

Snow opened the next box, her hands shaking, and found another, just as fresh and impossible as the first. She stared at all the boxes, dozens of them, all around the room, and remembered that the Queen had told her of the Prince's father, and the many wives that had disappeared.

And the Prince himself had a wife before Snow, and she, too, had disappeared.

Snow stared at the red curtain, and heard the terrible noises coming from the next room. She did not want to know, but she had to.

She pulled the curtain aside.

Her husband's face was buried in something that might have once been a woman, though all that was left of her now was meat. When Snow pulled the curtain he looked up from his meal, and she saw that his face had overnight grown a thick blue beard, and his eyes were as red as the blood that ran over his chin.

He smiled, and Snow thought it was a travesty to call such a thing a smile.

"Naughty, naughty girl," her husband said. "I told you to stay out of the east wing."

Snow ran.

She heard his laughter echoing behind her as she fled down the hallway, down the stairs and to the front door, but no matter how she tugged on the handle it would not open, and there was no hole for her magic key.

"Where are you running to, my little bride?" Prince Charming called from the top of the east wing stairs.

Snow ran for the opposite stair, not knowing what she would do or where she could go, only knowing that she had to escape, to stay out of his grasp.

As she passed the table she saw the poison ring sunk into the butter. Without really knowing why she grasped the ring (and a handful of butter with it) and kept running, up the west wing stairs.

"There is no escape, Snow White," her husband called. He sounded amused and unhurried and far too close behind her.

"None of my brides have ever escaped, no matter how

they scream and cry and run," he said. "I do like it when they run. Keep running, my little dove. It makes you all the sweeter when I catch you."

Snow fled to her room, thinking that she could lock the door on him again, but the magic had gone out of the key and the lock would no longer rebel against its master.

She backed away from the door as it swung open, her mind repeating the same phrase over and over – *What shall I do? What shall I do?* Butter seeped through her fingers and her heart hammered so hard she thought it might leave her body.

But it will leave my body. He will cut it from me and keep it in a box, a prize like all the others.

He seemed enormous as he pushed through the doorframe, twice as large as he'd been before, and his hands were red and sticky and reaching for her.

"There is nowhere for you to flee, so you should be a good girl and let me do what I wish to you, Snow White," he said. "I'm only going to do it anyway."

She saw all her terrors reflected in his eyes. The breeze from the open window behind her ruffled her white gown. His fingers curled, ready to tear it from her.

No, Snow thought. *I will not. I will not be a good girl ever again.*

He opened his mouth and bent toward her throat – to kiss? To bite? Snow never knew – and she took the fistful of butter and the poisoned ring inside it and shoved it all inside his maw.

He choked, then reflexively swallowed, and the butter made the ring slide down his gullet.

"What have you done?" he said, clawing at his own throat, tearing away long bleeding strips of skin. Smoke rose from his mouth and seeped out the corners of his eyes, and blackened veins rose under the surface of his face. "WHAT HAVE YOU DONE, SNOW WHITE?"

He lunged for her and she darted out of his grasp, revealing the open window.

Snow pushed him as hard as she could.

He screamed as he fell, and she heard his terror and his fury, and she was glad.

After a while he stopped screaming, and she was able to look out. Far below she saw his broken body on the rocks that surrounded the castle.

Off in the distance there was dust rising from the road. As Snow watched three figures emerged, riding fast – her brothers, coming to take her home.

TROLL BRIDGE

NEIL GAIMAN

They pulled up most of the railway tracks in the early sixties, when I was three or four. They slashed the train services to ribbons. This meant that there was nowhere to go but London, and the little town where I lived became the end of the line.

My earliest reliable memory: eighteen months old, my mother away in hospital having my sister, and my grandmother walking with me down to a bridge, and lifting me up to watch the train below, panting and steaming like a black iron dragon.

Over the next few years they lost the last of the steam trains, and with them went the network of railways that joined village to village, town to town.

I didn't know that the trains were going. By the time I was seven they were a thing of the past.

We lived in an old house on the outskirts of the town. The fields opposite were empty and fallow. I used to climb the fence and lie in the shade of a small bulrush patch, and read; or if I were feeling more adventurous I'd explore the grounds of the empty manor beyond the fields. It had a weed-clogged ornamental pond, with a low wooden bridge over it. I never saw any groundsmen or caretakers in my forays through the gardens and woods, and I never attempted to enter the manor. That would have been courting disaster, and besides, it was a matter of faith for me that all empty old houses were haunted.

It is not that I was credulous, simply that I believed in all things dark and dangerous. It was part of my young creed that the night was full of ghosts and witches, hungry and flapping and dressed completely in black.

The converse held reassuringly true: daylight was safe. Daylight was always safe.

A ritual: on the last day of the summer school term, walking home from school, I would remove my shoes and socks and, carrying them in my hands, walk down the stony flinty lane on pink and tender feet. During the summer holiday I would put shoes on only under duress. I would revel in my freedom from footwear until the school term began once more in September.

When I was seven I discovered the path through the wood. It was summer, hot and bright, and I wandered a long way from home that day.

I was exploring. I went past the manor, its windows boarded up and blind, across the grounds, and through some unfamiliar woods. I scrambled down a steep bank, and I found myself on a shady path that was new to me and overgrown with trees; the light that penetrated the leaves was stained green and gold, and I thought I was in fairyland.

A little stream trickled down the side of the path, teeming with tiny, transparent shrimps. I picked them up and watched them jerk and spin on my fingertips. Then I put them back.

I wandered down the path. It was perfectly straight, and overgrown with short grass. From time to time I would find these really terrific rocks: bubbly, melted things, brown and purple and black. If you held them up to the light you could see every color of the rainbow. I was convinced that they had to be extremely valuable, and stuffed my pockets with them.

I walked and walked down the quiet golden-green corridor, and saw nobody.

I wasn't hungry or thirsty. I just wondered where the path was going. It traveled in a straight line, and was perfectly flat. The path never changed, but the countryside around it did. At first I was walking along the bottom of a ravine, grassy banks climbing steeply on each side of me. Later, the path was above everything, and as I walked I could look down at the treetops below me, and the roofs of occasional distant houses. My path was always flat and straight, and I walked along it through valleys and plateaus, valleys and plateaus. And eventually, in one of the valleys, I came to the bridge.

It was built of clean red brick, a huge curving arch over the path. At the side of the bridge were stone steps cut into the embankment, and, at the top of the steps, a little wooden gate.

I was surprised to see any token of the existence of humanity on my path, which I was by now convinced was a natural formation, like a volcano. And, with a sense more of curiosity than anything else (I had, after all, walked hundreds of miles, or so I was convinced, and might be *anywhere*), I climbed the stone steps, and went through the gate.

I was nowhere.

The top of the bridge was paved with mud. On each side of it was a meadow. The meadow on my side was a wheatfield; the other field was just grass. There were the caked imprints of huge tractor wheels in the dried mud. I walked across the bridge to be sure: no trip-trap, my bare feet were soundless.

Nothing for miles; just fields and wheat and trees.

I picked an ear of wheat, and pulled out the sweet grains, peeling them between my fingers, chewing them meditatively.

I realized then that I was getting hungry, and went back down the stairs to the abandoned railway track. It was time to go home. I was not lost; all I needed to do was follow my path home once more.

There was a troll waiting for me, under the bridge.

"I'm a troll," he said. Then he paused, and added, more or less as an afterthought, "Fol rol de ol rol."

He was huge: his head brushed the top of the brick arch. He was more or less translucent: I could see the bricks and trees behind him, dimmed but not lost. He was all my nightmares given flesh. He had huge strong teeth, and rending claws, and strong, hairy hands. His hair was long, like one of my sister's little plastic gonks, and his eyes bulged. He was naked, and his penis hung from the bush of gonk hair between his legs.

"I heard you, Jack," he whispered in a voice like the wind. "I heard you trip-trapping over my bridge. And now I'm going to eat your life."

I was only seven, but it was daylight, and I do not remember being scared. It is good for children to find themselves facing the elements of a fairy tale – they are well equipped to deal with these.

"Don't eat me," I said to the troll. I was wearing a stripy brown T-shirt, and brown corduroy trousers. My hair also was brown, and I was missing a front tooth. I was learning to whistle between my teeth, but wasn't there yet.

"I'm going to eat your life, Jack," said the troll.

I stared the troll in the face. "My big sister is going to be coming down the path soon," I lied, "and she's far tastier than me. Eat her instead."

The troll sniffed the air, and smiled. "You're all alone," he said. "There's nothing else on the path. Nothing at all." Then he leaned down, and ran his fingers over me: it felt like butterflies were brushing my face – like the touch of a blind person. Then he snuffled his fingers, and shook his huge head. "You don't have a big sister. You've only a younger sister, and she's at her friend's today."

"Can you tell all that from smell?" I asked, amazed.

"Trolls can smell the rainbows, trolls can smell the stars," it whispered sadly. "Trolls can smell the dreams you dreamed before you were ever born. Come close to me and I'll eat your life."

"I've got precious stones in my pocket," I told the troll. "Take them, not me. Look." I showed him the lava jewel rocks I had found earlier.

"Clinker," said the troll. "The discarded refuse of steam trains. Of no value to me."

He opened his mouth wide. Sharp teeth. Breath that smelled of leaf mold and the underneaths of things. "Eat. Now."

He became more and more solid to me, more and more real; and the world outside became flatter, began to fade.

"Wait." I dug my feet into the damp earth beneath the bridge, wiggled my toes, held on tightly to the real world. I stared into his big eyes. "You don't want to eat my life. Not yet. I-I'm only seven. I haven't *lived* at all yet. There are books I haven't read yet. I've never been on an airplane. I can't whistle yet – not really. Why don't you let me go? When I'm older and bigger and more of a meal I'll come back to you."

The troll stared at me with eyes like headlamps.

Then it nodded.

"When you come back, then," it said. And it smiled.

I turned around and walked back down the silent straight path where the railway lines had once been.

After a while I began to run.

I pounded down the track in the green light, puffing and blowing, until I felt a stabbing ache beneath my ribcage, the pain of stitch; and, clutching my side, I stumbled home.

* * *

The fields started to go, as I grew older. One by one, row by row, houses sprang up with roads named after wildflowers and respectable authors. Our home – an aging, tattered Victorian house – was sold, and torn down; new houses covered the garden.

They built houses everywhere.

I once got lost in the new housing estate that covered two meadows I had once known every inch of. I didn't mind too much that the fields were going, though. The old manor house was bought by a multinational, and the grounds became more houses.

It was eight years before I returned to the old railway line, and when I did, I was not alone.

I was fifteen; I'd changed schools twice in that time. Her name was Louise, and she was my first love.

I loved her gray eyes, and her fine light brown hair, and her gawky way of walking (like a fawn just learning to walk which sounds really dumb, for which I apologize): I saw her chewing gum, when I was thirteen, and I fell for her like a suicide from a bridge.

The main trouble with being in love with Louise was that we were best friends, and we were both going out with other people.

I'd never told her I loved her, or even that I fancied her. We were buddies.

I'd been at her house that evening: we sat in her room and played *Rattus Norvegicus*, the first Stranglers LP. It was the beginning of punk, and everything seemed so exciting: the possibilities, in music as in everything else, were endless. Eventually it was time for me to go home, and she decided to accompany me. We held hands, innocently, just pals, and we strolled the ten-minute walk to my house.

The moon was bright, and the world was visible and colorless, and the night was warm.

We got to my house. Saw the lights inside, and stood in the driveway, and talked about the band I was starting. We didn't go in.

Then it was decided that I'd walk *her* home. So we walked back to her house.

She told me about the battles she was having with her younger sister, who was stealing her makeup and perfume. Louise suspected that her sister was having sex with boys. Louise was a virgin. We both were.

We stood in the road outside her house, under the sodium yellow streetlight, and we stared at each other's black lips and pale yellow faces.

We grinned at each other.

Then we just walked, picking quiet roads and empty paths. In one of the new housing estates, a path led us into the woodland, and we followed it.

The path was straight and dark, but the lights of distant houses shone like stars on the ground, and the moon gave us enough light to see. Once we were scared, when something snuffled and snorted in front of us. We pressed close, saw it was a badger, laughed and hugged and kept on walking.

We talked quiet nonsense about what we dreamed and wanted and thought.

And all the time I wanted to kiss her and feel her breasts, and maybe put my hand between her legs.

Finally I saw my chance. There was an old brick bridge over the path, and we stopped beneath it. I pressed up against her. Her mouth opened against mine.

Then she went cold and stiff, and stopped moving.

"Hello," said the troll.

I let go of Louise. It was dark beneath the bridge, but the shape of the troll filled the darkness.

"I froze her," said the troll, "so we can talk. Now: I'm going to eat your life."

My heart pounded, and I could feel myself trembling.

"No."

"You said you'd come back to me. And you have. Did you learn to whistle?"

"Yes."

"That's good. I never could whistle." It sniffed, and nodded. "I am pleased. You have grown in life and experience. More to eat. More for me."

I grabbed Louise, a taut zombie, and pushed her forward. "Don't take me. I don't want to die. Take *her*. I bet she's much tastier than me. And she's two months older than I am. Why don't you take her?"

The troll was silent.

41

It sniffed Louise from toe to head, snuffling at her feet and crotch and breasts and hair.

Then it looked at me.

"She's an innocent," it said. "You're not. I don't want her. I want you."

I walked to the opening of the bridge and stared up at the stars in the night.

"But there's so much I've never done," I said, partly to myself. "I mean, I've never. Well, I've never had sex. And I've never been to America. I haven't…" I paused. "I haven't *done* anything. Not yet."

The troll said nothing.

"I could come back to you. When I'm older."

The troll said nothing.

"I *will* come back. Honest I will."

"Come back to me?" said Louise. "Why? Where are you going?"

I turned around. The troll had gone, and the girl I had thought I loved was standing in the shadows beneath the bridge.

"We're going home," I told her. "Come on."

We walked back and never said anything.

She went out with the drummer in the punk band I started, and, much later, married someone else. We met once, on a train, after she was married, and she asked me if I remembered that night.

I said I did.

"I really liked you, that night, Jack," she told me. "I thought

42

you were going to kiss me. I thought you were going to ask me out. I would have said yes. If you had."

"But I didn't."

"No," she said. "You didn't." Her hair was cut very short. It didn't suit her.

I never saw her again. The trim woman with the taut smile was not the girl I had loved, and talking to her made me feel uncomfortable.

* * *

I moved to London, and then, some years later, I moved back again, but the town I returned to was not the town I remembered: there were no fields, no farms, no little flint lanes; and I moved away as soon as I could, to a tiny village ten miles down the road.

I moved with my family – I was married by now, with a toddler – into an old house that had once, many years before, been a railway station. The tracks had been dug up, and the old couple who lived opposite us used it to grow vegetables.

I was getting older. One day I found a gray hair; on another, I heard a recording of myself talking, and I realized I sounded just like my father.

I was working in London, doing A&R for one of the major record companies. I was commuting into London by train most days, coming back some evenings.

I had to keep a small flat in London; it's hard to commute when the bands you're checking out don't even stagger onto the stage until midnight. It also meant that it was fairly easy to get laid, if I wanted to, which I did.

I thought that Eleanora – that was my wife's name; I should have mentioned that before, I suppose – didn't know about the other women; but I got back from a two-week jaunt to New York one winter's day, and when I arrived at the house it was empty and cold.

She had left a letter, not a note. Fifteen pages, neatly typed, and every word of it was true. Including the PS, which read: *You really don't love me. And you never did.*

I put on a heavy coat, and I left the house and just walked, stunned and slightly numb.

There was no snow on the ground, but there was a hard frost, and the leaves crunched under my feet as I walked. The trees were skeletal black against the harsh gray winter sky.

I walked down the side of the road. Cars passed me, traveling to and from London. Once I tripped on a branch, half-hidden in a heap of brown leaves, ripping my trousers, cutting my leg.

I reached the next village. There was a river at right angles to the road, and a path I'd never seen before beside it, and I walked down the path, and stared at the partly frozen river. It gurgled and plashed and sang.

The path led off through fields; it was straight and grassy.

I found a rock, half-buried, on one side of the path. I picked it up, brushed off the mud. It was a melted lump of purplish stuff, with a strange rainbow sheen to it. I put it into the pocket of my coat and held it in my hand as I walked, its presence warm and reassuring.

The river meandered away across the fields, and I walked on in silence.

I had walked for an hour before I saw houses – new and small and square – on the embankment above me.

And then I saw the bridge, and I knew where I was: I was on the old railway path, and I'd been coming down it from the other direction.

There were graffiti painted on the side of the bridge: FUCK and BARRY LOVES SUSAN and the omnipresent NF of the National Front.

I stood beneath the bridge in the red brick arch, stood among the ice cream wrappers, and the crisp packets and the single, sad, used condom, and watched my breath steam in the cold afternoon air.

The blood had dried into my trousers.

Cars passed over the bridge above me; I could hear a radio playing loudly in one of them.

"Hello?" I said, quietly, feeling embarrassed, feeling foolish. "Hello?"

There was no answer. The wind rustled the crisp packets and the leaves.

"I came back. I said I would. And I did. Hello?"

Silence.

I began to cry then, stupidly, silently, sobbing under the bridge.

45

A hand touched my face, and I looked up.

"I didn't think you'd come back," said the troll.

He was my height now, but otherwise unchanged. His long gonk hair was unkempt and had leaves in it, and his eyes were wide and lonely.

I shrugged, then wiped my face with the sleeve of my coat. "I came back."

Three kids passed above us on the bridge, shouting and running.

"I'm a troll," whispered the troll, in a small, scared voice. "Fol rol de ol rol."

He was trembling.

I held out my hand and took his huge clawed paw in mine. I smiled at him. "It's okay," I told him. "Honestly. It's okay."

The troll nodded.

He pushed me to the ground, onto the leaves and the wrappers and the condom, and lowered himself on top of me. Then he raised his head, and opened his mouth, and ate my life with his strong sharp teeth.

* * *

When he was finished, the troll stood up and brushed himself down. He put his hand into the pocket of his coat and pulled out a bubbly, burnt lump of clinker rock.

He held it out to me.

"This is yours," said the troll.

I looked at him: wearing my life comfortably, easily, as if

he'd been wearing it for years. I took the clinker from his hand, and sniffed it. I could smell the train from which it had fallen, so long ago. I gripped it tightly in my hairy hand.

"Thank you," I said.

"Good luck," said the troll.

"Yeah. Well. You too."

The troll grinned with my face.

It turned its back on me and began to walk back the way I had come, toward the village, back to the empty house I had left that morning; and it whistled as it walked.

I've been here ever since. Hiding. Waiting. Part of the bridge.

I watch from the shadows as the people pass: walking their dogs, or talking, or doing the things that people do. Sometimes people pause beneath my bridge, to stand, or piss, or make love. And I watch them, but say nothing; and they never see me.

Fol rol de ol rol.

I'm just going to stay here, in the darkness under the arch. I can hear you all out there, trip-trapping, trip-trapping over my bridge.

Oh yes, I can hear you.

But I'm not coming out.

AT THAT AGE

CATRIONA WARD

When they come into the classroom, John thinks he's seeing double. They are exactly alike: gold and blue, hair and eyes. The boy is slightly taller, maybe. John looks the longest at the girl. Everyone is looking at them. They don't seem to mind. They are used to it. The teacher says their names and they smile politely. Daisy and Drew. John thinks, how stupid to give twins names that begin with the same letter, like characters from those old stories about boarding schools. Alice liked those kinds of books. John doesn't.

There is an empty seat next to him and he hopes and hopes. But obviously the teacher puts the girl at the very back of the class, and the boy sits next to John. A strange, delicate scent hangs about him, like the fruit bowl at home when those little flies start hanging over it.

John starts, because suddenly chair legs are scraping and there is a tumult of voices. The lesson is over. The boy is looking at him in a friendly way.

"You were sleeping with your eyes open."

"It was boring," John says. He doesn't sleep at night anymore but he doesn't want to talk about that.

John is thirteen. Sometimes he tells people he's sixteen. And sometimes they believe him because he is tall – though he has developed a hunch in recent months. He doesn't like to take up too much space, or be looked at. Just in case what's inside him might be visible on the outside.

He blinks. He is in the playground in the sunshine and the Drew boy is standing beside him with a friendly air. His skin and eyes are so clear that he seems almost pearlescent, lit from within. The upper school girls file past. It is the end of their break time. They look at Drew, little flashes of heat passing through the chain-link fence. Jealousy spears John deep in his stomach. They don't look at him like that, with his dull brown hair and normal eyes.

Drew says, "So, what is there to do around here?"

"Not much," says John. He doesn't bother to sound matey.

"Do you want to come to our house after school? There'll be no grown-ups home."

John says, "Nah."

"Oh, do," says Drew and John shrugs and says *OK*, to make him go away. He supposes it beats going home to his mother, her slow sorrow. He is tired, these days. Maybe that's why people believe him, when he says he's older.

* * *

Daisy is waiting outside the school gates. She walks alongside them in silence. Her hair falls over one eye in a white-gold sheaf. Drew says, "Where's the nearest place to buy beer?"

"There's the off-licence on the corner," John says. "But they ask for ID."

"Don't worry," Drew says.

John supposes Drew has a fake ID. The twins have money, that's obvious. He can pay for the good kind.

"I'll pay," Drew says, as if tracking John's thoughts. "Daisy and I will. We don't mind."

John stops in the little cobbled alley by the off-licence. "OK," he says. "Here you go."

"I'm not going in," Drew says. "You are."

John feels a spurt of irritation. "I can't," he says. "They know me and my mum. I thought you had an ID or something."

"No."

"Waste of time," John says and walks away.

"Wait." A soft, pale hand on his arm. Daisy smells like her brother but sweeter, like apple juice. "Please," she says. "We have an idea."

John stops. Her hand feels like it's sinking into his flesh, but not in a gross way.

"I know a trick you can use," Drew says. "It's like… hypnotism or something. It's that same guy who hypnotised the entire football stadium. Did you see that on TV?"

John is interested, in spite of himself. He did see the man hypnotising the football stadium full of people. It was cool.

He likes magic and all that stuff.

"All you have to do is lean in close, and say a word, and the other person will do whatever you want them to do."

"Yeah, right."

"I know it sounds mad," Drew says. "But it works, I swear."

"What's the word?"

Drew whispers in his ear. Afterwards John can't call the word to mind. It sounds something like *anuśru*, or *anushru*, but not really. It sounds like stone grating on stone, bones calcifying deep beneath the earth.

* * *

The door gives with a cheerful tinkle. Inside, the shop smells mineral and cool, like glass bottles or maybe coins. John's palms start sweating. His skin crawls with shock as he sees that it isn't the old man behind the counter; it's his wife. She is knitting and the sound of her needles seems to echo his speeding heart. *Click, click, click.* Mrs Berry has this way of looking at you, just like she is doing now, over the rim of her glasses.

He goes to the fridge anyway. The cans are blue and gold, so cold that they stick to his palm. The colours make him think of Daisy. He takes out a six-pack of something. It could be beer, cider. His eyes won't make sense of the label. His fingers aren't steady and he drops the cans onto the counter with a sharp sound. Mrs Berry looks at him.

"Proof of age, please," she says gently. She's not angry, it's worse than that. John sees that she pities him, she is thinking of

Alice and how sad it all is. His heart feels like a balloon that's been blown up too much and has reached breaking point.

He leans in close to her. The word drops from his mouth like a stone. Mrs Berry blinks and says, "Are you all right, John?"

He says the word again, panicking, and she takes the beer away from him. "I'll put this back in the fridge," she says. "You get home." She puts her hand on his, briefly. "I know you're having a rough time. It will pass, I promise. You've got to try and be a help to your mum, now."

Outside, John finds that he is trembling with rage. He runs to the alley where he left the twins. He seizes Drew and shoves him against the brick wall.

"You were making fun of me," he says, breathing hard. "The word didn't work."

Drew gives a shout of mingled surprise and laughter. "*Of course* it didn't work," he says. "What did you think? Honestly."

John stares at him for a moment. A feeling bubbles up inside him. It bursts out and he realises he is laughing too. How could he have believed that there was a magic word that made people do what you wanted? Honestly, it is pretty funny.

"Let's go to your house," he says.

The smile spreads slowly over Daisy's face like sunrise.

* * *

Daisy and Drew's house is in the new development on the other side of town. They walk there slowly, talking.

"You have a sister, John?" asks Daisy.

"A twin," John says. He doesn't feel like getting into the Alice thing right now. "She goes to a different school."

Where Drew and Daisy live, all the houses look the same. They are big and clean and anonymous. They don't have the pressing weight of sadness on them, because nothing has happened there yet. John wishes he and his mum lived here, and not in the small grey terrace filled with memories of loss. He worries about his mum. At least John gets to go to school during the day. She just sits.

They stop outside a white house, which looks just like the adjacent white houses, and all the other houses in the close. Drew opens the gate and they go up the garden path, which is so new that the crystals in the paving still sparkle in the afternoon sun.

Inside the front door is a large table, piled a foot deep in letters and bills.

"Woah," John says.

"The previous owners," says Daisy, drawing him on. "They didn't leave a forwarding address. I suppose we should just throw it all away."

The living room is like a large, cool cave, what his mum would call open plan. Everything is either white or shining. Daisy puts on music, which comes out of hidden speakers in the walls. Drew hands John a drink in a real martini glass, just like James Bond. The first swallow burns his throat, but after that everything starts to feel wonderful.

"Let's have a party," Drew says.

"Oh, do let's!" says Daisy.

John laughs, because sure, why not? A party, out of nowhere. "Won't your mum and dad mind?"

"Hester is out," Daisy says. "But she won't mind, anyway."

Drew takes out his phone and starts calling. In what seems like minutes, the doorbell rings and there are kids outside. John doesn't know any of them. They must be from other schools. It happens again, and again, and soon the white living room is filled with teenagers. Everyone's teeth seem really white, and the girls' clothes are amazing: dresses that seem ready to float off like clouds, flower crowns and bare feet.

John finds himself talking to an earnest boy wearing black, named Edmond. He has glasses and his dark hair is long, combed over one side of his face. Even so, John glimpses the scar beneath. It is long and vicious.

"How did you get that?" he asks. He knows that personal questions are rude but he feels so close to Edmond with his nervous eyes and sweet face.

Edmond tugs his hair. "It was a long time ago," he says. "Like, years and years ago."

"When you were a baby?"

"Kind of," Edmond says. Then he goes pale in the dim light. "I forgot to give them my letters." He disappears. John shrugs and wanders away through the party. The music gets louder and light effects play across the white walls. Blue, pink, gold. It's really nice. In fact, John feels better than he has done for months. The drinks don't seem to slow him down, but make him more alert, light him up. There is another full glass in his hand. He can't remember how it got there. Drew and Daisy are all right, he decides. Nicer than he expected. The strange smell that had hung about them seems to be gone, now.

* * *

When John gets home his mother is sitting at the kitchen table, as always. She stares at nothing.

"Mum?" he says quietly. She doesn't answer. Her fingers drum. There are little marks forming on the surface of the wood, where her fingernails hit the table all day long.

He goes up to his room. The door is ajar, showing the streetlight shining in. He thinks of the other empty room next door, the one they never go into. He can almost feel her, Alice, in the dark, behind the wall. He thinks with burning envy of Drew and Daisy – their easy good looks, their cool mother who lets them have parties, their white house where no ghosts lurk behind closed doors.

* * *

The next day in school Drew is beside him, all smiles and perfect skin.

"Do you want to come over for supper tonight?" he asks.

"Will your parents mind?"

"Hester won't," Drew says.

John says yes. He is grateful that he doesn't have to go home and get fish fingers out of the freezer. He usually overcooks them and they taste terrible. He has to wheedle his mother into eating a few, burned morsels.

"What's your address?" he asks Drew. "I've got football practice."

Drew looks blank. "Oh, don't worry about that," he says. "We'll wait for you. We can all walk home together."

"That's a hassle for you," John says in surprise.

"We don't mind."

For a moment John wonders why Drew doesn't know his own address. But the thought drifts off. It has been a long time since he was last happy.

* * *

Daisy cooks. She makes things John has only read about in old books; stuffed marrow followed by trifle. He didn't even know you could get marrow anymore. He eats everything he is given.

"Where are your parents?" he asks.

"There's only Hester," Daisy says. "She sort of adopted us."

"Is Hester here?" John asks, nervous. He is not good with parents. He always says something weird.

"Yes," Drew says. "She's asleep, just now. Right, Daisy?"

Daisy nods. John feels a twinge of sympathy. He knows what it is like to have a parent who sleeps all the time. They have a lot in common, he and the twins.

"How about you, John?" Daisy asks politely.

"It's only me and my mum," John says. "My dad left." Somehow it doesn't hurt, talking about it here, with his stomach full of trifle.

"How sad," says Daisy. "Well, I'm so pleased that we met. Friends are important, I think."

"I'm sorry I was rude when I met you both," John says in a rush. "I think maybe it reminded me of my sister, Alice. Seeing you together, I mean. We were close, like you. Before the accident."

Drew looks at Daisy. "Accident?" he asks.

"Yes." Tears touch John's eyelids for the first time since it happened. "I feel like half a person, now. So stupid."

Daisy says quietly, "So your twin is dead, John?"

"Yes," he says.

"I suppose I couldn't tell," Daisy says, "because you haven't let her go."

There comes a thump from upstairs, and then a groan, as though someone has fallen out of bed onto bare boards.

"What was that?" asks John.

"I don't know," says Daisy. "Cats on the roof, I expect. Better go and see about it, Drew."

"In a minute," Drew says.

Something moves across the ceiling above their heads. A heavy thing drags itself towards the stairs. The groan comes again, muffled, filled with pain.

"By Jove," says Drew. "It's late, John, you'd better be off."

John says goodbye and Daisy says goodbye too. She is polite, as always, but it's as if she's listening intently to something John can't hear.

As John goes through the hall, he quickly shuffles through some of the letters piled deep on the table. There must be two hundred, all addressed to different people in different parts of the country. He finds one addressed to an Edmond Booker in Halifax. It can't be the same Edmond he met at the party; Halifax is hundreds of miles away. But even so it makes John feel weird. He quickly goes out of the front door.

John goes down the sparkling granite path in the purple dusk. Sounds from inside the house are carried on the still night. The person who was moaning is now crying, perhaps pleading. Drew speaks to them. Or at least it sounds like Drew at first. Then John's not sure. It's an old, old voice.

"Leave him be," it says. "Get back in your hole."

* * *

When John gets home his mum is sitting in the kitchen, streetlight playing on her still face. John goes upstairs. He pauses on the landing, before Alice's door. After a moment he opens it and goes in. It is too warm, the air tastes stale and dusty.

He turns on the light and goes to Alice's bookshelf. He takes down a book with a bright, illustrated cover, showing five smiling children and a dog. These were Alice's favourites; tales of nineteen fifties schoolchildren caught up in extraordinary adventures of smugglers and robbers and secret islands. He opens the book and reads. It doesn't take long to find what he's looking for.

"By Jove," said Harry. "There's simply lashings and lashings of trifle."

* * *

The next day, in history, the seat next to John is empty. When he cranes his neck, he sees that there is a gap in the back row like a missing tooth. Daisy isn't at school either. John feels a moment of something – surely not disappointment? Then he feels electric. This proves that something is up. Where did those two come from anyway? He doesn't drift off in class today. His mind is filled with thoughts of time travel, or maybe vampires.

The moment the last bell sounds, John has his rucksack over his shoulder. He runs through the shady streets towards the new white houses. He doesn't know what he will say, but he is filled with certainty. They are doing something bad, he knows it. He is almost sure that they are keeping someone prisoner upstairs in their house. Maybe their mother, Hester. John suspects that what he's doing is dangerous, but it is a relief to feel something, even fear.

He turns into the close where the first houses reach pale and tall against the summer sky. As he goes, he begins to falter. Was it the second left or the third after the house with the yew tree in the garden? Everything looks the same. He doesn't see another living person. Most of the houses are empty – he can see wide expanses of pale bare boards through the windows. None of them have numbers on their gates. And he doesn't know the number, anyway. By the time the first stars show at the edges of the sky John is lost, penned in by empty white houses.

In the end he finds it by the noise. Pale pink and blue lights play on the windows, and the house seems to pulse with the beat. The twins are having another party. Well, he thinks, they can't say they were off sick. Against his will, John feels his heart and his feet speed up in time with the music.

He pushes the front door. It swings open. He quickly slips into the cupboard under the stairs. It is dark, which seems safer than the colourful lights. A damp mop tickles his arm, reassuring and real. He peers through the keyhole. The party seems to be well underway. Everyone swaying in the flashing air. But it seems less fun than the party John was at. In the warm glow cast by the drink, he hadn't noticed certain things. A lot of the kids seem to be hurt, or have old scars. One is missing a hand. And they drink and mingle but no one says more than hello to one another. Not like they're shy – as if they know each other too well to bother. Some of the children are dressed really weirdly. One girl wears a voluminous old-fashioned nightgown. A blond boy wears what looks like a three-piece suit. Another wears tights and there are large shiny buckles on his shoes.

The music dies and the lights come up. John thinks, *they know I'm here*, and his breath stops. But their attention is on Drew who stands in the centre of the room.

"It's time," he says.

"How many?" says a small girl in a shimmering white shift.

"Four, today."

The children bow their heads and someone sobs. But no one moves.

"Decide," Drew says, "or I'll choose." When no one moves he goes around the circle and pulls four into the centre. "You made me do it," he snaps at the little girl in the white shift, who has begun to cry.

The four make their way to the stairs in procession, heads lowered. They climb slowly and disappear out of sight, one by one, leaving silence behind them.

"Well, come on," Drew shouts. "Gracious, it's a party!" The music rises, and despite what he has just seen, John's heart begins to pound in time.

"That's how they first get us," says Edmond. "With the parties." He is standing in the cupboard next to John. "If you come once, you have to come back, no matter where or when it is. Time doesn't mean anything to them. Past or future, you have to come. Got to fill the room. Sometimes I hide when it's time to pick. Didn't know you had thought of it, too."

"What will Drew do to them upstairs?" asks John. He feels sick. He has heard of this. Kids lured in by gangs. It's called grooming. And then bad, bad things.

"Her body is old now, it wears out fast," says Edmond. "That's why she needs twins. Matching spare parts. My brother volunteered. She used him first."

Edmond's hair falls aside and John sees that his right eye is missing. Edmond's fingers explore the place where it was.

"Where's Daisy?" whispers John. He couldn't see her out in the party. He hopes she hasn't been taken upstairs. He is afraid for her.

"There isn't much Daisy left," Edmond says. "Not after all this time."

"Don't be weird," John says, frightened.

"Bodies are like houses to Hester," says Edmond. "She finds one she likes and keeps it, until it can no longer be fixed."

John wants Edmond to stop saying mad stuff so he shoves him hard. Edmond does not seem to notice. He is gazing past John at Drew who stands in the open cupboard doorway, golden hair slicked back on his head like an old film star. John sees that one of Drew's ears is missing.

"I hoped you wouldn't return," Drew says to John. "I persuaded her that she didn't need you. I even gave her something, to help her forget."

"You tell me what's going on, right now," John says. He clings to desperate remnants of hope – that all this is a mistake, a misunderstanding, that he is drunk or mad or in a dream.

"What has always gone on," Drew says, patient. "They have always taken children. People used to think they swapped them. Changelings, you know. Maybe that was confusion about the twin thing. They used to keep the children inside hills though, that's true enough. They've moved with the times since then."

All John's anger slides into one channel, hot. He understands that he is being mocked. It's that time outside the off-licence all over again. Everything that has been building since Alice died now fills the depths of him, licks up at the edges. "You think I believe that stuff?" He punches Drew hard in the face. He hears, but doesn't feel, the sharp crack of his knuckles against cartilage. Drew's nose explodes in a mist of red. He falls to the floor. John doesn't see Daisy until her hands are around his neck. Stars bloom and cloud across his vision.

"He's the only one who stood up for you," Daisy hisses in John's ear. "He betrayed Hester, trying to help you get away. You should be on your knees thanking him. But instead you've ruined his nose."

"Now you've done it," Edmond says. He tugs his hair over the gap where his eye should be and backs slowly into the shadows of the cupboard.

Drew looks at John with his ancient blue eyes. John wonders how he ever thought the two of them were the same age. "I tried to keep you out of it, old chap," Drew says. "You're not a twin, anymore, so you aren't useful. You could have lived a long life. But she's out of her hole now."

There is a sound like stone grinding against stone. The lights and the music fade. The children huddle into corners. The room is lit with greenish light. The walls move as John watches. They creak with the pain of growth. New twigs and branches thrust out from their lengths, tender leaves push forth painfully, become dark and glossy, then curl up, brown. A spray of white hawthorn bursts into the air, showering blossom. Everything buds and grows and withers and dies before John's eyes. Time churns at a sickening speed.

"Run," he turns to say to Daisy.

But something has happened to Daisy. Her face has become a hole with children in it. She is made of layer upon layer of time. She is older than anything else in the world. She is made of wood, with a face like a woman trapped screaming in a tree trunk. Then she is John's sister Alice, white and lovely in her grave clothes.

Vines race along the floor like snakes and curl up around the furniture legs, encasing them in sticky green. They flow towards Daisy and she catches them in her hands, strokes them like puppies and croons to them in a high voice. Then they wind their slim fingers around Drew.

"Don't fight it," whispers Daisy. But Drew does. He tears at the vines and shouts a word that sounds like *moksha*. She recoils, her green fingers loosen, only for a moment. Then she has him in her strangling grip once more. She takes his hand as the moss creeps green and living over his face.

"I'm sorry," the thing that was Daisy says.

"No," Drew says, "please!" Her fingers reach into his mouth, now, down his throat, and into him. It is over quickly.

Hester stands. She wears Daisy's body with animal grace. "Let that be a lesson to you all," she says. "Not to test me. Now I am going back upstairs with my new friend John. He's no good for repairs, but I think there is something to be done. He owes me a brother, after all. Come, John."

They go up, hand in hand. Hester drags Drew's corpse behind her and his head hits each step with a *crack*.

* * *

John opens his front door. His mother sits at the table. Moonlight plays in her hair, which is dark again, piled high and bound by a silver coronet. The scent of the garden fills the kitchen, oleander and wisteria are heavy on the air. A pond ripples at her feet. Water lilies open slowly at his glance. A golden fish kisses the sleek surface of the water then sinks back into the deep. A firefly wanders past his nose. John can see it, now – where his mum has been, all this time.

His mother turns to John and smiles. "Isn't it lovely?" she asks.

"Yes," he says. "Lovely, Mum." He squeezes her hand.

The first thing Hester did was take his mother's mind. That happened before he even met Daisy and Drew. There's an order to it. She removes the parents first. He thinks about all the other mothers and fathers sitting alone in their night-gardens, arrested in time and place. Ever since there have been people, there has been Hester. He wonders what the real Daisy was like. He is sure that some of her still lingers in her body, just as there is some John left in this body. No Drew, though. Drew is dead. John does not want to die.

John collects the letters and bills that have piled high on the table in the hall. He will take them to Hester, and they will all be answered and paid, and no one will disturb his mother as she sits in her night-garden. He looks about him and bids the house farewell. He won't be coming back here for some time.

He takes a moment to smooth his shining blond hair in the hall mirror. Even in the moonlight he can see the deep and perfect blue of his eyes. Time to go. He has a big day ahead. He starts his new school tomorrow. John closes the front door behind him, softly.

LISTEN

JEN WILLIAMS

They always knew when she was about to arrive. Erren didn't understand how that worked, but then, she didn't understand much about her life these days.

Gods help them, they were even excited. As Erren reached the outskirts of this newest settlement, she saw a handful of children sitting on a long, meandering fence, their faces bright with interest. When she drew closer, the dust from the long road kicking up little orange clouds around her feet, they began to shout shrill questions at her. Where had she come from? What would she play? Could she play a song that they wanted, if they asked?

Erren nodded at them politely and said very little. They would hear her song soon enough, unfortunately.

She followed the children, who took her to a large mound of a building, built from stone and mud and pitted with small, square windows that were little more than holes. The very top of it was covered in bright green grass and flowers, and a thin stream of grey smoke rose steadily from a hole she couldn't see.

Erren was fairly sure she'd never seen anything like it, but once she was taken inside she realised it was just another tavern, at heart like every other drinking hole she'd ever been inside: the strong smell of beer, the smoky twinkle of a fire.

"So you're the player," said the tavern keeper warmly. "Have you come far?"

Erren chose to ignore this question. They could never understand the answer.

"I'm the player," she agreed. "You'll listen to me?"

Every time she asked, a tiny bit of her hoped they would say no, but no one had yet. Of course they hadn't. The tavern keeper beamed all the wider, crossing her arms under her sizeable chest.

"We'll be glad to," she said. "We don't get much by way of entertainment around here. You'll have most of the village watching I expect, darlin'. Should I make you a space by the fire? How much room do you need?"

"Not much, I only have one set of pipes. But if I could beg some food, first...?"

She had learned to make sure she got fed before she played. It was hard to fight the urge to play; the need was like a hot, dry feeling on the back of her neck, a weight in her fingers, but if she concentrated very hard she could avoid it for around an hour or so. The tavern keeper brought her hot onion soup, good fresh bread and, to Erren's delight, a glass of berry-flavoured rum that reminded her sharply of her own impossibly distant home. But soon enough her fingers began to tingle, and the heat on her neck grew suffocating, like slim hands closing around her throat. She put the bowl and the glass to one side and reached into her pack for the pipes.

While she had been eating, the tavern had gradually filled with patrons until every seat was taken and more were standing, all eyes trained on her. They did not seem surprised by the pipes themselves, but then people rarely were. Erren often wondered if they assumed they were made of an especially pale wood, or a fine clay of some sort. Or perhaps they knew what they were, and didn't care.

Not looking at the men and women gathered – and children, gods help her, children too – she lowered her mouth to the ends of the pipes and gathered her breath.

* * *

When she left, under the grey-pink skies of almost-dawn, all life and warmth seemed to have bled away from the place. Erren hurried towards the gate, her head down, trying to hear only her footsteps on the dusty ground, but somewhere nearby a man was sobbing, a pitiless, despairing sound, and then just as she passed out of the gate, she heard an angry shout, and an answering wail.

But it didn't matter. Her feet were already calling her to her next destination, and she couldn't have stopped, even if she had wanted to.

* * *

The next place was larger, a village clustered on the banks of a river. At some point in her long walk, Erren had passed over a border – there had been wooden signs, painted with sigils that looked half-familiar – and this place was more prosperous. There was a good brick wall made of red clay, and at the edge of the wide river there were lots of small boats tethered; a lively trade was happening there, even at dusk. Erren saw crates of fish being carried away to market, thick rolls of wool being pressed into sacks. She couldn't see a tavern, although she was sure there must be one, so she headed to the little market square, following the ripe smell of river fish. It had been a long walk with no people in sight, and the urge to play now was overwhelming. There would be no food for her tonight, and no rest.

The setting sun had turned the sky a bruised orange by the time she found the little performance area. It was a wide square of flattened dirt, bordered on all sides by colourful bunting on poles, and within it a small, wiry man was standing on a stool while he juggled a set of wooden skittles. A couple of grubby children were watching him, identical expressions of boredom on their faces.

"Can I borrow your stool, friend?" asked Erren. The little man looked affronted, but he plucked his skittles from the air and stepped down onto the dirt.

"It's not my stool," he said, and then, "you won't get anyone listening tonight, girl. It's the wrong season for it, see. Everyone is down at the docks, getting the trade in."

Erren nodded, and sat down anyway. A few moments later the two grubby children were joined by another family and a trio of men dressed like guards. A few more minutes passed, and the crowd grew larger; women with dusty aprons, young girls with their hair tucked up under red caps, old men with thick knuckles. Erren watched them, unsurprised. It was all a part of it. There would always be an audience for her, wherever she went.

Ignoring the rumbling of her stomach, she pulled her pipes from her bag and set them immediately to her lips. She didn't want to look at these people, didn't want to be able to picture their faces later. With the barest exhalation, a series of low, haunting notes floated out across the square. Immediately, the gentle murmur of the audience died away, and an eerie silence fell over the space, broken only by Erren's lilting notes. Now, the music was building, growing more complex – a strange filigree of sounds, more than could have been produced by the breath of a single woman, perhaps – and the hush seemed to be breeding shadows. Despite the warm light of the early evening sky, pools of darkness were building at the feet of her audience, seeping out of the ground like oil. As yet, the people hadn't noticed; they were too busy watching her. Their faces were still, faintly bemused, as if they didn't understand what they were hearing.

Erren's fingers flew over the tiny holes in the pipes, teasing out new sounds, darker ones. At the back of the crowd, a baby began to cry.

"What is happening?" someone said, but their voice was thick, slurred almost, as if they had just woken from a deep sleep. The shadows around the audience's feet had bled together into one thing, becoming a kind of wide, dark stage between Erren and them. It was another thing Erren did not like to look at – that darkness was too flat, too unnatural under the good, sun-touched sky.

It was at that moment the first of the figures appeared. A bulge formed in the flat black stage, a crown pushing through to reveal a small, neat head. The girl had long, reddish hair, and she lifted her face up to the sky as if she had missed it, her thin lips parting to reveal small, yellowish teeth. Her skin was grey, and her eyes were empty sockets.

"What— What is..." The voice from the audience rose for a moment, struggling against the silence that had fallen over them, then fell silent again. The girl rose fully from the darkness and started to dance, twirling her arms around to the music, spinning on the spot. She danced as a child danced, and Erren guessed that she had likely been around nine years old, when she lived. Her dress was a drab brown thing but her feet were quick, and Erren thought it was possible she was even enjoying herself – she liked to tell herself that, when the nights were especially dark.

"Lizbet?" A woman with strawberry-blonde hair pushed abruptly to the front of the crowd, half-falling to her knees. "Gods help me. *Lizbet?*"

The music played on and another figure was rising from the

black. This one came faster, as if he couldn't wait to be free of the shadows; it was an old man, so painfully skinny that even Erren was shocked, despite everything she'd seen. Bones poked at skin that was a darker grey than the girl's, and his knees looked swollen and strange, too large for the sticks they were supporting. Just like the girl, he had dark holes where his eyes should be. Despite all that he danced, his elbows thrust out and his chin held up. Meanwhile, the woman at the edge of the audience had shuffled forward, her arms stretched out towards the dancing girl, not quite daring to touch the black stage that lay between them.

"Lizbet, my sweet? What… What's happening? Have you come back to us?"

The girl stopped dancing so abruptly it was as though she'd been struck. Her arms fell down to her sides, and she turned to the crowd, looking at them for the first time – or at least, her face was turned to them; she had no eyes to look at anyone. Erren's fingers kept moving over the pipes, and the music kept coming. There was no stopping now.

"Mother." Her voice was thin and reedy, a voice heard on the wind, half-imagined. "Did I like to climb?"

The woman lowered her arms. Behind the girl, the dead old man was still turning a jig, his long teeth bared at the sky.

"I… No, sweetheart. You liked to sit with your dolls, to talk to them. You didn't like to get your dress dirty." The woman's voice broke, and Erren saw that there were tears pouring down her cheeks. "You were a sweet girl, my little flower girl."

"Then why was I on that wall, Mother? Why was I up there at all?" She turned her head slightly, as if to address the slim, blond-haired figure standing next to her mother. The boy was rigidly still, all colour having drained from his face. "Perhaps you should ask Willem."

The woman's face seemed to collapse, and she turned to the boy next to her, but the girl was off dancing again, her slim grey arms turning and turning. By this time other figures were rising up through the dark, their eyeless faces tilted upwards to greet the evening sky, and the crowd were beginning to cry out, a desperate moaning noise, like children caught in a nightmare. One large man with broad shoulders and an unshaven face pushed his way angrily to the front.

"What's going on here?" bellowed the man, pointing a meaty finger in Erren's direction. "What are you bloody playing at with this… this abomination?"

Erren kept her head down and continued to play. The skinny old man, though, the one who had followed Lizbet out of the dark, turned to the large man.

"Abomination? A big word from you, Samuel, a very big word."

The man – Samuel, Erren assumed – curled his hands into fists, his face turning brick red.

"Shut up! You're not supposed—"

"My lad there, my Samuel," the skinny dead man raised his hands, fingers splayed, as if addressing the whole audience. "When I got ill, too ill to walk, to feed myself, he locked me in his backroom and let me starve. Left me to piss and shit myself, yes he did, until I died, starving and covered in filth." His grey lips peeled back in what Erren supposed might have been a smile. "Good, brave Samuel. All you kind neighbours who brought round stew and potatoes and bread for me? He ate it all himself. Yes he did. And when my cries became too bothersome, he tore up strips of cloth and stuffed them in his ears. I ask you, good people, who is the real abomination here?"

A muttering of anger from the crowd.

There were more. More dead men and women and children rose, and with each of them, a handful of painful secrets, devastating truths. The audience – their families, their friends – were unable to leave, rooted to the spot until each of the dead had been granted their say. Erren played all through the long night, her fingers and chest aching and her limbs cold, until eventually the dark stage gave up its last ghost, and as one they all began to fade with the rising sun. It wasn't over for the living though; already, fights had broken out, punctuated with screaming arguments and tearful confessions, and revenge had been sworn half-a-dozen times already.

When it was done, Erren stood up, wincing at the flood of tingling in her numb feet and legs, and shoved the pipes back into her pack. It was time to move on.

* * *

It was days until the next settlement, and finally she came to a clearing in a forest where she felt she could stop. Shaking with fatigue, Erren built a fire with the first twigs that came to hand, and soon she had a smoky flame going – enough to heat up some water, drink a small cup of something hot. In her pack were a few strips of dried meat, and she dunked these in the water until they were soft enough to chew. She sat mindlessly, staring at nothing. After a while, the shady clearing grew lighter. Soft yellow motes of light floated down from the tree-tops, and a warmth began to crawl across the mulchy ground. Erren squeezed her eyes shut briefly.

"No. Leave me alone. Isn't what you did to me enough?"

The light grew brighter, the movement of the motes more frantic, until a figure stepped out of it. She was tall, and achingly beautiful. Her skin was as green as a new leaf in spring, and a pair of curling horns sprouted from her forehead.

"I like to see how you're getting on, Erren."

"It's the same as it ever is," she said. "I go to these places, I play for them, and they suffer. They hurt each other, because of what I show them."

"All these little human cruelties." The horned woman nodded, seemingly pleased. "There's just so much of it, isn't there? How do you feel, when you see what they've done? All these normal people, capable of such awful things."

Erren didn't answer. Instead she was looking down at her hands.

"Let me see him," the horned woman said, her tone suddenly more serious. Erren, who could no more have dis-obeyed her than she could have flown up into the sky like a bird, removed the pipes from the pack and held them up. The green woman went to take them, then changed her mind. She stepped away instead, like an animal jumping back from an incoming blow, and Erren felt her own shame deepen despite her anger.

"I'm sorry," she said.

"Sorry? What use is that to me?" The woman shook her head slightly, and Erren put the pipes away again. "You didn't need any more meat, hunter. Not that day. Your pack was *full*."

"I know." It was a conversation they had had many times before. "But it was the most beautiful deer I had ever seen. I had to take it."

"You see something beautiful and you kill it." The horned woman looked at her now, and her eyes – yellow, like an unripe apple – were bright with anger. "I will show you what death means, mortal. What cruelty means."

"Then kill me." She forced herself to meet the horned woman's furious gaze. She wanted to stand, to face her directly, but she was afraid her legs wouldn't hold her after so many days of walking. "Bring this to an end."

"I will not kill you." She paused, then recited the old curse: "*The dead shall dance, wherever you go, and the living shall never harm you.* I can't kill you, Erren Keeneye, even if I wanted to."

"But you're not mortal!" Erren did stand up then, knocking over her tin cup of hot water. "You're a god! You can do whatever you like."

"A wood-spirit is all I am, hunter. More than you'll ever be, that's true, but an untouchable god?" She gestured tersely to Erren's pack, where the pipes lay hidden again. "My brother died easily enough, did he not? An arrow in his heart."

Erren had nothing to say to that. The horned woman walked away from her, and her light faded into the soft shades of twilight.

* * *

Days crumbled into months. The moon grew fat and thin again, over and over, and the seasons ceased to make any sense, winter tumbling into summer, spring leaping into autumn, and back again. Erren walked and around her the world changed, yet her skin stayed smooth and her limbs remained strong. She ached all the time, but it was the deep, familiar ache of work, something she remembered keenly from her days spent as a hunter in the woods, not the ache of the infirm or the ageing. The living couldn't touch her, and neither, it seemed, could life.

And the world changed. She passed over the remnants of battlefields, where the armour had yet to rust and the carrion birds were still enjoying themselves. The ghosts in the settlements near these places were rowdy and loud, full of their battle-rage and all the injustice of war. Buildings grew taller, more beautiful; she saw towers that seemed to pierce the sky, as thin as needles, and vast arenas where men and women raced in chariots. Wild woods and rocky landscapes gave way to cultivated fields and orchards, and on the people she saw clothes of all colours, fine silks and embroidery, gems and precious metals on fingers, at throats. Weapons, too, were changing: brittle swords became hardened steel, became impossibly lethal blades of a white metal she couldn't name.

In the next settlement she came to, Erren played in a handsome hall with six fireplaces, each taller than her. She travelled across the sea and played for the captain of the ship; men and women rose up through the darkness with seaweed in their hair and eels nestled in their eye sockets. On an entirely new continent, she played her pipes within a ring of huge standing stones the colour of tree bark, and the people there reminded her of the horned woman; their eyes were too bright, and they were tall and long limbed. They were a beautiful people, yet when their dead rose up through the shadows their faces turned ugly, frightened and filled with fury. They drew silver knives and stabbed each other.

Deep inside a mountain, Erren played her music for people who seemed half-rock to her. Their faces were mottled like marble, and all of them, down to the smallest children, carried pickaxes on their belts. When the dead had finished their dancing, the fight that came after was as brutal as Erren had ever seen, and when she finally left that place, dragging herself out of a tunnel, she washed her face and hands in the snow and watched the white turn to pink with the blood of others. When that was done, she began to make her way back down the incline only to fall by the side of the path, her stomach abruptly emptying itself. The blood, and the smoke, the screaming…

"It's too much!" She slumped against a boulder. It was freezing on the side of the mountain, but it didn't matter. It couldn't kill her. "I can't go any further. I just can't."

"But you must, and you will." A patch of warm sunlight to her left, and the horned woman was there. She stood close to her, looking down with an expression on her face that Erren hadn't seen before. "Those are the terms of the curse you are under. To play forever."

"How long has it been?" she asked, then swallowed. She was frightened of how broken her voice sounded. "Can you tell me that?"

"You mean, what small section of forever have you completed? Do you think knowing that would help you?" The forest spirit was frowning slightly, her hands held awkwardly behind her back.

"What of my family then? Everyone I left behind. What has happened to them?"

"Erren Keeneye, everyone you ever knew passed out of this world a very long time ago. I think that in your heart, you knew that already."

Erren dropped her head. There was a time when she had been too proud to cry in front of the horned woman, but that time had also passed. Sobs forced their way up through her throat. Inside she felt herself inch closer to a deep black pit, and she reached towards it eagerly; it would be a relief to lose herself in that darkness, even temporarily.

"I shouldn't be here," Erren said eventually. "Even you must be able to see that. My time has gone. I don't recognise this world anymore. Everything has changed so much. Surely this goes beyond the kind of punishment you imagined when you put this compulsion on me?"

The horned woman stepped back from her. Green and filled with her own summer light, she looked especially unreal against the grey and white and brown of the mountain. For the first time, she looked uncomfortable.

"I can't release you from it, Erren," she said. Her voice carried to the hunter easily, despite the howling winds. "I am a mortal, living thing, bound to this world as you are, and I can't raise a hand against you. Nor can I take the curse from you."

"Then why do you keep coming to see me?" Erren rubbed viciously at the hot tears on her cheeks, suddenly furious. The forest spirit opened her mouth to speak, so she spoke over her. "You've told me so many times that I didn't understand what I was doing when I killed your brother, that I didn't realise the full impact of my actions. Well, I don't think you did, either, when you made this curse. When you forced me to make those pipes out of your brother's bones, were you really thinking of *this*?" Erren gestured at the blood-stained snow.

But when she turned back to the woman, she had vanished. The small patch of snow where her feet had been was a puddle of water. Erren glared at it, and pulled her pack back on her shoulders. It was time to move again.

* * *

The years passed, and Erren became reckless. When she had time to eat, she requested the strongest alcohol from her hosts, and drank as much as she could before the urge to begin playing the pipes overwhelmed her. She shouted warnings to her audience as they gathered – though they were ignored – and when fights happened after she played, she ran into the midst of them for as long as she could, hoping that a stray axe would strike her down. But nothing did. Blades, arrows, bolts and, eventually, bullets, all found ways around her, as though she existed in a cocoon of safety.

On one evening, late in the latest of a thousand summers, she played her pipes under a full moon in an exquisite palatial garden. The place was filled with night-blooming flowers, and people crushed in from all sides to see her, their faces lit with pastel light from the colourful paper lanterns strewn in all corners. From what she had gathered, the palace belonged to a young prince and his most favoured cousins, who sat in gilded chairs just opposite her.

"Play on then!" called the young prince, half-laughing to the cousin on his right. "I've been told your music is the greatest this world has ever seen."

The reedy sound of the pipe music floated out across the garden, and the grass turned black, so thick with shadows it was like looking into a void. One by one, figures emerged, their faces turned up to the starlight, and each one of them was a young woman. They danced together for a while, their grey limbs moving gracefully across the dark. Erren found herself moved by it, by their carefully spaced steps, and the way they reached for each other's hands. Eventually, when the crowd had grown restless, they all turned as one to look at the young prince with their sightless eyes.

One at the front spoke for them. "We all came to this palace as servants. We all met our ends in the secret rooms here. The prince speaks sweetly, and promises much, but he has the appetites of a beast."

There was an uproar. Erren stood, shoving her pipes away into her pack even as a number of armed guards swarmed from the inner palace gates. The prince had evidently invited the common people of his lands to the gardens, and it was these people who had given up their daughters to him, again and again. From the speed of their outrage, Erren thought they must have suspected the prince of his crimes for many years, but had never quite had the courage to confront him with it. Her dancing ghosts had finally given them the push they needed.

On her way out, taking the quieter paths back down towards the city, she saw the prince again. His clothes were torn and his nose was bloody. He had been separated from his guards somehow.

"You! Bard. Take me down through the city, smuggle me out. I will pay you well for it, woman."

She looked at him. From the way he crouched he was clearly frightened, yet the look he gave her was direct, confident. As far as he was concerned, there was no way she would disobey him.

"You value no life but your own," she told him. "You saw something beautiful, and you had to spoil it. And now justice has caught up with you." She raised her voice to call to the crowds still up in the gardens. "He's down here! He's alone! Come and get him."

As she walked away down through the quiet paths to the city, she looked back once to see the pastel lights of the paper lanterns, and the horned woman was there, an eerie beacon in the dark. She was watching Erren, and for the strangest moment she wanted to raise a hand to the wood-spirit – to acknowledge her in some way. But instead Erren turned her back and walked on into the night.

* * *

For a long time, Erren walked and walked and found no people at all. There were long stretches of grasslands, endless purple hills, deep forests where mushrooms grew as tall as trees; all of it passed her by without her hearing another human voice. For the very first time in her long life, she began to wonder if she might be lost, but the sense of following a path never left her, and so she kept moving, her eyes scanning the horizon for chimney smoke or the familiar structures of men.

She came to a place where the earth appeared to have been split in two. Huge cliffs of shining black stone rose to either side of her, and the ground under her feet was a dense layer of brittle yellowed rocks – when she looked at them more closely, she saw that they were bones, the skulls of millions of tiny animals. The chasm led down into the centre of the world, deeper and deeper until the sky above her turned blue-black and was pierced with strange, multi-coloured stars. Time – always an unreliable companion on her journey – seemed to come untethered entirely, and she couldn't have said how long she spent in the chasm. Years, certainly. Centuries? It seemed very possible.

"Where are you sending me?"

The horned woman never answered.

Eventually, she emerged into a vast throne room filled with pools of water as dark as wine. All around the vast space, men and women stood talking quietly, or playing musical instruments. Except that Erren knew immediately that these were not people such as she knew them; each was twice her height, and they glowed with their own interior light. Some of them had the heads of animals, and one man with a long, golden beard had a pair of eagle's wings sprouting straight out of his back. They watched her come with eyes that looked emptier than those of the dead.

"Well?" the winged-god thundered. "You have come all this way. Will you play, or not?"

Erren hesitated. The urge to play was as strong as it had ever been, but it seemed absurd to drag her old bone pipes from her pack when she could see harps made of gold, a flute that shone the colour of moonlight. The music of the gods teased her, made her feel drunk. *I'm not supposed to be here*, she thought again.

But she couldn't resist forever. She sat down in front of them and began to play. The darkness came, as it ever did, and slowly, slowly, new figures began to rise out of the shadows. They were as fearsome as the gods who watched them, vast figures with golden skin, with ebony skin, with faces so beautiful it was difficult to look at them. They danced, solemnly and without the joy that came so naturally to humans, and one by one, their stories came.

The hero who journeyed home from a decade-long war, only to find that the woman he had married had been bewitched, and opened her bed – and their kingdom – to another god.

The goddess who had given her own heart to save her son, only for the witch-god to burn it, gaining all her power.

The children who had been eaten by the all-father, one by one, lest they rise up one day and defeat him.

All of the betrayals, the murders, the violations, all of them were trotted out, and even the gods had to sit and listen to them all. Erren watched them over the top of her pipes, and saw the furious looks that passed between them, the slow draining of colour from certain faces. When it was over, the man with the eagle wings looked down at her. His feathers were turning black.

"We have been at peace for centuries, woman, and you've brought us war on the notes of a beggar's pipe. Do you think you'll leave here alive?"

Erren laughed. It felt strange in her mouth, a fruit she hadn't tasted before.

"No mortal can kill me," she said.

"What do you think we *are*?" answered the winged-man.

* * *

It was quick, at least.

There was a sensation of movement, a feeling of falling and a quick burst of pain across her chest. The next moment, Erren was some feet away, looking down at her own crumpled body. The winged-god was already stepping over her, summoning a vortex of shimmering light into his outstretched hand. He had his eyes on a man on the other side of a marble pool, who was raising his own trident. The gods were dropping their instruments and reaching for swords and axes.

A soft voice at her elbow. "So, it's over then."

The green woman was there with her. Erren wasn't surprised to see her.

"Finally." The relief was so large it was difficult to comprehend. Instead she looked up at the sky. The huge stars that boiled there, blue and green and red, were gradually winking out of existence. A giant wolf, bigger than anything she had ever seen, was eating the moon. "What is happening?"

"Just the end of all things. Shall we leave? I can take you far from here, if you wish."

Erren nodded, and took the horned woman's hand. It was cool against her skin. "Somewhere quiet, I think. No music, and no dancing."

"Oh I think I can guarantee it."

Above them, the sky quietly tore itself to pieces.

HENRY AND THE SNAKEWOOD BOX

M.R. CAREY

I was sitting in the window of a charity shop in East Barnet when Henry Mossop wandered by. I was not particularly well placed. The assistant (clueless little puke-stain that he was) had wedged me into a corner, between an eye-wateringly ugly vase and a plate commemorating the wedding of Prince Charles and Lady Diana Spencer.

I didn't give Henry a second glance as he lumbered into view. He wasn't the kind of person who invited second glances. He was basically a random jumble of limbs with a head the shape of a turnip. Greasy black hair like some kind of mycelial growth. Clothes that belonged together, but only on a bonfire.

Second glance or not, though, Henry was a receptive soul, and fortunately he lingered long enough for me to make contact. I think it was the plate that caught his eye at first – not because he was a royalist, but because he was a romantic. He got all misty-eyed, and he leaned in so close his breath fogged up the outside of the glass. You just know he had "Candle in the Wind" playing in 5.1 surround sound in the ideal theatre of his mind.

I went around to the back of that theatre, found the fire door, jimmied it open and slipped inside. It took about ten seconds, all told. What can I say? I'm good at this stuff.

Hey, Henry, I said. *Hey. Look. Down here. Track left from the plate until you hit the… no, no, you went too far. Back to the right a bit. Little more. Perfect. Hi there.*

In spite of this greeting, which was quite verbose by my standards and very circumstantial, Henry looked around in case I was talking to someone else who was standing behind him.

No, I said. *You. I'm talking to you. Jesus! Henry, I used your actual name.*

"Sorry."

Forget it. Just, you know, focus a little. This is important.

"Um… How come you can talk?" Henry asked.

I talk the same way you do. Well, not the exact same way. I don't have a mouth, obviously. But I form concepts in my mind using words as semantic counters, and string them together into intelligible statements.

"But you're a box!"

No, I'm really not. Common misconception. I look like a box, but really I'm a… you know, I'd prefer we leave the nuts and bolts stuff off to one side just for now. I was about to put a proposition to you.

Henry scratched his head, the immemorial gesture of the comically bemused. "A what?"

Proposition. Bargain. Offer. Deal. Chance of a lifetime, et cetera.

Slightly Faustian, but still good. Well, good's a slippery concept, but compared to most of these arrangements, I'm offering you the golden ticket.

Henry clung to one of the few words he'd understood, and parsed it as best he could. "A special offer?"

Yes, Henry. That. Exactly. A very, very special offer.

"What is it, then?"

Wishes.

"Wishes?"

Absolutely. You want money? Sex? A free Netflix subscription? More sex? Superpowers? Kinky sex? Whatever it is that gets your endorphins flooding, I can supply it. In frankly ridiculous abundance.

Henry thought about this. For a value of the word "thought", anyway. He wasn't exactly a championship contender at that particular activity. "Are you a fairy?" he asked.

Holy shit, I thought. This is the motherlode. But my terms and conditions are strict. I'm not allowed to lie. *No, Henry. Not a fairy, exactly. Kind of like that, but… yeah, not like that at all. Different. Very different. Chalk and cheese.*

Henry gave me a suspicious look. A look that said he wasn't the kind of man who gets taken in by talking boxes with slick sales pitches and dodgy credentials. "What are you, then?" he asked.

And since he'd asked, I had to answer. *I'm a demon.*

That's make-or-break for some people. Henry could have just taken to his heels and fled, and I would have had to let him go. You can't force these things. Especially when your material extrusion has been locked into the shape of a snakewood box with a hen and chicks painted (quite badly) on the lid. I'm not equipped for high-speed chases. Not on this plane. If you were to meet me on the fields of Tartarus, that would be a different thing entirely. And the meeting would be brief.

But Henry didn't run. He just nodded. His vacant expression didn't change.

Informed consent is important in these matters, so I tried again. *A demon*, I said. *You know. As in devil. Imp. Hellspawn. That kind of number.*

"Okay. But you grant wishes the same way a fairy does."

I do. Better than a fairy, even. Our current package includes unlimited wishes. The normal ceiling of three is waived for premier wish-makers like yourself. You can even wish for more wishes, although with a baseline of infinity you've probably got all you need. We've also removed the temporary restriction on timeline-altering wishes. You can mess with causality all you like.

Henry clapped his hands together. His innocent face was suffused with growing excitement. "A fairy in a box!" he said. "So cool! So cool!"

Demon. So let's seal the deal, Henry. Go on into the shop and buy me. I'm four pounds ninety-nine, but you can recoup that immediately by wishing for it back. I wouldn't want you to be out of pocket here. Go on.

The word "pocket" – a good, old-fashioned noun denoting a physical thing – got a reaction at last. Henry searched his various pockets for notes and coins, eventually coming up with a sizeable heap. "Is this enough?" he asked.

Yes, Henry. That's thirty-five and some odd change. Just give the nice lady the blue one there, on the top, and she'll give you back a penny. Plus me. Oh, but Henry, before you complete the purchase…

He was just about to enter the shop. He stopped. "Yeah?"

I'm a demon, but I'm not Maxwell's demon. You feel me?

He shook his head. "Uh-uh."

Well, okay then, we'll cover that part later. Do what you need to do, man. Let's make this happen.

And we did. I was proud of the little guy. He negotiated the transaction without a hitch, and was even given a plastic bag to carry me home in. Technically that should have cost an additional 5p, but the woman behind the counter saw no reason to press the point. She was sorry for Henry, seeing him as someone intrinsically harmless and basically adrift on the currents of life. The same assessment I'd made, essentially, but whereas I wanted to form a parasitic attachment to him in order to exploit that naivety for my own unspeakable ends, she just felt a little motherly. I guess it would be a boring world if we were all the same.

Once we were back at Henry's place, I encouraged him to take a test drive, as it were. *Something small*, I said. *To make sure it works.* Okay, Henry said. He screwed his eyes tight shut and wished for a goldfish. A nanosecond later, there it was, swimming its little heart out. Henry hadn't wished for a tank or water, but I threw those in anyway – along with some sand and rocks to cover the bottom, a blue LED strip to provide a little atmosphere and a filtration pump shaped like a

Spanish galleon. I could have just let the goldfish gasp out its last unavailing breaths on the linoleum – the literal-minded jobsworth gambit, as we call it – but that stuff is for losers. I mean it's fun up front, in a dopey slapstick kind of way, but it makes for diminishing returns. I wanted Henry to trust me, or at least to trust the process. To feel like he could go for gold.

Meanwhile, a couple of continents away, an Indian textile worker's bike lost a wheel on a downward stretch. The poor guy face-planted in the road and a car went over him before he could stop. A real mess, I can tell you.

Oblivious of this compelling human drama, Henry gave a little warble of glee. "I'll call him Goldy!" he said.

You can call him Ivan the fucking Terrible for all I care, I thought. Just keep the wishes coming.

Which he did. As I'd hoped, that first demo, modest as it was, was enough to prime the pump. In short order, Henry wished for a second goldfish, an OLED television, a recliner armchair facing said television, two more goldfish, a DVD collection of the works of Oliver Postgate (*Noggin the Nog*, *The Clangers*, *Bagpuss*, all the greats) and a meal of sausages and chips followed by Ambrosia creamed rice. Oh, and some money. Enough to live on, he said, which I interpreted liberally. He'd been laid off some months before from his job (insert air quotes) cleaning the toilets at the Spires mini-mall, and was as near to destitution as made no difference.

This was still small stuff, to be sure, but small stuff can have big effects if you get the leverage right. A fuse blows in a Cape

Town suburb. In the darkness someone trips and screams. A rock shatters a window. Before you know where you are, you're knee-deep in collateral damage. I've done this stuff before, in case that wasn't clear.

I got to know Henry pretty well, during this time. After all, we were housemates. Living under the same roof, sharing all of life's hurly-burly in a way that would make an excellent TV sitcom. I learned about his no-good father (abusive, then abominable, then absent), the shit he took from sociopathic schoolmates, his mother's untimely... I'll spare you. It was as boring as it sounds. The guy was a punchbag with a face. Good raw material, terrible company. I suffer for my art, is all I'll say on that score.

But now we were really gathering momentum. You always do, with unlimited wishes. The whole three-and-you're-done deal was intended to land your wish-maker in a mess of unintended consequences and leave them there. Small potatoes, for a simpler time. Once we got our heads around the fine print in the laws of thermodynamics, we redefined our goals.

Not that Henry was straining at the leash, exactly. Far from it. He needed a lot of nudging and coaxing along the way. *So, Henry,* I said, about three days in. *Tell me something.*

"Yes, box?"

This is a big house for just one guy. Have you always lived here by yourself?

"No, my mum used to live here with me."

Got you. Wow, was it tough on you when she died?

"I missed her lots. I still do. She always looked after me."

I'm sure.

"I had a dog, too. Her name was Princess." His eyes went wide. "Oh!" he said. "Oh!"

What?

"I could… I could wish for…"

Anything, man. Anything at all. Do it to it.

It came out all in a rush. "I wish Princess was alive again!"

I would have preferred the mother, frankly, and that was what I was angling for. More energy to play with, because a human timeline is a bigger, more complicated thing. But a dog's better than nothing. Princess appeared in the middle of the living room, tail going like a hairy metronome set to *prestissimo*, and bounded into Henry's lap.

Elsewhere, at the same time and not coincidentally, a sinkhole swallowed a house in Buenos Aires. I'd been meaning to do that for a while. The guy in the house was kind of a secular saint, with a limpidly beautiful, giving soul, and he pissed me the hell off.

Much more importantly, Henry's wish had opened up the alternate timeline window. I reached back into the past and tweaked a few things – most notably the *Ermächtigungsgesetz* in the German Reichstag in 1933, which now passed handsomely instead of failing by one vote. Abracadabra! A world war that hadn't happened now suddenly had. The bad guys lost, but they got in some sick licks before they went down and the ripples didn't stop for decades. I was on a roll.

Henry may have been slower than treacle on an ice shelf, but he was starting to see at least some of the endless possibilities. If he could have his dog back, he could have some of the other comforts of yesteryear too. He still fought shy of bringing Mummy back from the dead. Maybe he'd caught a re-run of "The Monkey's Paw" on *Thirty-Minute Theatre* when he was a kid, and it had left him with a vestigial sense of how badly wrong that transaction might go. But he could and did wish for lost toys, dead pets and the snows of fucking yesteryear. The dead pets in particular were a trial to me. The house was full of dogs, cats, hamsters and budgerigars, some of which had severe toilet-training problems and no respect at all for my mid-gloss finish.

But I endured all this with a philosophical patience. The flipside was mine, and the sky was now the limit. Literally. I filled it up with greenhouse gases, flipping the whole world onto a timeline where they'd discovered renewable energy very late and mostly ignored it. The biosphere was taking a pounding, extreme weather events were happening every other day, and the fun was only just getting started.

At the same time, I advanced the careers of bigots, hate-mongers and rabble-rousers, giving them the platforms they needed to spread their messages in a mainstream context. Rational discourse went out of style, and out of the window. Facts became an irrelevance. Hucksters and charlatans were revered as gods. It was a whole thing.

Maybe I overplayed my hand a little. I thought Henry was too lost in his ever-growing menagerie even to notice the state of the world. But one morning I noticed him looking out of the window with what is sometimes called a corrugated brow. Corrugated cardboard, in Henry's case.

What's the matter, champ? I asked him.

"Everyone's so unhappy, box."

Human condition. Don't worry about it.

"But they're more unhappy than they used to be."

Not good, I thought. Not good at all. Better find some way to change the subject before…

"Why, box? Why are they so unhappy?"

Too late. Now he'd asked, I didn't have a choice. Terms and conditions, et cetera. Under the geas, under the thumb. Fortunately, I reflected, the Brainless Wonder here was not remotely equipped for this ride. He just did not have the cognitive kit.

Well, I said, *here's the thing, Henry. You remember when we first met? I told you I was a demon.*

"I remember."

But I also said that I wasn't Maxwell's demon. That was me trying to find a simple way of expressing a fairly difficult concept. It's about entropy, and while I'm happy to try to explain I seriously doubt you'll understand a word of it.

"Tell me!"

Okay, then. Sit down and pin your ears back, man. Give it your best shot.

Henry did his best to look attentive. He looked ridiculous.

Maxwell was just this guy, you know? Physicist. Mathematician. Serious public masturbator, but that's by the by. Nobody ever caught him at it. Anyway, he got interested in the second law of thermodynamics. The one that says things fall apart, and no take-backs.

Maxwell tried to come up with a take-back. Wanking never comes to good, in my experience. Or even when it does, it leaves a mess. Come to think of it, that's as good an example of the second law of thermodynamics as any. In a closed system, entropy – disorder, dysfunction, mess – must always increase. It's not an accident that the stars burn out and the quarks stop twitching and your freezer rolls over and dies in a heatwave. It's the nature of things. It's built-in.

But hey, Maxwell says. Let's posit a box, with two compartments. Atoms zinging around every which way. A turbulent system. A shit-storm. Like your bedroom, Henry, only without the one-eyed teddy bear. Or leave the bear in the mix, if that helps. It's just a thought experiment.

And now let's posit a trapdoor, in the middle of the box. In the wall that separates the two compartments. And a demon, sitting right next to the trapdoor, with his little clawed hand on the doorknob. He can be holding your teddy bear, if you like. Whenever an atom zings past this little guy, he chooses whether or not to let it through. If it's quick – and therefore hot – he opens the door. If it's slow, and cold, he cold-shoulders it. Door stays shut.

And so, over time, atom by atom, the box sorts itself out. One half of it gets hot, the other cools down.

"Why does that matter?" Henry asked.

I was surprised. That sounded like a pertinent question. Spooky. Just an accident, though, surely.

It matters, Henry, because entropy has decreased. Order has been created, with no expenditure of energy. It's magic, kind of. A friendly miracle. It means the universe doesn't have to end up as a frozen, unavailing slab of shit-fuck-all. There's a chance it might work out okay after all.

But – stay with me, Henry – I'm not that demon. I'm a different kind of demon altogether. I like entropy. Fuck, I am all about that stuff. You could say I'm an entropy factory. Where Maxwell's demon dusts the ornaments on the sideboard and puts out the milk bottles, I take a meat cleaver to the sideboard and use the milk bottles for Molotovs. You follow?

Henry frowned hard, like he was seriously trying to. "No."

Well, that was a relief. A yes would have worried me a lot.

Well look, Henry, I said. I grant wishes, right? That, in a way, is anti-entropic. Or it could be. It reorganises the universe in line with the desires of one of its current inmates, which increases order. Admittedly, that's a gift that's usually squandered on trifles. But it's a fucking awesome thing, intrinsically. Who wouldn't want a piece of that action? You can see why people sign up. But the recoil is a killer.

"What's recoil?" Henry asked, with the same look of intellectual constipation.

Like, from a gun, Henry. When you shoot a gun, and you go over on your back. Because the energy that pushes that tiny little bullet a thousand yards is more than enough to push a much bigger object – you – into a hilarious somersault that lands you on your arse-bone. I do that. Only I do it better. Every time I grant a wish, I throw out a curse. And the curse is about a thousand times bigger than the wish was. I use the probabilistic power loosened by the wish to mess with the whole world on a scale that – no, I shouldn't boast, but it's good stuff. Which is to say, bad stuff. Bad stuff that gets me off.

It was a long speech. I made it long on purpose, knowing that Henry's attention span was short. But after I was finished,

I could tell by the way the muscles of his face kept moving that he was trying to have a thought.

Don't sweat it, Henry, I said. *Please don't. You know what Oscar Wilde said. Ignorance is like a delicate exotic fruit. Touch it and it's fucked to shit.*

"But…" Henry said.

No, man, no. Don't do this to yourself. Just wish for something really nice, and let your brain drift off again. You can never have too many puppies, right?

"No, but…"

Bu-bu-bu-bu-baa-baa-baaaaa! Let's focus on what we do best. What would make you happy right now? Tell me, and I'm all over it.

"But if making me happy makes everyone else sad…"

Shit! I'd broken Henry. How was that even possible? He was a one-piece moulding in high-impact stupid.

No, I insisted. *Henry. Listen to me. Unhappiness is the human condition. These people, if you don't make them miserable, they feel like they're missing out. And if it isn't this, trust me, it's just gonna be something else. Hey, remember the little fuckers who tortured you at school? Well, multiply them by a billion and that's the human race. You don't owe them anything, except maybe a little payback.*

Henry shook his head. Meaning he had the temerity and hitherto unsuspected balls to disagree with me. "My mum said you've got to reach out and help a stranger in need. She said we're put here in this world to be good to each other."

Did she now? Wow! Quite the shitheap philosopher, your mum. Now let's go along to get along. Make a wish. A nice big one. What do you say?

Henry didn't answer. He had a face on him like a mule with a thistle up its crack.

Henry, I insisted. *You've got to make a wish, man. You'll feel better for it, and so will I.*

More mule/thistle musings followed. I was about to intervene, when Henry beat me to the draw.

"I wish—"

Finally! You had me worried there, champ. Let's hear it.

"I wish I was smart enough to understand everything you just told me."

Well, shit.

It's not a conditional thing, in case you were going to ask. You can't just grant this wish and then filter out that other one. The system's not designed that way. The defaults kick in, and the energy flows. A million tiny cogwheels turn. Reality shifts into a new shape, with a lot of creaking and clanking and the occasional hiss of escaping probability.

Understanding suffused Henry's face. It wasn't pretty.

"You used me," he said.

That's an insulting way of putting it, Henry. We used each other, surely. I got to tilt the world on its axis, you got puppies. But if you're not happy with the deal, we can end it at any time. Right now, even. Your call.

"You gave me trivial gifts, and syphoned off... what, the existential residue? Then you used that power to make life significantly and irreversibly worse for millions of people."

Billions, I think you mean. I like that phrase, existential residue.

That's a neat way of putting it. Again, we can annul our bargain at any time, and there won't be any hard feelings on my side. What do you say? Go our separate ways?

"No."

Again, shit. Henry's boosted brain was taking aim, and I was in the crosshairs. There was a reason why I'd chosen him in the first place. He was – what's that phrase of Lenin's? Oh yeah, a useful idiot. And now he was standing there having deep thoughts. Right at me. I didn't like it one bit.

"So a wish that creates a small increase in happiness for one person creates a recoil effect – a curse – that causes misery for millions."

And now I can see that doesn't work for you. Respect. Say the word, Henry, and I'm out of here.

"Would that work the other way? If I made a wish that caused me pain, would the recoil be a general increase in happiness?"

Shit, for the third and last time.

Yes, I said. I couldn't lie. Couldn't hide it. He'd found my kryptonite.

Henry sat down. He stared at the snakewood box that is my material extension. He ran his finger along the forward edge of my lid.

"Settle in," he told me. "It's going to be a long night."

He wasn't kidding. It *was* a long night, a long morning, a long week, a long… Things have gotten long. Let's leave it at that.

My relationship with Henry has never been the same since that terrible, fucked-up day. I mean, it has its upsides. I get to roast the smart-arsed little bastard alive, in both figurative and literal ways. Whenever my rooted dislike of him, and the things he's making me do, gets to be too much, I can take out every ounce of my frustration on him. No rules, no limits.

But every time I do, the world gets that much closer to Utopia. He suffers, and the recoil churns up great waves of serendipity, joy and goodwill. The architecture of reality refines itself, relentlessly, into something dazzling and delightful and awe-inspiring, an omni-dimensional temple that sings in angelic harmonies when the winds of limbo break on its marbled vistas. It's sickening.

The other demons laugh at me behind my back. There goes Goody Two-Hooves, they say, with his magic wand and his sparkly tutu, bringing gifts for all the little girls and boys. Henry Mossop's pet. The archangel Fucknuts. The fairy from the top of the Christmas tree.

I've been drinking a lot. Two or three bars every night. Any place where they'll serve a beer or ten to a snakewood box. Last night I bumped into Maxwell's demon and we got wrecked together.

He told me, it was never about thermodynamics for him. He was doing what he loved.

SKIN

JAMES BROGDEN

Nearly home – she'd so nearly made it home.

Hannah couldn't have put her finger on the exact moment she became aware of the *shuffle-slump* of footsteps dragging on the pavement a dozen yards behind, following her. The night bus had dropped her in the aquarium brightness of shop-windows and headlights up on the main road, and she'd turned the corner onto her street, which was always perfectly well lit, with her house only a few doors down from the corner. If it had been any further, or darker, she'd have taken a taxi. It didn't seem possible that anybody could have been aware of her long enough to want to follow her.

Unless whoever it was had been on the bus too, watching her the whole time.

She tried to remember what the other passengers had looked like, but she'd sat at the front, near the driver, nice and safe.

Shuffle-slump. Shuffle-slump.

It was blustery and cold, the wind tugging at her coat.

She walked faster, brisk but not hurrying, she told herself, past terraced houses with bay windows and light spilling from around drawn curtains. Their front yards were tiny; if it came to it she could reach over any one of their gates and tap on the window, ask for help. Except that it was obviously just a harmless old man behind her and what kind of an idiot would she look, knocking on a stranger's door for that?

— *shuffleslumpshuffleslump* —

His pace had quickened to match hers.

She dug her hand into her coat pocket, finding her house keys and clutching them with a key between each knuckle. Two more doors – number 47 with their Christmas lights still up, and then number 49 with its wheelie bin sprawling like a drunkard and the low hedge that always had litter jammed into it – and she'd be home.

"Hannah!" he called. Jesus, how did he know her name? She bashed the front gate open with her thighs, three strides up the path to her front door, the security light suddenly dazzling, her key out in her other hand and slotting into the lock when he called again.

"Hannah, wait, please, I need to talk to you!"

And here, suddenly, was the strangest thing of all: she recognised his voice.

She stopped in the act of turning the key, and looked back over her shoulder. "Robin?"

He'd stopped out on the pavement, hands jammed in his pockets, his face hidden in the shadow of a heavy, dark hoodie.

A gust of wind swirled around them, making the litter in the street dance. He nodded.

"Robin, is that you? Jesus, Rob, you scared the fuck out of me!"

"I'm sorry," he mumbled. This wasn't like him; the Robin Saunders she'd known would never have apologised in such humble tones. He looked and smelled like he'd been sleeping rough. Now that she looked more closely, she saw that he was dressed in creased sweatpants and filthy trainers splitting at the soles – clothes in which the Rob of old would never have been seen dead – and the odour that rolled off him was thick and pungent. "That's what I've come to say," he continued. "That I'm sorry. For everything."

"Well…" She found herself at a loss for words. "Good, then." She turned the key and started to open her front door.

"And also!" he added, taking a step forward, but he then seemed to regret his eagerness and shuffled back again, ducking his head. Either that or he was trying to keep out of the light. She still couldn't see his face. "To say that I've made something for you. A present. To make amends."

She continued to open the door slowly, edging in. "You've made me a what?" His words made no sense. "I haven't seen you for six months and you turn up now and… I'm sorry, what? A present? What are you talking about?"

"Please…"

Another gust of wind tugged at them, momentarily pulling his hood away from his face. He snatched it back, but not before she'd caught a glimpse of his features that made her gasp in shock and reel backwards through her doorway. He looked like he'd been ravaged by some kind of flesh-eating disease, patches of his skin pocked and cratered and shiny with scar tissue, unless that was – dear God, was that *bone?*

"Oh my God, Rob, what's happened to you?"

He lurched away, tugging the edge of the hood as far down over his face as it would go, and now she noticed that he was wearing gloves, as if whatever had happened to him had affected not just his face but his entire body. "I'm sorry," he said. "I shouldn't have come. This was a mistake." He started to go, and she really should have let him, but there was something so pathetic about him compared to the arrogance of the man she'd known that she found herself feeling sorry for him, and despite her better judgement she called out, "Wait!"

He paused, hunched against the chill.

"I can't let you in," she said. "It's too late and I've had a long day, and it's just… No, not tonight."

"I understand." A car drove past and he flinched in the glare of its headlights.

"But come back tomorrow, and we'll talk."

He nodded.

"I need to know—" She stopped suddenly. It was too much to go into, here on the doorstep. "We need to talk." It was lame, but all she could offer.

"Thanks, Hannah," he mumbled, and left.

She went inside, locked the door, then immediately went into the front room and peered through a crack in the curtains to see if he was still lurking out there on the street, maybe hiding in the shadows of next door's hedge. But he seemed to have genuinely disappeared. Expelling a huge sigh of relief, she dumped her bag in the hall and went through to the narrow galley kitchen where she knew there was a half-finished bottle of red wine on the counter. She poured herself a generous glass, took it and the bottle back into the living room, plonked herself down on the sofa and then just sat there, staring into the sane, orderly silence of her empty home.

"Fuck," she said quietly.

Sipping her wine, she took out her phone and started scrolling back through the history of her Instagram feed. A week might be a long time in politics, so it was said, but six months was virtually a geological age in social media. She'd deleted all her pictures of him and the two of them together – they'd only had a few dates so there weren't that many to begin with – but there they were in the feeds of her friends, along with their congratulatory comments like *"Girl he's GORGEOUS you done GOOD"*, *"Oh come on, he must be gay"*, and *"Does he have any brothers?"* He was (or had been, at any rate) fantastically good-looking, it had to be admitted: hazel eyes, stylishly careless dark hair, flawless skin the colour of lightly toasted cinnamon, and a body that was toned but not overly muscular. Her last few dates before Rob had been with men whose idea of dinner conversation seemed to consist of talking entirely about themselves and what they hated about their jobs, football teams, or favourite television programmes she'd never heard of. She'd been so surprised to find herself in the company of a man who actually paid attention to her and seemed to want to make an effort that she'd mistaken his vanity for self-confidence, and ignored the alarm bells until it was almost too late.

As she scrolled through the images, feeling that same mixture of confusion and self-blame, she became aware of an itching on her left knee, and that she'd been unconsciously scratching at it for some time. The skin was red and flaking, and a drift of silvery bits littered the sofa cushion underneath.

"Ugh, pratt," she scolded herself. Falling into old bad habits again. She brushed the bits away and went upstairs to the bathroom to find her pot of Dermalex.

She'd first met Rob at a private dermatologist's clinic on the Hagley Road, where she was having a check-up for her psoriasis – not that she told him that, of course. It was embarrassing and ugly and only localised to a few places like her knees and elbows, which were easily hidden, and why would you tell the gorgeous man sitting next to you in the waiting room that you were there because bits of you were flaking off like some kind of disgusting troll-like creature? She'd made up something about having a suspicious-looking mole examined, and he'd shown her a picture on his phone of that old cartoon of the guy in the doctor's surgery with a small furry critter in sunglasses and a trench coat sitting on his shoulder, and they'd laughed. As it happened he actually was there to have a mole removed himself, he explained, and showed her an almost invisible blemish on the left side of his chin. To her mind it didn't seem serious enough to need attention, but then she wasn't the doctor and it was Rob's money to spend and who was she to judge? When he asked her if she was doing anything afterwards and could he buy her a coffee, she almost refused because he was so obviously out of her league – but then she found that a small, brave part of her had taken control and was nodding yes, that would be lovely, thanks.

So there was coffee, and a week after that there was dinner, and three dinners after that there was a concert at the Symphony Hall. He was a senior credit analyst for a large multinational which had relocated its British headquarters from London to the Midlands, and she fantasised about taking him to meet her parents, because he was exactly the sort of handsome and successful young man that her mother aspired to seeing take her wallflower of a daughter down the aisle, and exactly the sort of prospective son-in-law who would take her father to task for his right-wing, *Daily Mail*-inflamed politics and still be respected for it.

The photographs of their dates were still there like ghosts in her friends' timelines. They haunted her with fragments of forgotten conversations, and her skin tingled at recalling the light touch of his hand on her arm as he helped her out of a taxi, or his leg brushing hers as they sat in their seats for the concert. He was never less than respectful and attentive, but looking at the images now she saw the hints of what had been hiding there, like blemishes on the smooth façade of his charm. The way he dipped his head slightly down and to one side in every picture, as if he knew which was his best angle and presented it instinctively. The way he had, at the end of one taxi ride home with her head resting on his shoulder, plucked fastidiously and with a tiny frown of distaste at the single stray hair she'd left on his jacket.

He hid it well, but he was a vain man. She didn't appreciate exactly how vain until the first and only time she went back to his apartment.

They were kissing even as they made it into the hall, one of his hands in the small of her back and the other tugging at her dress zip, but she broke from him long enough to ask him where his bathroom was; Feminine Mysteries and all that, she said, hoping that it sounded humorously arch but fearing that she just came across as pompous. He smiled, showed her and said that he'd be in the living room making them a drink.

The bathroom, like the rest of the apartment and the man who owned it, was tastefully and expensively decorated. It was more of a wet-room, with a shower head the size of a dinner plate and a natural slate floor, chromed fittings and a huge mirrored medicine cabinet over the sink. She took care of her own business and then, out of no impulse more noble than naked curiosity, had a quick snoop in the cabinet. She refused to tell herself that she was looking for evidence of another woman in his life, but all the same felt a swift shiver of relief when she found none. What she did find, on the other hand, was an Aladdin's cave of male skincare products. There were moisturisers, wipes, balms and exfoliants, chemical peels and oil control serums, depilatory creams, anti-shine lotions, charcoal purifying daily face washes, and something called a hydra-energetic anti-fatigue system. There was a whole shelf glittering with stainless steel implements that would have shamed a dentist's surgery: scissors, tweezers, clippers, cuticle trimmers, blackhead extractors, razors (safety and disposable), and on the topmost shelf something that looked like a Hallowe'en mask for a robot costume, complete with wires and a battery pack. Presumably he wore that at night, though hopefully not every night – she thought that if she woke up next to that she'd scream the place down.

Then the thought of being in his bed took over and she went back out to pick up from where they'd left off.

Ten minutes later, they were on the sofa and she had her fingers clenched in his hair and her mouth locked on his as he slipped a hand up under the hem of her dress and around the back of her thigh. She crooked her knee up onto his leg and his hand slipped behind her knee before she realised where it was going and what it would find, and her bright spark of panic coincided exactly with his exclamation of shock as he pulled away sharply.

"What the hell was that?" he demanded.

Confused and red-faced with embarrassment, she pulled away to her own end of the sofa, tugging the hem of her dress back down. "It's just a patch of dry skin," she murmured. "Thanks for mentioning it."

As exciting as it had been to be dating again after such a long time, it had the unfortunate side-effect of making her psoriasis flare up again. The Dermalex was mostly keeping it under control, but there was no disguising the scaliness that his fingers had met. Her skin itched, but it was nothing compared to the burning mortification she felt.

"That's more than just dry skin," he replied, staring in accusation at a single silvery flake which lay between them on the dark leather of the sofa cushion. He stared at his hand, muttered "Ohmigod", then dashed into the bathroom, from where she heard the sound of running water.

Her humiliation flared into anger. "It's not contagious, you know!" she yelled. "Jesus, Rob, what's your problem?"

"My problem?!" he yelled back from the other room. "What about *your* problem? What is it, Hannah? What have you got?"

By this time she had grabbed her things together and was heading for the hallway, but she stopped by the open bathroom door. He was at the sink, scrubbing furiously at his hand. "It's psoriasis, okay?" she said. "I've got fucking psoriasis. Happy now?"

He moaned and scrubbed harder. "How could you not tell me you had something so grotesque?" he demanded. "How could you lie to me like this?" All the charm and erudition had fled his voice; he sounded just like any other drunken dickhead standing outside a club bellowing about what he thought he was entitled to.

"*Lie to you?*" Anger tipped over into humiliated outrage, and she felt the heat start to rise inside her. The condition, mild as her own case was, had still been a nightmare for her since as early as she could remember. School had been especially bad, and physical education lessons most of all. She'd endured all manner of bullying and name-calling – "Scabbers" had been the most popular one. Cornflakes had been tipped in her hair, and pencil shavings in her food. Rumours had been started that it was a sexually transmitted disease she'd caught by being a slut. Online it was even worse. She thought she'd left it behind with childhood, but here it was again: the same ugly face of petty cruelty, just dressed up more smartly. Now the rage burned hotter, directly behind her navel, spreading and growing through her belly as she started to sweat.

"You have no idea what *grotesque* is!" she shot back. "You have no idea what it's like, feeling bits of yourself falling off. Well I hope it *is* fucking contagious. I hope that every time you look in the mirror you see how *grotesque* you are. I hope that you see every little spot and freckle and that they drive you mad until you have to cut them out of your own fucking skin!"

At that, the fire inside her exploded in a tsunami that roared up to her scalp and down to her feet, only to flash outwards and into him, leaving her empty, dazed and breathless. She didn't wait for Rob's response but staggered out of his apartment, more confused now than angry and embarrassed.

That had been the last she'd seen or heard of Rob until this evening. She finished her wine and took herself to bed, but lay awake in the darkness, wondering if he was out there on the street again, watching. She stared at the images on her phone, seeing only the ruin of his face, half-lit by streetlights. Dear God, had he taken her at her word? Her grandmother used to tell stories about the women in her family and the things that they could do, but of course Hannah hadn't believed them. Who would? The notion that she might actually have cursed him was ridiculous.

Because as monstrous as Rob had become, what did that then make her?

She went back through the photographs again, re-reading the comments and her own replies, squirming at the smug, self-congratulatory tone with which she'd bragged to her friends about the gorgeous man she'd caught. *Look at me! See? I'm popular!* If he'd been a vain man obsessed with his own appearance, what had she done but feed that? The least she could offer him now was a chance to explain himself.

The next morning she called in sick at work and waited.

She didn't realise how much on edge she was until a tentative knock on her front door, faint though it was, jolted her like an electric shock. Through the door's frosted glass pane she saw a blurred shape shuffling back and forth, and she hesitated with her hand on the lock. She could ignore him, pretend she wasn't in, and hope that whatever revelations he brought disappeared with him. But she needed to know what had happened. She needed to know if it was somehow her fault. Hannah unlocked the door and opened it.

Rob still had his hood up, but there was no disguising his mutilations in the clear morning light – indeed, from the defiant way that he held his jaw it seemed that he had no intention of hiding from her.

But oh, what damage had been wrought to that jaw, and the face above it.

What little skin was left sat uneasily beside patches of exposed muscle and tendon, yellow gristle marbling the red, and the glimpses of naked bone at his forehead and cheeks last night hadn't been her imagination. He had no eyelids; his eyeballs were naked and staring, and she couldn't imagine why he wasn't completely blind. His lips (she remembered the touch of them and shuddered) resembled thick rubber bands, and his nose was little more than a cavity with a few scraps of cartilage. The scarring extended down his throat and below the collar of his stained t-shirt; was his whole body like this? It explained why his voice had sounded so nasal and muffled last night. He looked like a crude imitation of one of those plastinated "Bodyworlds" exhibits, made by an amateur with palsied hands and the rusty lid of a tin can instead of a scalpel. With such injuries he should have been in intensive care, but here he was all the same. His lips thinned in something which might have been intended as a smile, and when she saw the workings of his anatomy pull that smile into existence she nearly slammed the door shut again.

"Hi Hannah," he said.

"Rob-Robin," she managed.

"I know." He gestured at himself. He was wearing lavender-coloured surgical gloves. Presumably his hands were just as bad. She tried not to recall the touch of those fingers cupping her face, stroking her skin. "I can't imagine how this must look to you."

She grimaced.

"Thank you for letting me come back," he continued. "I wouldn't have blamed you if you'd told me to piss off."

That was still very much on the cards as far as she was concerned. He clearly wasn't in his right mind. The door was still on its chain.

"What—" She faltered, swallowed, tried again. "Oh Rob, what have you done to yourself?"

"What have *I* done? Nothing I didn't have coming to me, I know that now. But it was your words, Hannah, that made me do this."

"Oh no." She shook her head vehemently and started to close the door. "This isn't my fault."

"No, of course not! I know that! That's not what I'm saying! *Please!*" She tried to shut the door on him but he got a foot in the gap to prevent her. She slammed it anyway and he grunted in pain but didn't budge.

"I'll call the police," she warned.

"Hannah," he begged, and the pleading in his voice was more naked than his ruined flesh. "You were right! Absolutely right to say what you did! After you went I took a good hard look at myself – I mean literally – and all I could see was the ugliness. Every mole, every blocked pore, every wrinkle. They were *all* I could see, and they were everywhere, and I knew that I had to cut them out of me, so that's what I did. I did it because you told me to! I couldn't stop myself! I kept cutting and cutting until it was all gone. Please, you have to understand – you have to *see!*"

"Oh, I can see well enough," she said. "Get your foot out or I swear to God——"

"NO!" He shoved the gap wider, snapping the chain, and then he was over the threshold and in her hallway, advancing on her with his mutilated hands in their surgical gloves. She screamed and tried to run, but even in his condition he was too fast. He caught her by the staircase and wrapped his arms around her from behind. "I'm not going to hurt you," he said, his breath fervid in her ear. "But I'm not going to let you ignore this, either.

"You did it, deep down you know you did. You made me do this to myself. Don't get me wrong!" he added hastily. "It was a good thing, a right thing, but you know you have to see all of it. You can run and call the police if you want, but I'll be long gone by the time they get here, and you'll never know. Or you can come with me and let me show you. I'm only asking for an hour of your time. Then you'll never see me again, I swear."

He was as good as his word, and let her go.

She ran.

But she only got as far as the kitchen, her hand on the back door.

She stopped, paused, and looked back. He wasn't chasing her. It seemed that his efforts to break in and restrain her had cost him because he was leaning against the wall, shuddering and gasping in pain. She could easily escape and call the police, or pick up a knife and drive him out of her home. She did neither. She edged back towards him warily.

"One hour," she said.

He nodded, as if even talking was beyond him now, and staggered from the house.

She followed.

He took her to his old apartment. They went by alleyways and empty side-streets where there were fewer people to see him – though he'd pulled a kind of wraparound scarf over his face anyway – and through service yards to a set of back stairs which led up to his door. She found herself surprised that he was still living in the same place, as if his strange affliction should have made it impossible for him to maintain a home, but realised that she'd never known anything about his domestic arrangements. For all she knew he might have owned the place outright, and not needed a job to pay for it. He couldn't possibly be working in his current state, after all. It occurred to her then that she'd never really known anything substantial about him. Had she really only dated him because he was handsome and attentive and looked good next to her in photos that her friends and family would have liked? Had she actually been no less shallow than he?

Once inside, it became clear that he wasn't maintaining

anything. Far from the clean, elegant apartment she'd seen, it was rank with filth and stank like an abattoir.

"I couldn't just throw it away, you see," he explained, leading her down a hallway piled with old stacks of newspapers. Scurrying things fled from their approach, deeper into the shadows. "That would have felt like a betrayal of everything I was learning."

"What… what were you learning?" she asked, stepping gingerly.

He stopped and looked back, his lidless eyes gleaming. "What I was," he replied, and led her on. "A vain, superficial man obsessed with the perfection of his outer appearance, and blind to the ugliness inside. It took you to make me understand, to bring that out of me, so that I could cut it out of myself. But throwing it away? No, that would have been an even worse denial."

They were at the doorway to the bathroom, the last place she'd seen him as a normal human being, scrubbing at his flesh in horror and staring at his reflection. A meagre light seeped through the murk-smeared window, enough to see that the chrome fittings were tarnished, the slate floor mottled with old blood, and the porcelain of the sink unit streaked ochre with it. The medicine cabinet was still there – in fact it was probably the only clean thing in the whole place, one gleaming oval wiped out of its filthy surface. Scattered around it, beside the sink and on the floor, were the rusted and bloodstained implements from inside, the ones that he'd used to cut away the ugliness that her curse had forced him to see. And, hanging on an ordinary coat hanger from the shower head, something which she at first took to be a ruined dry cleaning bag, or else the discarded husk of some monstrous insect.

"There," he whispered. His face was averted, as if he couldn't bear to look at it. "You see?"

She saw.

It was the curd-yellow of old skin rinds and overgrown toenails, strips and shreds of it curled and browning at the edges but laboriously sewn and glued back together into a crude approximation of where each had been cut from his body; a man-suit of his own scarred skin. Some parts were recognisable − here an eyelid, there a nipple, elsewhere a swirl of knuckle − but the rest was a harlequin motley of wart-gnarled and blood-blackened flesh, utterly loathsome. She backed away, hands to her mouth in horror.

"I cut it away, but I had to put it back together, to see myself as you saw me."

Then she looked at the muscles and tendons of his face, testament to the physical torture that he'd put himself through to atone for his vanity − and suddenly saw the beauty of his offering; what nobility his suffering had brought to light.

When he reached for her, she didn't shrink away, but went willingly into his arms and kissed him. He gasped a little; he was raw, and it must have hurt, but he let her explore the softness of his flesh, the quivering velvet of his muscles, the smoothness of naked bone.

"I'm sorry," she said, surprised to find tears on her cheeks. "Sorry I made you do this to yourself."

"I'm not. It's just…" He faltered.

"Just what?"

His whisper was so faint, a hair against her cheek. "It hurts."

Now, with her body pressed against his, she felt the heat deep within him. Not the burning of infection – though Lord knew he should have been dead from that long ago – this felt familiar. It was the rage and hurt that she had thrown into him on the night he'd shamed her six months ago. It was still in him, keeping him alive and forcing him to commit atrocities upon himself. He hadn't just brought her here to show her the results of that; every straining sinew in him was begging for release.

He wasn't the monster here.

"I'm so sorry," she repeated, weeping, and she took the fire back, drawing it out of him and into herself where it belonged, in a slow-pulsing multi-petalled bloom behind her navel. He sighed and sagged in her arms, but the fire gave her strength and she held him up, because it was time to start learning to do something better with that strength. She kissed him goodbye and carried his body into the bedroom and laid him down in the darkness, but found that she could still see him quite clearly.

Here, in this place, he shone.

FAITH & FRED

MAURA McHUGH

They found the skulls on the third day of renovation.

Owen had just bashed in the plasterboard with the sledgehammer his contractor, Bald Jim, had handed him with a, "Let her rip, lad."

Owen had bridled at the "lad", since he was nearing thirty, but the heft of the scarred sledgehammer in his gloved hands gave him a tactile joy, which overrode his pride. Assaulting the wall was deeply satisfying: the hard swing, the protesting sound as the pitted metal head smashed through the cheap panelling, and the aftershock down his arms.

Dust and chip fragments flew up and obscured the view at first. Gradually, daylight from the big windows behind them lanced through the widening jagged opening that Owen had created. They knew this had been a closet of some kind before a previous owner walled it up, but it was wasted space, and Owen was determined to use every inch of Caldwere Farmhouse. From its dilapidated rooms he would create a home for someone willing to pay a good price.

Bald Jim tapped him on the shoulder to indicate it was time to relinquish the weapon, and Owen reluctantly handed it back to the brawny older man. Brute force had done its job, now was the time for the finesse of experts.

Bald Jim propped the tool against the wall, and selected a smaller hammer. He pried at the opening, splintering it open further until he suddenly hopped back, alarmed.

"Flippin' 'eck," he said.

"What is it?" Owen stepped into the miasma, squinting. Something gleamed white in between metal bars. He fished his phone out of the thigh pocket in his combat trousers and swiped on the torch app. He was aware of Bald Jim's solid presence behind him.

Two human skulls stared at him from inside an old metal cage fashioned from flattened iron strips. The cage sat on a simple wooden table.

"Holy shit!" Owen said, his voice hushed, as he directed the light around the space. He leaned forward, inhaling a mouldy reek, and immediately regretted not wearing a dust mask.

Sitting in front of the cage was a white card inscribed with fluid copperplate writing, obscured by a layer of dust.

He reached in warily and retrieved the card.

Here be Faith & Fred.
Keep them homestead,
Lest they wail.

"That's us buggered," said Bald Jim after he scanned the text.

He walked to the double windows, dipping into the May sunlight, and pulled out an old-school battered mobile phone from one of his many pockets.

"I'll call the cops."

"What?"

"Do you think this is the first frightener I've found in one of these old gaffs?" He shook his head. "Occupational hazard."

"What'll they do?"

Bald Jim tipped back his hardhat and stared through the glass, across the flat green fields, to the blue line indicating the distant shore.

"They'll take your new friends for tests. Ask questions. Bring in boffins. There'll be paperwork for sure. It'll be a right pain in the arse."

The words stirred a panic in Owen. He imagined the room being shut down, and the disruption to their schedule. The news would get out in the area, and maybe become a viral story online.

He noticed that Bald Jim kept well away from the hole punched in the wall, and cast unhappy glances in that direction. If this bloke was nervous because of a spooky find, how would the other workers react? Or potential buyers?

Owen had little margin for mistakes. His new leaf had been turned over too recently, and there were plenty of people longing to see him screw up again.

"Does anyone else have to know?"

Bald Jim turned away from the calm vista, levelled a hard stare at Owen, but said nothing. Leaving a gap into which Owen rushed.

"It's probably a nineteenth-century parlour entertainment. We know from the plans that it's been shut up for at least a hundred years. It's not some CSI Holderness situation…"

Bald Jim nodded and let Owen continue.

"If I wrap these up and dispose of them, then no one need be any the wiser." He reached for his wallet. "Why don't you take the rest of the day off?"

He counted off six fifty-pound notes and held them out.

Bald Jim considered the money for a drawn-out moment. Owen oozed a fresh sheen of sweat.

"Aye," he said, "the missus would love a fancy meal out." He pointed at the hole. "I want no sign of those when I'm back, mind." He slipped the notes into his back pocket, and walked to the door, his boots thumping across the bare boards.

At the entrance he paused and added, "Thaddy – Thadeus – Ogram runs The Adder's Knot. His family's been hereabouts since the Ark. He might know something about…" And he jerked his head at the problem.

From where Owen stood, mote-suffused rays slanted into the recess and illuminated the empty eye sockets of the dead couple, lending them shining new orbs. Gooseflesh erupted across his arms. The black gaps between their aged teeth grinned at him.

"I'll take care of it," he promised.

Bald Jim left, and Owen heard him calling to Roger and Tall Jim. A mumble of voices ensued, followed by doors slamming, and cars driving down the long lane to the main road.

Owen strode to where Bald Jim had left the hammer, grabbed it and laid into the edges of the gap, cursing as he did, venting his frustration.

He was panting by the time it was wide enough to pull out the cage.

It was awkward, arcing his body into the hidden space and latching his hooked fingers into the sharp metal grid. His legs pressed against the remaining plasterboard as he strained to lift and negotiate the cage through the uneven rent.

A shattering *crack*: the rest of the wall collapsed and he pitched into the closet, slamming down into the cage, knocking it off the table.

He fell completely inside the cavity, his face and chest landing on the cruel edge of the cage. Fireworks exploded across his vision. Beneath him, the skulls knocked around like snooker balls. Perhaps rolling with mirth.

He yelped, in fear and in pain, breathing in the dank smell of a previous century and old pacts.

A fury erupted and he rose in a flurry of thrashing arms and yelled curses.

"Fucking typical!" he screamed and hauled the cage out of the broken wall, dumping it on the ground, and kicking it several times until it was on the far side of the room. The skulls had moved about, but he noticed something else on their ivory surfaces: splatters of red dots.

The stream of damp on his forehead alerted him to the cut. He reached up to touch it and his fingers returned to his view dripping with vivid scarlet blood. His old phobia surged alive at the sight of it. His chest constricted while his legs softened like loops of overcooked noodles.

He needed to get away, desperately.

Owen wobbled a couple of steps towards the doorway before he fainted.

* * *

He woke to twilight and pain.

Moving cautiously, he tested his arms and wrists, which must have broken his fall: sore, bruised, but not sprained or broken, thankfully. He sat up. His legs and feet checked out, but his forehead thumped an agonising beat, and his right collarbone radiated trouble. Gingerly, he touched his temple and felt the crusted scab. He whooshed out a few breaths, feeling the horror rise in him again, which was rapidly pursued by his disgust at his weakness. It prompted a maelstrom of memories replaying his worst moments: his younger sister Poppy defending him in school because the bullies learned they could make Owen faint if they cut him; avoiding any chance of conflict by playing sick and hiding; warping into a cynical little prick who mastered mimicking others and performing idiotic stunts to make his "friends" laugh; picking on Poppy relentlessly as a teen, trying to wear down her strength so they could be equally frail.

He clutched his hands to his head and moaned a little, because that sin hurt him more than anything else. He banished the past to deal with the present.

The room was deeply shadowed as the world dimmed into a rose-violet hush. The birds were not singing their farewells to the sun.

Owen looked over at the crevasse in the wall, a slash of black that seemed to bleed darkness into the room. He did not know what constituted concussion, but he wondered if he had it. It never sounded good when the concerned doctors talked about it as they shone a flashlight into the eyes of their patients on the telly.

He got onto one knee and levered himself off the floor at a sedate pace. The room tilted and distorted for a moment and he heaved in a breath to steady himself. The cage lay in crooked darkness, only visible due to a patch of white lattice.

A skull doily, Owen thought, and a fizz of weird laughter tickled his mouth, but he kept it contained rather than break the suffocating silence.

A city boy, Owen had trouble with the pervasive quiet at the farmhouse, especially at night. Worse still were the erratic unfamiliar noises that startled him out of the oppressive lull at odd moments: a fox yipping; the squeaking of hunting bats; owls hooting to each other. Whenever he went outside for a smoke break, and was engulfed in a soothing cigarette pall, dark shapes could suddenly flit about in the sky or zip low to the ground. The countryside was too full of unruly, strange life for him. He had set up a monastic existence in the bedroom upstairs, but he kept his wireless headphones on most of the time, listening to music and podcasts, or watching films. Anything to avoid confronting his jittery solitude.

He approached the cage and dragged it from its concealment and into the starlight squares cast by the windows. There was a latch at the front, and it lifted easily. Owen opened the door and considered what to do next. The idea of touching the skulls made his fingers draw back towards his palms involuntarily.

"Man up," Owen whispered, and immediately hated that the phrase had passed his lips. It was a spiteful invective that had been thrown at him by his old man on many occasions.

He reached in and pulled out one of the skulls: it was cool to the touch and surprisingly solid. The bottom jawbone was attached to the skull by twists of copper wire. For some reason he thought this one was Faith. He left her on the wide window seat and retrieved her brother.

He sat Fred beside her and wondered why he thought of them as siblings.

Owen stood in front of them, looking at their dark sockets, brimming with secrets.

"What's your story, then?"

They stared at him, smiling, steadfastly mute.

Behind them, through the window, two shadows flapped by.

Turn on a light, you idiot!

He darted to the switch, but the yellow light of the lone bulb dangling from the ceiling made it worse. A jaundice afflicted the space.

But it showed him the hammer lying on the ground where he'd dropped it earlier. He picked it up and its weight gave him confidence. Owen approached the skulls and made a practice swipe in front of them. As if to threaten them.

They were unimpressed.

He hesitated, wondering if there was a better way to deal with this problem, and considered that these long-dead people probably deserved better treatment. But plenty of people die alone, forgotten, and unburied. His own great-Uncle Spencer had died in this house and had not been discovered for a month. Which was how he came to inherit the place.

They'd had their life. Now he wanted his, the one where he became an older brother Poppy could respect.

He raised the hammer and brought it down on Faith's crown. She burst apart into skittering shards.

He laughed, and pulverised Fred.

He fetched a dustpan, swept up their pieces, and dumped them into a black bin bag. Afterwards he moved the cage into his bedroom, covered it with a dust cloth, and sat his second-hand lamp on it. Then he went outside, under the pitiless vault of stars, and walked to the skip. Owen pushed the bag of bone bits deep under the assorted rubble, and strolled back to the house, whistling.

* * *

In his dream Faith and Fred were teenaged twins with black curls, dark eyes, and deeply tanned skin that bore the marks of torture and beating. They stood upon a makeshift gallows, the noose around their necks. Hatred burned in Faith's bruised eyes as she glared at the Magistrate standing in the throng of baying townspeople.

"Obadiah Creaser: none of your line shall prosper. You, who swore to care for and shelter us, will never be quit of us now. We shall call out your sins to the Almighty forever."

Then the terrible sound of two snapping necks followed by howls of jubilation from the crowd.

The shrieks continued as the faces of the watching people twisted and morphed into distended caricatures. It was a cacophony of righteous wrath.

Owen bolted upright in his bed, sweating, the sound ringing in his ears, and his heart thudding quickly.

The screams continued. Two voices sounding their anguished fury.

Owen leapt up, disorientated but desperate to end the horrible din. It was close, but not upstairs.

He slammed on the light and found shoes to slip on. Owen stumbled downstairs, flicking on every light switch he passed, urgently needing to push back the darkness. All the time the screams assaulted his ears, and kept the images of the twin children dangling, dying before an audience vivid in his mind.

He had to make it stop.

Owen nearly tripped over a box of tiles in the disassembled kitchen, but he noticed at the last second and jumped it before flinging open the back door.

Here, the noise was a piercing pain.

The reassembled skulls of Faith and Fred sat on the doorstep, screaming.

Owen reeled as reality crashed into disbelief.

They continued to voice their anger to the heavens.

Panicked, he ran over, gathered them up, and stepped back into the kitchen.

They fell silent instantly.

Breathing hard, he stood inside the threshold and looked out the door at the forbidding night. A chilly breeze swept past his bare ankles.

He glanced down at the skulls cradled in his arms, and walked through the doorway into the yard. Their cries pealed out again.

Owen marched back into the kitchen and laid the skulls upon the small, paint-stained table he was using until the room was kitted out properly.

The skulls locked their protests behind their teeth.

For a long time Owen stared at the de-fleshed heads and pondered his next move. Finally, he scooped them up, carried them to his bedroom, and put them back in their cage.

He covered it again with the thick cloth and returned to the kitchen to brew coffee and wait for the dawn.

* * *

Bald Jim didn't discuss the previous day's events with Owen again, although he asked about the plaster on his forehead. Owen described falling over the box of tiles in the kitchen during a midnight foray for snacks, and Bald Jim promptly moved the obstacle and lectured Owen on tripping hazards. Satisfied he had taught Owen a lesson, Bald Jim and his crew got back to work, moving through the tasks on their schedule. They had weeks of work left to do, and every day there was a new minor crisis or bill to pay. Owen had little time to dwell on the skulls' unnatural behaviour, but whenever his thoughts idled their cries reverberated in his mind.

He startled when a table saw shrieked, thinking it was the skulls again, but instead it was the reassuring sight of Roger, wearing protective earmuffs, cutting floorboards. He thought of the twins' skulls, sitting covered in his bedroom. Listening to a new generation of people readying the house for occupation. He considered all the various families they had haunted, until they were boarded up. How many people had they eavesdropped upon? How many people had gone about their daily business unaware that the dead twins spied upon them?

That evening he drove to The Adder's Knot in the nearby hamlet. It was a small but well-appointed pub that had made some concessions to the twenty-first century. It had wi-fi and a good local cider, but the few regulars in that night were elderly couples and bachelor men who were territorial about their seats.

Thaddy was in his sixties with a huge pock-marked nose and red cheeks. He eyeballed Owen as soon as he entered, and moved along the varnished oak counter to greet him.

"What'll it be?" he asked, a touch gruffly.

Owen ordered a soft drink, and quickly added, "And whatever you're having for yourself," once he saw Thaddy's spectacularly bushy eyebrows rise in surprise to meet his unruly hair.

"You're Spencer's nephew?"

"Ah, great-nephew. Owen, pleased to meet you."

Thaddy placed the glass clinking with ice in front of Owen. "Not a drinker?"

Owen considered being evasive but guessed Thaddy wouldn't abide bullshit. "Yeah, I'm sober. It doesn't agree with me."

Thaddy nodded solemnly as he poured himself a whisky. "A man should know his limits."

Owen imagined this was a subtle warning that The Adder's Knot wasn't a place for a heart-to-heart. Instead they discussed rugby for an hour.

Eventually they got onto the subject of local legends and folk tales. Thaddy had a couple of whiskies in him and the customers had thinned out. There was only a tiny wizened man in a cap nursing half an ale at a table in front of the telly.

"Spencer knew plenty about local history," Thaddy said. "He was an old git – rest in peace – but he liked reading." Thaddy shook his head as if this was a shocking habit. "He even wrote a couple of pamphlets."

"What?"

Owen had only met Uncle Spencer once, when he was ten, so he knew little about him.

"There's got to be some of them knocking about in his – your – house. Library might have a copy. Spencer was right proud of them."

Thaddy rose stiffly from his stool behind the bar and reached for the hanging bell. He rang it twice. "Time, gents! Finish up, please."

Owen drove through the deserted, hedged lanes to his house, and after a quick sandwich headed up to bed. He tugged back the cloth to peer into the jail and check on the prisoners.

They didn't appear to have moved. They made no sound.

He sat down in front of them, cross-legged, and told them all about his pub outing.

* * *

That night he dreamed of Faith and Fred as children, living with their mother in a small house on a farm near a copse. The children played in the woods in a little lean-to they built, and in it they hung a variety of trinkets and tokens they had found or crafted. Fred had a talent for carving figures in wood. They were uncannily like the subjects he chose: a badger, a crow, a toad, his sister and his mother. Their woodland father. Faith's voice was unearthly, divine. When she sang, the birds marvelled.

The twins devised special games and chants. They charmed the moths and snails. They played with their huge, grey cat, which was a cunning mouser. She often brought them mauled birds and rodents as offerings. The children buried them in a little graveyard they created and erected twig crosses as markers. They conducted their own burial rites in their green cathedral, singing odd hymns with angelic voices.

And when the little family visited the village, which was rarely, a stream of whispers followed them.

* * *

Owen woke up, his head muggy, his shoulder tender, and his mood poignant. He knew some of the tragedy waiting for the family. They just wanted to be left alone. Why couldn't people let others be?

Later, to the tune of hammering and banging, Owen dug through the boxes of books and knick-knacks he had earmarked for charity shops. He hadn't looked too closely at any of their titles since to his eyes they were a bunch of boring history books, a subject he'd failed in his GCSEs.

He almost missed the slender volume despite his thoroughness. It was slotted inside a large hardback book about the history of the Viking invasion. It had a woodcut print on the cover depicting a couple of crooked imps playing the drums and fiddle for dancing hags in pointed hats. It was titled *Tales of Vanished Villages* and there was his grand-uncle's name: Spencer Creaser.

Owen brewed a mug of coffee, heavy with milk, and retired to his bedroom to read. He'd left a corner of the cage uncovered so Faith and Fred could get some air while he was out of the room. He pulled the cloth back further so the pair had a better view. He showed them the book.

"Spencer was an author. Fancy that." He felt strangely proud of the man. As if his relative's literary achievement somehow opened a possibility for his future. Like he could have that same talent in his veins.

He read the preface, in which Spencer credited his grandmother for his interest in history and folklore: *She had a story for every croft and bole, and none were the same. She collected the skeins of the past and wished them rewoven.*

Owen regarded the index. One category was "Fairies, Boggles, and Wee Folk". But the section that arrested him was "Screaming Skulls".

Much to his surprise there were several examples. Skeletons that were restless and loud in graveyards were disinterred and returned to their homes, and over time, most of their bones were lost, until only the skulls remained.

Some of the early peoples of England were head-hunters and kept skulls as trophies. Many cultures consider them the receptacle of the vital spirit. The practice of pilgrimage to visit decorated saints' bones in jewelled reliquaries remains popular. In other lands they are brought out each year, to be fed and feted. Sometimes they communicate prophecies or act as guardians of ancestral knowledge. To hear their voices is a sign of someone attuned to a peculiar realm.

Owen looked up from the pages and regarded the skulls. They looked back at him. He frowned. *What a shite superpower.*

142

He skimmed through the stories until he spotted an entry that caused his pulse to speed up: *Caldwere Farm.*

It is said that Caldwere Farm became the property of a widow of striking beauty, who had twin children called Faith and Fred.

Owen blinked and read the words again. They were real. He glanced over at the skulls in their draped shrine. From below he heard a barrage of hammering, and voices raised. Something shifted, as if the house's axis had moved minutely. "That's got it," he heard Tall Jim shout. Then all was quiet again.

Owen returned to reading.

The family lived quietly, a day's walk from the seaside village of Withensea (long since fallen into the waves). The children played in the woods and rarely went to church. In the evening lights were seen flickering through the close-knit trees. Strange songs floated on the air. They had an eerie way of speaking as one and were reported to ask impious questions. As innocents, they must have been damned by their mother. Something had to be done to save them.

Their mother was taken, tested, and confessed to being in league with Satan. She was hanged, and the local magistrate, Obadiah Creaser, ensured the twins witnessed their mother's wrecked form led up to the gibbet and her neck stretched.

Obadiah was granted guardianship of the children and their land, but no amount of godly care could reform their wildness. The girl was particularly obdurate. The Magistrate prayed privately with her every evening, but the child's screams of defiance were heard by all in the fine new farmhouse he built upon the land.

Several people testified that she became wanton and led her brother into terrible betrayals against God's natural order. During their trial the twins protested this vehemently, although the girl was no longer a maiden. Seven years after their mother's hanging, the twins were dragged up before the village and hanged by the same noose.

Owen stopped, his face wrinkled with revulsion. This man, Obadiah, was an ancestor who had profited from a terrible abuse of his position of authority. Owen did not want to look upon the twins again, so he returned to the final paragraphs.

Faith cursed Obadiah and all his line from the gallows. "You, who swore to care for and shelter us, will never be quit of us now. We shall call out your sins to the Almighty forever." Their bodies were buried, unmarked, outside the graveyard, but people nearby complained of rending screams every night, until finally the exhausted neighbours gathered, dug up the decaying twins, and dumped them on Caldwere Farm.

Over the years only the skulls survived. The Creasers never declined, but never prospered. And each time a relative attempted to sell on or destroy the skulls, they returned to cry their bloody truth until they, and their caretakers, returned home.

Owen gasped, and glanced at the skulls. He knew he could not remove them. But, surely he could *leave* them? He had been considering digging a special grave in the cellar, where he could bury them so he could move on.

He knelt in front of the two skulls and placed his face close to their hard features.

"I didn't do this to you! You can't take it out on me."

They regarded him silently. Judging him, Owen felt.

He flipped the cloth back over their cage.

"It's not my fault!" he hissed at them.

He stood up too fast and his head ached.

You will take care of us.

Owen froze.

You, or another.

His breath hitched in his chest, and he took a step back, as if he could evade the thought.

"No," he said, softly.

You'll hear us always, lad, no matter how far you run. We'll sing our special songs. The ones that charm snakes and spiders. That attract ill luck and ill will. You'll come back.

You, or another.

He had planned to sell the house and split the money with Poppy. And then he'd travel and move somewhere far from those who knew his old, weak self. He'd be a fresh person, someone freed from expectations and old stories.

It felt as if giant chains had fallen from above and landed upon his shoulders to anchor him in his past. He would be fastened forever in fucked-up, irresponsible Owen.

He dropped to the floor with a thud.

Owen reached forward with unsteady fingers and drew the curtain up.

Inside their shadowed cell the two skulls gleamed with pleasure.

"Please," he entreated.

You, or another.

THE BLACK FAIRY'S CURSE

KAREN JOY FOWLER

She was being chased. She kicked off her shoes, which were slowing her down. At the same time her heavy skirts vanished and she found herself in her usual work clothes. Relieved of the weight and constriction, she was able to run faster. She looked back. She was much faster than he was. Her heart was strong. Her strides were long and easy. He was never going to catch her now.

* * *

She was riding the huntsman's horse and she couldn't remember why. It was an autumn red with a tangled mane. She was riding fast. A deer leapt in the meadow ahead of her. She saw the white blink of its tail.

She'd never ridden well, never had the insane fearlessness it took, but now she was able to enjoy the easiness of the horse's motion. She encouraged it to run faster.

It was night. The countryside was softened with patches of moonlight. She could go anywhere she liked, ride to the

147

end of the world and back again. What she would find there was a castle with a toothed tower. Around the castle was a girdle of trees, too narrow to be called a forest, and yet so thick they admitted no light at all. She knew this. Even farther away were the stars. She looked up and saw three of them fall, one right after the other. She made a wish to ride until she reached them.

She herself was in farmland. She crossed a field and jumped a low stone fence. She avoided the cottages, homey though they seemed, with smoke rising from the roofs and a glow the color of butter pats at the windows. The horse ran and did not seem to tire.

She wore a cloak which, when she wrapped it tightly around her, rode up and left her legs bare. Her feet were cold. She turned around to look. No one was coming after her.

She reached a river. Its edges were green with algae and furry with silt. Toward the middle she could see the darkness of deep water. The horse made its own decisions. It ran along the shallow edge but didn't cross. Many yards later it ducked back away from the water and into a grove of trees. She lay along its neck, and the silver-backed leaves of aspens brushed over her hair.

* * *

She climbed into one of the trees. She regretted every tree she had never climbed. The only hard part was the first branch. After that it was easy, or else she was stronger than she'd ever

148

been. Stronger than she needed to be. This excess of strength gave her a moment of joy as pure as any she could remember. The climbing seemed quite as natural as stair steps, and she went as high as she could, standing finally on a limb so thin it dipped under her weight, like a boat. She retreated downward, sat with her back against the trunk and one leg dangling. No one would ever think to look for her here.

Her hair had come loose and she let it all down. It was warm on her shoulders. "Mother," she said, softly enough to blend with the wind in the leaves. "Help me."

She meant her real mother. Her real mother was not there, had not been there since she was a little girl. It didn't mean there would be no help.

Above her were the stars. Below her, looking up, was a man. He was no one to be afraid of. Her dangling foot was bare. She did not cover it. Maybe she didn't need help. That would be the biggest help of all.

"Did you want me?" he said. She might have known him from somewhere. They might have been children together. "Or did you want me to go away?"

"Go away. Find your own tree."

* * *

They went swimming together and she swam better than he did. She watched his arms, his shoulders rising darkly from the green water. He turned and saw that she was watching. "Do you know my name?" he asked her.

"Yes," she said, although she couldn't remember it. She knew she was supposed to know it, although she could also see that he didn't expect her to. But she did feel that she knew who he was – his name was such a small part of that. "Does it start with a W?" she asked.

The sun was out. The surface of the water was a rough gold.

"What will you give me if I guess it?"

"What do you want?"

She looked past him. On the bank was a group of smiling women, her grandmother, her mother, and her stepmother too, her sisters and stepsisters, all of them smiling at her. They waved. No one said, "Put your clothes on." No one said, "Don't go in too deep now, dear." She was a good swimmer, and there was no reason to be afraid. She couldn't think of a single thing she wanted. She flipped away, breaking the skin of the water with her legs.

She surfaced in a place where the lake held still to mirror the sky. When it settled, she looked down into it. She expected to see that she was beautiful, but she was not. A mirror only answers one question and it can't lie. She had completely lost her looks. She wondered what she had gotten in return.

* * *

There was a mirror in the bedroom. It was dusty so her reflection was vague. But she was not beautiful. She wasn't upset about this and she noticed the fact, a little wonderingly.

It didn't matter at all to her. Most people were taken in by appearances, but others weren't. She was healthy; she was strong. If she could manage to be kind and patient and witty and brave, there would be men who loved her for it. There would be men who found it exciting.

He lay among the blankets, looking up at her. "Your eyes," he said. "Your incredible eyes."

His own face was in shadow, but there was no reason to be afraid. She removed her dress. It was red. She laid it over the back of a chair. "Move over."

She had never been in bed with this man before, but she wanted to be. It was late and no one knew where she was. In fact, her mother had told her explicitly not to come here, but there was no reason to be afraid. "I'll tell you what to do," she said. "You must use your hand and your mouth. The other – it doesn't work for me. And I want to be first. You'll have to wait."

"I'll love waiting," he said. He covered her breast with his mouth, his hand moved between her legs. He knew how to touch her already. He kissed her other breast.

"Like that," she said. "Just like that." Her body began to tighten in anticipation.

He kissed her mouth. He kissed her mouth.

* * *

He kissed her mouth. It was not a hard kiss, but it opened her eyes. This was not the right face. She had never seen this man before and the look he gave her – she wasn't sure she liked it.

Why was he kissing her, when she was asleep and had never seen him before? What was he doing in her bedroom? She was so frightened, she stopped breathing for a moment. She closed her eyes and wished him away.

He was still there. And there was pain. Her finger dripped with blood and when she tried to sit up, she was weak and encumbered by a heavy dress, a heavy coil of her own hair, a corset, tight and pointed shoes.

"Oh," she said. "Oh." She was about to cry and she didn't know this man to cry before him. Her tone was accusing. She pushed him and his face showed the surprise of this. He allowed himself to be pushed. If he hadn't, she was not strong enough to force it.

He was probably a very nice man. He was giving her a concerned look. She could see that he was tired. His clothes were ripped; his own hands were scratched. He had just done something hard, maybe dangerous. So maybe that was why he hadn't stopped to think how it might frighten her to wake up with a stranger kissing her as she lay on her back. Maybe that was why he hadn't noticed how her finger was bleeding. Because he hadn't, no matter how much she came to love him, there would always be a part of her afraid of him.

"I was having the most lovely dream," she said. She was careful not to make her tone as angry as she felt.

WENDY, DARLING

CHRISTOPHER GOLDEN

On a Friday evening at the end of May in the year Nineteen Hundred and Fifteen, Wendy spent her final night in her father's house in a fitful sleep, worried about her wedding the following day and the secrets she had kept from her intended groom.

The room had once been a nursery, but those days were all but forgotten. She had stopped dreaming the dreams of her girlhood years before, such that even the echoes of those dreams had slid into the shadows in the corners of the room. Now it was a proper bedroom with a lovely canopy over the bed and a silver mirror and an enormous wardrobe that still gave off a rich mahogany scent though it had stood against the wall for six years and more.

Some nights, though… Some nights the tall French windows would remain open and the curtains would billow and float. On those evenings the moonlight would pour into the room with such earnest warmth it seemed intent upon reminding her of girlhood evenings when she would stay up whispering to her brothers in the dark until all of them drifted off to sleep and dreamt impossible things.

Wendy had lived in the nursery with Michael and John for too long. She ought to have had her own room much sooner, but at first their father had not wanted to give up his study to make another bedroom and later – when he'd changed his mind – the children were no longer interested in splitting up. By then Wendy had begun to see the Lost Boys, and to dream of them, and it seemed altogether safer to stick together.

That day – the day before her wedding – there had been a low, whispery sort of fog all through the afternoon and into the evening. Several times she stirred in her sleep, uneasy as she thought of Jasper, the barrister she was to wed the following afternoon. She quite relished the idea of becoming Mrs. Jasper Gilbert, and yet during the night she felt herself haunted by the prospect. Each time her eyes flickered open, she lay for several moments staring out at the fog until she drifted off again.

Sometime later, she woke to see not fog but moonlight. The windows were open and the curtains performed a ghostly undulation, cast in yellow light.

A dream, she thought, for it must have been. She knew it because the fog had gone. Knew it because of the moonlight and the impossibly slow dance of those curtains, and of course because the Lost Boys were there.

She lay on her side, half her face buried in the feather pillow, and gazed at them. At first she saw only three: two by the settee and one almost hidden in the billow of the curtains. The fourth had a dark cast to his features that made him seem grimmer, less ethereal than the others, though he was the youngest of them. She had not seen them in years, not since her parents had gotten a doctor involved, insisting that the Lost Boys were figments of her imagination. She had never forgiven John and Michael for reporting her frequent visits with the Lost Boys to their parents, a grudge she had come to regret in the aftermath of Michael's death in a millinery fire in 1910. How she had loved him.

By the time of the fire it had been years since she had seen the Lost Boys. After the fire, she had often prayed that it would be Michael who visited her in the night.

"Wendy," one of the Boys whispered now, in her moonlit dream.

"Hello, boys," she said, flush beneath her covers, heart racing. She wanted to cry or scream but did not know if it was fear she felt, or merely grief.

As if grief could ever be *merely*.

She recognized all four of them, of course, and knew their names. But she did not allow herself to speak those names, or even to think them. It would have felt as if she welcomed them back to her dreams, and they were not welcome at all.

"You forgot us, Wendy. You promised you never would."

She nestled her cheek deeper into her pillow, feathers poking her skin through the fabric.

"I never did," she whispered, her skin dampening. Too hot beneath the covers. "You were only in my mind, you see. I haven't forgotten, but my parents and Doctor Goss told me I must persuade my eyes not to see you if you should appear again."

"Have you missed us, then?"

Wendy swallowed. A shudder went through her. She had not.

"As I'm dreaming, I suppose it's all right that I'm seeing you now."

The Lost Boys glanced at one another with a shared, humorless sort of laugh. More a sniff than a laugh, really. A disapproving sniff.

The moonlight passed right through them.

The nearest of them – he of the grim eyes – slid closer to her.

"You were meant to be our mother," he said.

Wendy couldn't breathe. She pressed herself backward, away from them. It was their eyes that ignited a terror within her, those pleading eyes. She closed her own.

"Wake up, Wendy," she whispered to herself. "Please wake up."

"Don't you remember?" the grim-eyed one asked, and her lids fluttered open to find herself still dreaming.

"Please remember," said another, a lithe little boy with a pouting mouth and eyes on the verge of tears.

"No," she whispered.

The hook. Soft flesh against her own. The pain. Blood in the water.

Her body trembled as images rushed into her mind and were driven back, shuttered in dark closets, buried in shallow graves.

"Stay away," she whispered. "Please. My life is all ahead of me."

She did not know if she spoke to the Lost Boys or to those images.

"My fiancé is a good man. Perhaps when we are wed, we can take one or two of you in. He is kind, you see. Not like—"

A door slammed in her mind.

"Like who, Wendy?"

Hook, she thought. *My James*.

"No!" she screamed, hurling back her bedcovers and leaping from the bed, hot tears springing to her eyes. "Leave me, damn you! Leave me to my life!"

Fingers curved into claws, she leapt at the nearest of them. Passing through him, chill gooseflesh rippling across her skin, she fell to the rug and curled up into herself, a mess of sobs.

In the moonlight, she lay just out of reach of the fluttering curtains and cried herself into the sweet oblivious depths of slumber.

When she woke in the early dawn, aching and chilled to the bone, she crept back beneath her bedclothes for warmth and comfort and told herself that there would never be another night when she needed to fear bad dreams. For the rest of her life she would wake in the morning with Jasper beside her and he would hold her and kiss her until the last of sleep's shadows retreated.

The sun rose to a clear blue morning.

No trace of fog.

* * *

The world only began to feel completely real to Wendy again when the carriage drew to a halt in front of the church. Flowers had been arranged over the door and on the steps, and the beauty of the moment made her breath catch in her throat. A smile spread across her lips and bubbled into laughter and she turned toward her grumpy banker of a father and saw that he was smiling as well – beaming, in fact – and his eyes were damp with love for her, and with pride.

"Never thought you'd see the day, did you, Father?" Wendy teased.

George Darling cleared his throat to compose himself. "There were times," he allowed. "But here we are, my dear. Here. We. Are."

He took a deep breath and stepped out of the carriage, itself also festooned with arrangements donated by friends of Wendy's mother who were part of the committee behind the Chelsea Flower Show. A pair of ushers emerged from the church, but Wendy's father waved them back and offered his own hand to guide her down the carriage steps.

George stepped back. He'd never been sentimental, and now he seemed to fight against whatever emotions welled within him. Amongst those she expected, Wendy saw a flicker of uneasiness.

"You look beautiful," he told her.

Wendy knew it was true. She seldom indulged in outright

vanity, but on her wedding day, and in this dress... well, she would forgive herself. Cream-white satin, trimmed in simple lace, it had been one of the very first she had laid eyes upon and she had loved it straight away. Cut low at the neck, with sleeves to the elbows, it had a simple elegance reflected in the simplicity of the veil and the short train. Her father helped gather her train, spread it out behind her, and took her hand as they faced the church.

"Miss Darling," said one of the ushers, whose name she'd suddenly forgotten. She felt horrible, but it seemed that her thoughts were a jumble.

"I'm about to be married," she said, just to hear the words aloud.

"You are, my dear," George agreed. "Everyone is waiting."

The forgotten usher handed her a wreath of orange blossoms and then the other one opened the church door, and moments later Wendy found herself escorted down the aisle by her grumpy-turned-doting father. A trumpet played and then the organ, and all faces turned toward her, so that she saw all of them and none of them at the same time. She smelled the flowers and her heart thundered and she began to feel dizzy and swayed a bit.

"Wendy," her father whispered to her, his grip tightening on her arm. "Are you all right?"

Ahead, at the end of the aisle, the bridesmaids and ushers had spread out to either side. The vicar stood on the altar, dignified and serious. Her mother sat in the front row, her brother John stood amongst the ushers. And there was Jasper, so dapper in his morning coat, his black hair gleaming, his blue eyes smiling.

She no longer felt dizzy. Only safe and sure.

Until the little boy darted out from behind a column – the little boy with grim eyes.

"Stop this!" he shouted. "You must stop!"

Wendy staggered, a terrible pain in her belly as if she were being torn apart inside. She gasped and then covered her mouth, glancing about through the mesh of her veil, certain her friends and relations would think her mad – *again. They would think her mad again.*

But their eyes were not on her. Those in attendance were staring at the little boy in his ragged clothes, and when the second boy ran in from the door to the sacristy and the vicar shouted at him, furious at the intrusion, Wendy at last understood.

The vicar could see the boys.

They could *all* see.

"Out of here, you little scoundrels!" the vicar shouted. "I won't allow you to ruin the day—"

The grim-eyed boy stood before Jasper, who could only stare in half-amused astonishment. That sweetness was simply Jasper's nature, that indulgence where any other bridegroom would have been furious.

The third boy stepped from the shadows at the back of the altar as if he had been there all along. And, of course, he must have been.

"No, no, no," Wendy said, backing away, tearing her arm from her father's grip. She forced her eyes closed, because they couldn't be here. Couldn't be real.

"Wendy?" her father said, and she opened her eyes to see him looking at her.

He knew. Though he had always told her they were figments and dreams, hadn't he seemed unsettled whenever she talked of them? *Spirits*, he'd said, *do not exist, except in the minds of the mad and the guilty.*

Which am I? she'd asked him then. *Which am I?*

Jasper clapped his hands twice, drawing all attention toward him. The unreality of the moment collapsed into tangibility and truth. Wendy breathed. Smelled the flowers. Heard the scuffling and throat-clearing of the stunned members of the wedding.

"All right, lads, you've had your fun," Jasper said. "Off with you!"

"Wendy Darling," one of the boys said, staring at Jasper, tears welling in his eyes. "Only she's not 'darling' at all. You don't know her, sir. She'll be a cruel mother. She'll abandon her children—"

"Rubbish!" shouted Wendy's father. "How dare you speak of my daughter this way!"

Wendy could only stare, not breathing as Jasper strode toward the grim-eyed boy and gripped him by his ragged shirtfront. She saw the way the filthy fabric bunched in his hands and it felt as if the curtain between dream and reality had finally been torn away.

"No," she said, starting toward Jasper... and toward the boys. "Please, don't..."

Her fiancé glanced up, thinking she had been speaking to him, but the boys looked at her as well. They knew better.

"She's had a baby once before," a pale, thin boy said, coming to stand by Jasper, his eyes pleading. "Go on. Ask her."

"Ask her what became of that child," said the grim-eyed boy.

Shaking, Wendy jerked right and left, trapped by all of the eyes that gazed upon her. Jasper frowned, staring at her, and she saw the doubt blooming in him, saw his lips beginning to form a question. Her father still glared angrily at the boys, but even he had a flicker of hesitation. In the front row, Mary Darling stepped from the pew and extended a hand toward her daughter.

"Wendy?"

Shaking her head, Wendy began to back away from those who loved her, retreating down the aisle. She tripped over her silken train and when she fell amongst the soft purity of its folds, she screamed.

"Ask her!" one of the boys shouted. Or perhaps it had been all of them.

Thrusting herself from the ground, whipping her train behind her, she ran. Her whole body felt flushed, but she caught a glimpse of her left hand as she ran and it was pale as marble. Pale as death. At the back of the aisle, a few crimson rose petals had fallen, petals meant to be scattered in the path of husband and wife after the ceremony. To her they were blood from a wound.

She burst from the church, an abyss of unspoken questions gaping behind her, and she fled down the steps in fear that if she did not run, that yawing silence would drag her back. Pain stabbed her belly and her heart slammed inside her chest. Her eyes burned and yet strangely there were no tears. She felt incapable of tears.

At the foot of the steps she tore off the train of her dress. When she glanced up, horses whinnied and chuffed. Her wedding carriage stood waiting. The driver looked at her with kind eyes and his kindness filled her with loathing.

"Wendy!"

Jasper's voice. Behind her. She dared not turn to look at him.

Racing across the street, she darted down a narrow road between a dressmaker's and a baker's shop. At a corner, she nearly collided with two more of the Lost Boys – *names, you know their names* – and she turned right to avoid them, racing downhill now. Another appeared from an alley to her left, but this boy was different from the others. He'd been badly burnt, skin and clothing charred, and unlike the rest he had no substance, flesh so translucent that she could see the stone face of the building behind him.

She wailed, stumbling in anguish, and fell to the street. Her dress tore and her knee bled, so that when she staggered to her feet and ran screaming – grief carving out her insides – a vivid red stain soaked into the satin and spread, the petals of a crimson rose.

"Mother," the burnt boy said behind her.

She did not look back, but glanced once at the windows of a pub as she bolted past. In the glass she saw their reflections, not only the burnt boy but the others as well, one with his head canted too far, neck broken, another beaten so badly his features were ruined.

Moments before she emerged from between two buildings, she realized where she had been going all along. Had she chosen her path or had they driven her here? Did it matter?

Wendy stared at the bank of the Thames, at the deep water rushing by, and all the strength went out of her. Numb and hollow, she shuffled to the riverbank.

Somewhere nearby, a baby cried.

Glancing to her left, she saw the bundle perhaps a dozen feet away, just at the edge of the water. The baby's wailing grew louder and more urgent and she started toward it.

She knew the pattern on its blanket. His blanket.

Kneeling on the riverbank, her bloodstained dress soaking up the damp, she reached out to pull the blanket away from the infant's face. His blue face, bloated and cold, eyes bloodshot and bulging and lifeless.

The sob tore from her chest as she reached for the child, lifted it into her arms and cradled it to her chest. Still she could not weep, but she pressed her eyes tightly closed and prayed for tears.

The bundle in her arms felt too light. Gasping for breath, she opened her eyes.

"No, please," she whispered as she unraveled the empty blanket. The empty, sodden blanket.

"Mother," a voice said, so close, and a hand touched her shoulder.

Wendy froze, breath hitching in her chest. This was not the burnt boy or the grim-eyed child from the church. This was another boy entirely.

Still on her knees, she turned back to see his face. Nine years old, now, his skin still blue, eyes still bloodshot and lifeless. Her boy.

"Peter," she whispered.

He thrust his fingers into her hair and she screamed his name – a name she had never spoken aloud before today. Wendy beat at his arms and clawed at his face as he dragged her to the water and plunged her into the river. She stared up at him through the water and his visage blurred and changed, became the face of his father, James, the butcher's boy. He'd earned his nickname with the bloodstained hook he used in handling the sides of meat in the shop down the street from the Darlings' home.

Her chest burned for air, the urgency of her need forcing her to strike harder at the face above her, which now became her own face, only nine years younger. The hands that held her beneath the water were her own, but she was no longer herself – instead she was a tiny infant, so newly born he still bore streaks of blood from his mother's womb. An infant conceived by a mother and father who were only children themselves, carried and borne in secret – a secret safeguarded by her brothers in the privacy of the room they shared, a secret which destroyed her relationship with them forever. A secret made possible by a father's neglect and a mother's denial.

Peter, she thought.

Starved for air, thoughts and vision dulling, diminishing, slipping away, Wendy opened her mouth and inhaled the river.

Blackness crept in at the corners of her eyes, shadows in her brain, and she realized that she had stopped fighting him. Her arms slipped into the water and her hair pooled around her face. Bloodstained white satin floated in a cloud that enveloped and embraced her.

The hands on her now were larger. A man's hands. They dragged her from the river and for a moment she saw only darkness, a black veil for a cruel mother.

"Wendy," said an urgent voice.

She saw him then. Not the little drowned boy, but Jasper, her intended. He knelt over her, desperate and pleading and calling her name.

Gathered around him on the riverbank were the Lost Boys, those cast aside children, each murdered by his mother. Those dead boys she had met once before, on the night she had drowned her Peter in the Thames, when they had pointed trembling fingers and told her she would carry the black curse of murder all her days, that she might be allowed to approach happiness but never achieve it. They were the stain on her soul. They had been visible to the people in the church, dark dreams come to life, but now they were unseen once more. Jasper wept over her, unaware of their presence…

Wendy could only watch him, standing a short distance away. Her dress felt dry now, but the bloodstain remained.

"No," she whispered, as the darkness retreated from her thoughts and she understood what she saw.

Jasper knelt there, mourning her, grieving for the life they might have had. Wendy saw her own lifeless body from outside, her spirit as invisible to him as the Lost Boys. Others began to run toward the riverbank – her parents and her brother John, the vicar's wife and Jasper's brother, an aunt and uncle. They seemed like ghosts to her, these living people, their grief distant and dull.

The Lost Boys circled around her, dead eyes now contented.

"Mother," Peter whispered, taking her right hand.

Another boy took her left hand. She glanced down and saw the grim eyes that had so unsettled her in her dreams.

"You promised to be a mother to us all, forever," the grim-eyed boy said.

Wendy blinked and turned toward the river. Somehow she could still see the swaddled infant floating on the water, sodden blankets dragging it down, just as it had on that night nine years ago.

"Forever," said Peter.

They guided her gently into the river, where the dark current swept them all away.

FAIRY WEREWOLF VS.
VAMPIRE ZOMBIE

CHARLIE JANE ANDERS

If you're ever in Freeboro, North Carolina, look for the sign of the bull. It hangs off the side of a building with a Vietnamese noodle joint and an auto mechanic, near an alley that's practically a drainage ditch. Don't walk down that alley unless you're brave enough not to look over your shoulder when you hear throaty noises behind you. If you make it to the very end without looking back, hang a left, and watch your footing on the mossy steps. The oak door at the bottom of the stairs will only open if you've got the right kind of mojo.

If it does open, you'll find yourself in Rachel's Bar & Grill, the best watering hole in the Carolinas. My bar. There's only one rule: if there's any trouble, take it outside. (Outside my bar is good, outside of town is better, outside of reality itself is best of all.) I have lots of stories about Rachel's. There are names I could drop – except some of those people might appear. But there is one story that illustrates why you shouldn't make trouble in my bar, and how we take care of our own. It's also the story of how the bar got its mascot.

There was this young woman named Antonia, who went from a beautiful absinthe-drinking stranger to one of my regulars inside of a month. She had skin so pale it was almost silver, delicate features, and wrists so fine she could slide her hand into the wine jug behind the bar – although she'd have to be quick pulling it out again or Leroy the Wine Goblin would bite it off. Anyway, she approached me at closing time, asking if I had any work for her. She could clean tables, or maybe play her guitar a few nights a week.

If you've ever been to Rachel's, you'll know it doesn't need any live music, or anything else, to add atmosphere to the place. If there's one thing we got in spades, it's atmosphere. Just sit in any of the plush booths – the carvings on the wooden tables tell you their stories, and the stains on the upholstery squirm to get out of the way of your butt. From the gentle undulation of the ceiling beams to the flickering of the amber-colored lights to the signed pictures of famous dragons and celebrity succubi on the brick walls, the place is atmosphere city.

But then I got to hear Antonia sing and play on her guitar, and it was like the rain on a midsummer's day right after you just got your first kiss or something. Real lyrical. I let her play at Rachel's one night, and I couldn't believe it – the people who usually just guzzled a pitcher of my "special" sangria and then vamoosed were sticking around to listen to her, shedding luminescent tears that slowly floated into the air and then turned into little crystalline wasps. (The sangria will do that.)

So after Antonia got done singing that first night, I came up to her and said I guessed we could work something out, if she was willing to wipe some tables as well as getting her Lilith Fair on. "There's just one thing I don't get," I said. "It's obvious you're Fae, from the effect you have on the lunkheads that come in here. And you're a dead ringer for that missing princess from the High Court of Sylvania. Princess Lavinia." (Sylvania being what the Fae call Pennsylvania, the seat of their power.) "It's said his supreme highness the Chestnut King weeps every night, and would give half the riches of Sylvania to have you back. The drag queen – Mab – her eyeliner has been smudgy for months. Not to mention the lovestruck Prince Azaron. So what gives?"

"I cannot ever return home," Antonia (or Lavinia) wept. "I regret the day I decided to venture out and see the world for myself. For on that day, I encountered a curse so monstrous, I cannot ever risk inflicting it on any of my kin. I cannot undo what is done. The only way I can protect my friends and family is to stay far away. I am forever exiled, for my own foolishness. Now please ask no more questions, for I have tasted your sangria and I'm afraid my tears would sting you most viciously."

I said no more, although I was consumed with curiosity about the curse that kept the fairy princess from returning to the Seelie Court in Bucks County. I didn't learn any more – until a few weeks later, when the Full Moon arrived.

Antonia appeared as usual, wearing a resplendent dress made of the finest samite and lace (I think it was vintage Gunne

171

Sax). She muttered something about how she was going to play a shorter set than usual, because she felt unwell. I said that was fine, I would just put the ice hockey match on the big-screen TV. (Did I mention the big-screen TV? Also a big part of the atmosphere. We do karaoke on Fridays.) Anyway, she meant to play for an hour, but she got carried away with this one beautiful dirge about lovers who were separated for life by a cruel wind, and it grew dark outside, just as her song reached a peak of emotion.

And something strange happened. Her hands, so teeny, started to grow, and her guitar playing grew more frenzied and discordant. Hairs sprouted all over her skin, and her face was coarsening as well, becoming a muzzle. "NO!" she cried – or was it a howl? – as her already pointy ears became pointier and her hair grew thicker and more like fur. "No, I won't have it! Not here, not now. 'Tis too soon! By my fairy blood, I compel you – subside!" And with that last word, the transformation ceased. The hair vanished from her hands, her face returned to normal, and she only looked slightly huskier than usual. She barely had time to place her guitar in its case, leaving it on the bar, before she fled up the wooden staircase to the door. I heard her ascending into the alley and running away, her panting harsh and guttural.

Antonia did not return for three days, until the Moon was on the wane. When next she sang for us, her song was even more mournful than ever before, full of a passion so hot, it melted our internal organs into a fondue of longing.

Now around this same time, I was thinking about franchising. (Bear with me here, this is part of the story.) I had gotten a pretty good thing going in Freeboro, and I wanted to open another bar over on the other side of the Triad, in the town of Evening Falls. The main problem was, you don't want to open a bar aimed at mystical and mythological patrons in the same strip mall as a Primitive Baptist church, a nail salon and a Bar-B-Q place, right on Highway 40. And Evening Falls only had a few properly secluded locations, all of which were zoned as purely residential, or only for restaurants.

Now, chances are, if you've been to Rachel's, you've already heard my views on the evils of zoning. But just in case you missed it... [Editors' note: the next ten paragraphs of this manuscript consist of a tirade about zoning boards and the ways in which they are comparable to giant flesh-eating cane-toads or hornetaurs. You can read it online at www.monstersofurbanplanning.org.]

Anyway, where was I? Franchising. So I know some witches and assorted fixers, who can make you believe Saturday is Monday, but it's hard to put a whammy on the whole planning board. So I thought to myself, what can I do to win these people over? And that's when I remembered I had my very own enchanting fairy singer, with just a spark of the wolf inside her, on the payroll.

Antonia's eyes grew even huger, and her lip trembled, when I asked her to come and play at a party for the scheming elites of Evening Falls. "I cannot," she said. "I would do anything in

173

my power to help you, Rachel, but I fear to travel where I may be recognized. And my song is not for just anyone, it is only for the lost and the despairing. Can't I just stay here, in your bar, playing for your patrons?"

"Now look," I said, plunking her down on my least carnivorous barstool. "I've been pretty nice to you, and a lot of people would have called the number on the side of the thistle-milk carton to collect the reward on you already. Fairy gold! The real kind, not the type that vanishes after an hour. Not to mention, I put up with the constant danger of you biting my patrons and turning them into werewolves. Which, to be fair, might improve their dispositions and make them better tippers. But you know, it's all about one hand washing the other, even if sometimes one of those hands is a tentacle. Or a claw. Although, you wouldn't really want one of the Octo-priests of Wilmington to wash any part of you, not unless you want strange squid-ink tattoos sprouting on your skin for years after. Where was I?"

"You were attempting to blackmail me," Antonia said with a brittle dignity. "Very well, Rachel. You have shown me what stuff your friendship is made of. I shall play at your 'shindig.'"

"Good, good. That's all I wanted." I swear, there should be a special fairy edition of *Getting To Yes*, just for dealing with all their Fae drama.

So we put together a pretty nice spread at this Quaker meeting hall in Evening Falls, including some pulled-pork barbecue and fried okra. Of course, given that most of these people were involved in local zoning, we should have just let them carve up a virgin instead. I mean, seriously. [The rest of this section is available at www.monstersofurbanplanning.org – The Editors.]

Where was I? Oh yes. So it was mostly the usual assortment of church ladies, small-time politicians, local business people, and so on. But there were two men who stood out like hornetaurs at a bull fight.

Sebastian Valcourt was tall, with fine cheekbones and a noble brow, under a shock of wavy dark hair that he probably blow-dried for an hour every day. He wore a natty suit, but his shirt was unbuttoned almost to the navel, revealing a hairless chest that was made of money. No kidding, I used to know a male stripper named Velcro who was three-quarters elf, and he would have killed for those pecs.

The other startlingly beautiful man was named Gilbert Longwood, and he was big and solidly built, like a classical statue. His arms were like sea-cliffs, and his face was big and square-jawed – like a marble bust except that his eyes had pupils, which was probably a good thing for him. When he shook my hand, I felt his grip and it made me all weak in the knees. But from the start of the evening, both Gilbert and Sebastian could only see one woman.

Once Antonia began to play, it was all over – everybody in that room fell for her, and I could have gotten planning permission to put a bowling alley inside a church. Afterwards, I was talking to Gilbert, while Sebastian leapt across the room like a ballet dancer, landing in front of Antonia and kissing her hand with a sweeping bow. He said something, and she laughed behind a hand.

"You throw an entertaining party," said Gilbert, trying not to stare at Sebastian's acrobatic courtship over in the corner. "I don't think I've seen half these people show any emotion since the town historian self-immolated a few years ago." His voice was like a gong echoing in a crypt. I never got Gilbert's whole story, but I gathered he was the son of a wealthy sculptor, part of Evening Falls' most prominent family.

At this point, Gilbert had given up all pretense that he wasn't staring at Antonia. "Yeah," I said. "I discovered that girl. I taught her everything she knows. Except I held back a few secrets for myself, if you get my drift and I think you do." I winked.

"Please excuse me, gracious lady," Gilbert said. When he bowed, it was like a drawbridge going down and then up again. He made his way across the room, navigating around all the people who wanted to ask him about zoning (jackals!) on his way to where Sebastian was clinking glasses with Antonia.

I couldn't quite get close enough to hear the conversation that followed, but their faces told me everything I needed to know. Sebastian's mouth smiled, but his amber-green eyes burned with desire for Antonia, even as he made some cutting remark towards Gilbert. Gilbert smiled back, and let Sebastian's fancy wit bounce off his granite face, even as he kept his longing gaze on Antonia's face. For Antonia's part, she blushed and looked down into the depths of her glass of Cheerwine.

You could witness a love triangle being born, its corners sharp enough to slice you open and expose your trembling insides to all sorts of infections, including drug-resistant staph, which has been freaking me out lately. I always wash my hands twice, with antibacterial soap and holy water. Where was I? Right, love triangle. This was an isosceles of pure burning desire, in which two men both pined for the same impossibly beautiful, permanently heartbroken lady. My first thought was: There's got to be a way to make some money off this.

And sure enough, there was. I made sure Antonia didn't give out her digits, or even so much as her Twitter handle, to either of these men. If they wanted to stalk her, they would have to come to Rachel's Bar & Grill. I managed to drop a hint to both of them that what really impressed Antonia was when a guy had a large, heavy-drinking, entourage.

I didn't have to turn on the big-screen TV once for the whole month that followed. Sebastian and Gilbert, with their feverish courtship of Antonia, provided as much free entertainment as ten *Married With Children* marathons. Maybe even eleven. Sebastian gave Antonia a tiny pewter unicorn, which danced around in the palm of her hand but remained lifeless otherwise. Gilbert brought enough flowers that the bar smelled fresh for the first time since 1987.

This one evening, I watched Gilbert staring at Antonia as she sat on her stool and choked out a ballad. She wore a long canvas skirt, and her feet were crossed on the stool's dowel. He looked at her tragic ankles – so slender, with tendons that flexed like heartstrings – and his big brown eyes moistened.

And then Sebastian arrived, flanked by two other weirdly gorgeous, unnaturally spry men with expressive eyes. Every time you would think their eyebrows couldn't get any more expressive, or their gazes more smouldering, they'd kick it up another notch. Their eyebrows had the dramatic range of a thousand Kenneth Branaghs – maybe a thousand Branaghs per eyebrow, even. The other two smiled wan, ironic smiles at each other, while Sebastian kept his gaze fixed on the tiny trembling lips and giant mournful eyes of Antonia.

A few weeks – and a few thou worth of high-end liquor – later, both Sebastian and Gilbert began to speak to Antonia of their passion.

"A heart so grievously wounded as yours requires careful tending, my lady," Gilbert rumbled in his deep voice. "I have strong hands, but a gentle touch, to keep you safe." His sideburns were perfect rectangles, framing his perfectly chiseled cheekbones.

"I fear..." Antonia turned to put her guitar in its case, so the anguish on her face was hidden from view for a moment. "I fear the only thing for a condition such as mine is solitude, laced with good fellowship here at Rachel's. But I shall cherish your friendship, Gilbert."

Soon after, Sebastian approached Antonia, without his cronies. "My dear," he said. "Your loveliness outshines every one of those neon beer signs. But it is your singing, your sweet sad tune, which stirs me in a way that nothing else has for decades. You must consent to be mine, or I shall have no choice but to become ever more mysterious, until I mystify even myself. Did I say that out loud? I meant, I'll waste away. Look at my eyebrows, and you'll see how serious I am."

"Oh, Sebastian." Antonia laughed, then sighed. "Had I even a sliver of a heart to give, I might well give it to you. But you speak to a hollow woman."

Blah blah blah. This went on and on, and I had to re-order several of the single malt whiskeys, not to mention all the mid-range cognacs, and Southern Comfort.

Who can say how long this would have gone on for, if both Sebastian and Gilbert hadn't turned up on an evening when Antonia wasn't there? (You guessed it: The Full Moon.) The two of them started arguing about which of them deserved Antonia. Gilbert rumbled that Sebastian just wanted to use Antonia, while Sebastian said Gilbert was too much of a big ugly lug for her. Gilbert took a swing at Sebastian and missed, and that's when I told them to take it outside.

Soon afterwards, we all tromped outside to watch. Sebastian was dancing around like Prince on a hot griddle, while Gilbert kept lashing out with his massive fists and missing. Until finally, Gilbert's forearm caught Sebastian in the shoulder, and he went flying onto his ass. And then things got entertaining: Sebastian's face got all tough and leathery, and fangs sprouted from his mouth. He did a somersault in mid-air, aiming a no-shadow kick at Gilbert – who raised his boulder-sized fist, so it collided with Sebastian's face.

After that, the fight consisted of Gilbert punching Sebastian, a lot. "Stupid vampire," Gilbert grunted. "You're not the first bloodsucker I've swatted."

By this point, Sebastian's jaw was looking dislocated. Those expressive eyebrows were twisted with pain. "I'm not... your average... vampire," he hissed. Gilbert brought his sledgehammer fist down onto Sebastian's skull.

Sebastian fell to the ground, in an ungainly pile of bones. And he smiled. "The more beat up I get... the harder to kill... I get," he rasped. And then he stood on jerky legs, his flesh peeling away.

Sebastian's smile turned slack and distended. Instead of his usual witticisms, he said but one word: "Braiiiiiinnsss..."

Gilbert kept punching at Sebastian, but it did no good. Nothing even slowed him down. Sebastian thrashed back at Gilbert with a hideous force, and finally he hit a weak point, where Gilbert's head met his neck – and Gilbert's head fell, rolling to land at my feet.

Gilbert's severed head looked up at me. "Tell Antonia... my love for her was true." And then the head turned to stone. And so did the rest of his body, which fell into several pieces in the middle of the dark walkway.

Sebastian looked at me, and the couple other regulars who were watching. He snarled, with what remained of his mouth, "Braaaaaaaiiiiiinnsss!"

The nearest patron was Jerry Dorfenglock, who'd been coming to Rachel's for 20 years. He had a really nice, smooth bald head, which he'd experimented with combing over and then with shaving all the way, Kojak-style, before deciding to just let it be what it was: two wings of fluffy gray hair flanking a serene dome. That noble scalp, Sebastian tore open, along with the skull beneath. Sebastian reached with both hands to scoop out poor Jerry's gray matter, then stopped at the last moment. Instead, he leaned further down and sunk his top teeth into Jerry's neck, draining all the blood from his body in one gulp.

A moment later, Sebastian looked away from the husk of Jerry's body, looking more like his normal self already. "If I—" He paused to wipe his mouth. "If I eat the brains, I become more irrevocably the zombie. But if I drink the blood, I return to my magnificent vampiric self. It's always hard to remind myself. Think of it as the blood-brain barrier between handsome rogue... and shambling fiend." The other patron who'd been watching the fight, Lou, tried to make a break for it, but Sebastian was too fast.

I looked at the bloodless husks of my two best customers, plus the chalky pieces of poor Gilbert, then back at Sebastian – who now looked as though nothing had ever happened, except for the stains on his natty suit. I decided being casual was my best hope of coming out of this alive.

"So you're a half-vampire, half-zombie," I said as if I was discussing a *Seinfeld* rerun. "That's something you don't see every day, I guess."

"It is an amusing story," Sebastian said. "When I was a mortal, I loved a mysterious dark beauty, who grew more mysterious with every passing hour. My heart felt close to bursting for the love of her. At last, she revealed she was an ancient vampire, and offered me the chance to be her consort. She fed me her blood, and told me that if I died within twelve hours, I would become a vampire and I could join her. If I did not die, I could return to my mortal life. She left me to decide for myself. I went out to my favorite spot on the edge of Stoneflower Lake, to ponder my decision and savor my last day on Earth – for I already knew what choice I would make. But just then, a zombie climbed out of the lake bottom, where it had been terrorizing the bass, and bit me in the face. I died then and there, but as the vampire blood began to transform me into an eternal swain of darkness, so too did the zombie bite work its own magic. Now, I remain a vampire, only as long as I have a steady diet of restoring blood."

"That's quite a story," I said. I was already trying to figure out what I would do with Lou and Jerry's bodies, since I had a feeling Sebastian would regard corpse cleanup as woman's work. "You should sell the TV movie rights."

"Thanks for the advice." Sebastian looked into my eyes, and his gaze held me fast. "You will not speak to anyone of what you have seen and heard tonight." As he spoke, the words became an unbreakable law to me. Then Sebastian sauntered away, leaving me – what did I tell you? – to bury the bodies. At least with Gilbert, it was just a matter of lugging the pieces to the Ruined Statue Garden a couple of streets away.

By the time I got done, my hands were a mess and I was sweating and shaking and maybe even crying a little. I went back to the bar and poured myself some Wild Turkey, and then some more, and then a bit more after that. I wished I could talk to someone about this. But of course, I was under a vampiric mind-spell thingy, and I could never speak a word.

Good thing I've got a Hotmail account.

I put the whole thing as plain as I could in a long email to Antonia, including the whole confusing "vampire who's also a zombie" thing. I ended by saying: "Here's the thing, sweetie, Sebastian is gonna think you don't know any of this, and with Gilbert out of the way, he'll be making his move. Definitely do NOT marry him, the half-zombie thing is a *dealbreaker*, but don't try to fight him either. He's got the thing where the more you hurt him, the more zombie he gets and then you can't win; he's got you beat either way. And not to mention, the full moon is over as of tomorrow morning, so you got no more wolf on your side. Just keep yourself safe, okay, because it would just about ruin me to see anything happen to you – I mean you bring in the paying customers, don't worry, I'm not getting soppy on you. Your boss, Rachel."

She came in the next day, clutching Gilbert's head. Her eyes were puffy and the cords on her neck stood out as she heaved a sob. I handed her a glass of absinthe without saying anything, and she drained it right away. I made her another, with the sugar cube and everything.

I wasn't sure if Sebastian's mind control would keep me from saying I was sorry, but it didn't. Antonia shrugged and collapsed onto my shoulder, weeping into my big flannel shirt, Gilbert's forehead pressing into my stomach.

"Gilbert really loved me," she said when she got her breath back and sat down on her usual music-playing stool. "He loved me more than I deserved. I was... I was finally ready to surrender, and give my heart away. I made up my mind, while I was out running with the wolves."

"You were going to go out with Gilbert?" I had to sit down too.

"No. I was going to let Gilbert down easy, and then date Sebastian. Because he made me laugh." She opened her guitar case, revealing a bright sword made of tempered Sylvanian steel with the crest of Thuiron the Resolver on the hilt, instead of a guitar. "Now I have to kill him."

"Hey, hey, hey," I said. "There are some good reasons not to do that, which I cannot speak of, but hang on, let me get a notepad and a pen and I'll be happy to explain—"

"You already explained." She put her left hand on my shoulder. "Thanks for your kindness, Rachel."

"I don't—" What could I say? What was I *allowed* to say? "I don't want you to die."

"I won't." She smiled with at least part of her face.

"Are you starting your set early tonight? I have a request," Sebastian said from the doorway at the top of the short staircase leading into the bar, framed by the ebbing daylight. "I really want to hear some Van Morrison for once, instead of that—"

Antonia threw Gilbert's head at Sebastian. His eyes widened as he realized what it was, and what it meant. He almost ducked, then opted to catch it with one hand instead, to show he was still on top of the situation. While he was distracted, though, Antonia was already running with her sword out, making a whoosh as it tore through the air.

Antonia impaled Sebastian, but missed his heart. He kicked her in the face, and she fell, blood-blinded.

"So this is how it's going to be?" Sebastian tossed the head into the nearest booth, where it landed face-up on the table. "I confess I'm disappointed. I was going to marry you and *then* kill you. More fairy treasure that way."

"You—You—" Antonia coughed blood. "You never loved me."

"Oh, keep up." Sebastian loomed over Antonia, pulled her sword out of his chest, and swung it over his head two-handed, aiming for a nice clean slice. "I'll bring your remains back to Sylvania, and tell them a lovely story of how you and I fell in love and got married, before you were killed by a wild boar or an insurance adjuster. Hold still, this'll hurt less."

Antonia kicked him in the reproductive parts, but he shrugged it off. The shining sword whooshed down towards her neck.

"Hey!" I pumped my plus-one Vorpal shotgun from behind the bar. "No. Fighting. In. The. Bar."

"We can take it outside," Sebastian said, not lowering the sword.

"Too late for that," I said. "You're in my bar, you settle it how I choose."

"And how's that?"

I said the first thing that came into my head: "With a karaoke contest."

And because it was my bar, and I have certain safeguards in place for this sort of situation, they were both bound by my word. Sebastian grumbled a fair bit, especially what with Antonia being a semi-professional singer, but he couldn't fight it. It took us a couple hours to organize, including finding a few judges and putting an impartiality whammy on them, to keep it a fair competition.

I even broke open my good wine jug and gave out free cups to everybody. Once his nesting place was all emptied out, Leroy the Wine Goblin crawled onto the bar and squinted.

Antonia went first, and she went straight for the jugular – with showtunes. You've probably never seen a fairy princess do "Don't Tell Mama" from *Cabaret*, complete with hip-twirling burlesque dance moves and a little Betty Boop thing when she winked at the audience. Somehow she poured all her rage and passion, all her righteous Sarah McLachlan-esque anger, into a roar on the final chorus. The judges scribbled nice high numbers and chattered approvingly.

And then Sebastian went up – and he broke out that Red Hot Chili Peppers song about the City of Angels. He'd even put on extra eyeliner. He fixed each of us with that depthless vampire stare, even as he poured out an amazing facsimile of a soul, singing about being lost and lonely and wanting his freakin' happy place. Bastard was going to win this thing.

But there was one thing I knew for sure. I knew that he'd have to shut his eyes, for at least a moment, when he hit those high notes in the bridge about the bridge, after the second chorus.

Sure enough, when Sebastian sang out "Under the bridge downtown," his eyes closed so his voice could float over the sound of Frusciante's guitar transitioning from "noodle" mode to "thrash" mode. And that's when I shot him with my plus-one Vorpal shotgun. Once in the face, once in the chest. I reloaded quick as I could, and shot him in the chest again, and then in the left kneecap for good measure.

It wasn't enough to slow him down, but it did make him change. All of a sudden, the lyrics went, "Under the bridge downtown, I could not get enough... BRAIIIIINSSSS!!"

He tossed the microphone and lurched into the audience. The three karaoke judges, who were still enchanted to be 100 percent impartial, sat patiently watching and making notes on their scoresheets, until some other patrons hauled them out of the way. Leroy the Wine Goblin covered his face and screamed for the safety of his jug. People fell all over each other to reach the staircase.

"I shall take it from here." Antonia hoisted her sword, twirling it like a Benihana chef while Frusciante's guitar-gasm reached its peak. She hacked one of Sebastian's arms off, but he barely noticed.

She swung the sword again, to try and take his head off,

and he managed to sidestep and headbutt her. His face caught the side of her blade, but he barely noticed, and he drove the sharp edge into Antonia's stomach with his forehead. Blood gushed out of her as she fell to the ground, and he caught it in his mouth like rain.

A second later, Sebastian was Sebastian again. "Ah, fairy blood," he said. "There really is nothing like it." Antonia tried to get up again, but slumped back down on the floor with a moan, doubled up around her wounded stomach.

I shot at Sebastian again, but I missed and he broke the shotgun in half. Then he broke both my arms. "Nobody is going to come to karaoke night if you shoot people in the face while they're singing. Seriously." I tried not to give him the satisfaction of hearing me whimper.

Antonia raised her head and said a fire spell. Wisps of smoke started coming off Sebastian's body, but he just shrugged. "You've already seen what happens if you manage to hurt me." The smoke turned into a solid wall of flame, but Sebastian pushed it away from his body with a tai-chi move. "Why even bother?"

"Mostly," Antonia's voice came from the other side of the firewall, "just to distract yooooooooooo!" Her snarl became a howl, a barbaric call for vengeance.

There may be a sight more awesome than a giant white wolf leaping through a wall of solid fire. If so, I haven't seen it. Antonia – for somehow she had managed to summon enough of her inner wolf to change – bared her jaws as she leapt. Her eyes shone red and her ears pulled back as the flames parted around her and sparks showered from her ivory fur.

Sebastian never saw it coming. Her first bite tore his neck open, and his head lolled off to one side. He started to zombify again, but Antonia was already clawing him.

"Don't— Don't let him bite you!" I shouted from behind the bar.

Sebastian almost got his teeth on Antonia, but she ducked. "BRAIIINNSS!"

She was on top of him, her jaws snapping wildly, but he was biting just as hard. His zombie saliva and his vampire teeth were both inches away from her neck.

I crawled over to the cooler where I kept the pitchers of sangria, and pulled the door open with my teeth. I knocked pitchers and carafes on the floor, trying to get at the surprise I'd stored there the night before, in a big jar covered with cellophane wrap.

I hadn't actually buried *all* of Lou and Jerry.

I pulled the jar out with my teeth and wedged it between my two upper arms and my chin, then lugged it over to where Antonia and Sebastian were still trying to bite each other. "Hey," I rasped, "I saved you something, you bastard." And I tipped the jar's contents – two guys' brains, in a nice balsamic *vinaigrette* – into Sebastian's face. Once he started guzzling the brains, he couldn't stop himself. He was getting brain all over his face, as he tried to swallow it all as fast as possible. Brains were getting in his eyes and up what was left of his nose. There was no going back for him now.

Antonia broke the glass jar and held a big shard of it in her strong wolf jaws, sawing at Sebastian's neck until his head came all the way off. He was still gulping at the last bits of brains in his mouth, and trying to lick brain-bits off his face.

It took them an hour to set the bones on my arms and I had casts the size of beer kegs. We put Sebastian's head into another jar, with a UV light jammed inside so whenever the Red Hot Chili Peppers come on the stereo, he gets excited and his face glows purple. I never thought the Peppers would be the most requested artist at Rachel's. I never did get permission to open a second bar in Evening Falls, though.

As for Antonia, I think this whole experience toughened her up, and made her realize that being a little bit wild animal wasn't a bad thing for a fairy princess. And that Anthony Kiedis really doesn't have the singing range he thinks he has. And that when it comes to love triangles and duels to the death, you should always cheat. And that running away from your problems only works for so long. There were a few other lessons, all of which I printed out and laminated for her. She still sings in the bar, but she's made a couple of trips back to Sylvania during the crescent moon, and they're working on a cure for her. She could probably go back and be a princess if she wanted to, but we've been talking about going into business together and opening some straight-up karaoke bars in Charlotte and Winston-Salem. She's learning to KJ. I think we could rule the world.

LOOK INSIDE

MICHAEL MARSHALL SMITH

I'm going to tell a little fib to start off with. Don't worry – I'll let you know what it was, later on. I'll leave you with the truth, I promise.

But I'll tell you the other stuff first.

And I'm pregnant.

* * *

When it started, I'd been out for the evening. A work dinner, which meant a few hours in an Italian restaurant in Soho while my boss rambled about the challenges facing his company in these tough economic times, and was fairly good about not glancing down my blouse.

It wasn't a long dinner, and even after taking the tube back I was home by half-past nine. I own a very small house in an area of North London called Kentish Town, not far from the station and the main road. Kentish Town is basically now an interstice between the nicer and more expensive neighbourhoods of Hampstead, Highgate and Camden, but before it was subsumed into urban sprawl it had been a place of slight note, open country enlivened by the attractive River Fleet – sourced in springs up on Hampstead Heath but long-ago so snarled and polluted that it was eventually lost, paved over for its entire length and redirected into an underground sewer.

My narrow little house stands close to where it once ran, in the middle of a short mid-Victorian terrace, and is three (and a bit) storeys high with a scrap of garden out back halved in size by a galley kitchen extension put in by the previous owner. Originally, so I was told by said owner, the houses were built to home families of men working on the railway line. It's remarkably unremarkable except for the fact that one side of my garden is bounded by an old stone wall, inset into which is a badly weathered stone plaque mentioning St. John's College. A little research turned up the fact that, hundreds of years before, the land that these houses was built on – and a chunk of Kentish Town itself – had belonged to the College, part of Cambridge University. Why a college would have owned a garden a hundred miles away is beyond me, but then I've never understood the appeal of reality television or Colin Firth, either, so it's possible I'm just a bit dim.

Here endeth the tour.

It's a very small house but I'm lucky to have it at all, given London's lunatic house prices. Well – not *just* lucky. Oh, how my friends took the piss, when I bought my first flat and shackled myself with a mortgage straight out of university; but now I've been able to swap up to a place with an actual staircase, and they're still renting crappy two-bed apartments in neighbourhoods where not even hipsters want to live, it's not so bloody funny, it appears (except to me, of course).

Once indoors I hung up my coat, kicked off my shoes, and undid the top button of my skirt in an effort to increase my physical comfort in a post-pasta universe. Thus civilianised, I wandered through the living room (an epic journey of exactly five paces) and into the kitchen, where I zoned out while waiting for the kettle to boil. I'd drunk only two glasses of wine but I was tired, and the combination put me into a fuzzy trance.

Then, for no reason I was conscious of, I turned and looked into the living room.

The kettle had just finished boiling, sending a cloud of steam up around my face, and yet there was a cold spot on the back of my neck.

Someone's been in my house.

* * *

I knew it without doubt. Or felt I did. I've always believed it a romantic notion (in the sense of "sweet, but deluded") that you would somehow know if someone had been in your house: that the intrusion of a stranger would leave some tangible psychic trace; that your dwelling is your friend and will tattle on an interloper.

A house is nothing more than walls and a roof and a collection of furnishings and objects – most chosen on the grounds of economy, not with boundless attention or existential

193

rigour – and the only difference between you and every other person on the planet is that you're entitled by law to be there. And yet I knew it.

I knew someone had been in my house.

What if he's still here?

The kitchen extension has a side door, my back door, I guess, which leads into the garden. I could open it, slip out that way. I couldn't get far, though, as the neighbours' gardens are the other side of high fences (in one case built upon the remains of that old wall).

I didn't like the idea for other reasons, too.

It was my bloody house and I didn't want to flee from it, not to mention I'd feel an utter tit if I was discovered trying to shin my way over a fence into a neighbour's garden on the basis of a "feeling". That's exactly the kind of shit that gives women a bad name.

I reached out to the door, however. I turned the handle, gently, and discovered it was unlocked.

I knew the *front* door had been locked – I'd unlocked it on my return from dinner. All the windows in the kitchen were closed and locked, and from where I stood, still frozen in place, I could see the big window at the front of the living room was locked, too.

There was, in other words, only one possible way in which someone could have got into the house – and that was if I'd left the back door unlocked when I left the house that morning.

I didn't know anything about the tactics of house-breaking, but suspected that you'd leave your point of entry open (or at least ajar) while you were on the premises, to make it easier to affect a rapid exit if the householder returned home. You wouldn't close it.

My back door had been closed. Which meant hopefully he wasn't still on the premises.

I relaxed, a little.

I tip-toed back through the living room to the bottom of the stairs, and peered up them, listening hard. I couldn't hear anything, and I know from experience that the wooden floors up there are impossible to traverse without a cavalcade of creaks – that sometimes the damned things will creak in the night even if there's no one treading on them, especially the ones on the very top floor.

"Hello?"

I held my breath, listening for movement from above. Nothing. Absolute silence.

I went on a cautious tour of the house: the bathroom and so-called guest room on the first floor; the bedroom and clothes-storage-pit on the next; and finally the minuscule "attic" room at the very top, situated up its own stunted little flight of five stairs. According to the previous owner, this would originally have been intended for a housemaid. She'd have needed to be a bloody tiny housemaid.

The space was so small that any normal-sized person would have to sleep curled-up in a ball. She wouldn't have been able to stand up in the space, as I'd confirmed only the day before. I'd finally got round to hoicking out and charity-shopping a few old boxes of crap that had been languishing in there since I moved in. During the process I straightened at one point without thinking, banging my forehead on the dusty old beam hard enough to break the skin, causing a drop or two of blood to fall to the wooden floorboards.

I could still see where they'd fallen, but at least the tiny room was tidy now.

And empty, along with all the other rooms.

The whole house looked exactly as it had when I left that morning, i.e. like the lair of a twenty-eight-year-old professional woman who – while not a total slattern – isn't obsessed with tidiness. Nothing out of place, nothing missing, nothing moved. Nobody there.

And there never *had* been, of course. The sense I believed I'd had, the feeling that someone had been inside, was simply wrong.

That's all.

* * *

By the time I reached the ground floor again I was wondering whether I was actually going to watch television after all (my intended course of action) or if I should have a bath and go to bed instead. Or maybe just go straight to bed, with a book. Or magazine. I couldn't quite settle on a plan.

Then I thought of something else.

I shook my head, decided it was silly, but wearily tromped toward the kitchen. Might as well check.

I flicked the kettle back on to make a cuppa for bed (having decided on the way it was now late enough without spending an hour half-watching crap television, and showering tomorrow morning would do just fine, given the emptiness of my bed). Once a teabag was in the cup waiting, I turned my attention to the bread bin.

My mother gave this to me, a moving-in present when I bought the house. It's fashioned in an overtly rustic style and would look simply fabulous if placed within easy reach of an Aga in a country kitchen (which my mother has, and would like me to have too, preferably soon and in the company of an only moderately boring young man who would commute from there to a well-paid job in the City while also helping me to start popping out children at a steady clip). In my current abode the bread bin merely looks unfeasibly large.

I don't actually eat bread either, or not often, as it gives me the bloat something chronic. I was therefore confident that it should be empty of baked goods but for a few crumbs and maybe a rock-hard croissant.

Nonetheless this is what I had come to check.

I lifted the handle on the front, releasing a faint scent of long-ago sliced bread. Then I let out a small shriek, and jumped back.

The front of the bin dropped to the counter with a clatter that sounded very loud. I blinked at the interior, then cautiously reached out.

Inside my bread bin was a note. I took it out.

It said:

It's very pretty. And so are you

* * *

I need to backtrack a little here.

Years ago, in the summer after I left college, I went on a trip to America. I can't really describe it as "travelling", as I rented a car and stayed in motels most of the time – rather than heroically hitch-hiking and bunking down in vile hostels or camping in the woods, dodging psycho killers, poison oak and ticks full to bursting with Lyme Disease – but it was me out there on my own for two months, and so it qualifies for the word "trip" in my book.

In the middle of it I lodged for five days with some old friends of my parents, a genteel couple called Brian and Randall who lived in decaying grandeur in an old house in a small town near the Adirondack Mountains of New York State, the name of which escapes me. It was a pleasant interval, during which I learned that Mozart is not all bad, that my mother had once vomited for two hours after an evening sampling port wines, and that you can perk-up cottage cheese no end by stirring some fresh dill into it. Fact.

I noticed something the first night. Randall had gone upstairs to bed. Brian, by a slender margin the more butch of the two, sat up with me a while longer, conferring advice on local sights worth a visit (almost none, according to him).

As we said goodnight in the kitchen, I noticed that he checked the house's back door was shut (without locking it, however), and hesitated for a moment in front of a small, wooden box affixed to the wall opposite it, before giving it a little tap.

The next morning I was up early, and as I made myself a cup of tea (Brian and Randall were fierce Anglophiles, having spent several years living in Oxford, and had a bewildering array of hardcore teas to choose from) I drifted over and took a look at the wooden box.

It was small, about two inches deep, nine inches wide and six inches tall. There was a hinged lid on the top and upon this had been painted the words *LOOK INSIDE!*

I didn't feel that I could or should, however, and it was a couple of days later – after I'd seen Brian go through his late-night ritual twice more – that I finally asked him about it. He rolled his eyes.

"Silly idea," he muttered. He gestured for me to come over. "See what it says?"

"'Look Inside'," I said.

"What does that make you want to do?"

"Well… look inside."

He smiled. "Good. Go ahead."

I opened the little box. Inside was an envelope. I looked at Brian. "Go on," he said.

I pulled it out. The envelope was unsealed. I removed from it a cheerful greetings card that had the words *WELCOME, FRIEND* printed clearly on the front. Inside was another envelope, a little smaller than the first. I let this be for a moment, and read the message that had been inscribed on the card:

> *Dear Uninvited Visitor,*
>
> *Welcome to this house. We have called it ours for a long time now, and we like it very much. We hope you will find good use for what is in this card, and that it will be sufficient incentive for you to go on your way, without further loss or damage to our dear home. If so, you leave with our thanks, and our very best wishes.*
>
> *Regards,*
>
> *Randall & Brian*

I frowned, and looked up at Brian.

"Look inside the second envelope," he said.

I put the card down and opened the envelope. Inside, held together by a large paperclip with a smiley face on it, were bills totalling two hundred and sixty dollars.

"We started with a hundred," Brian said. "And have raised it by twenty every year. So it must be seven years, now, I suppose. No, eight. Time does trot along, doesn't it?" He gestured vaguely to indicate the house as a whole. "Nobody's going to break in through the front door," he said. "It's right on the main street, and in a town this small people keep a friendly eye on each other's properties. Someone could come around the side, but breaking windows is such a chore and prone to be noisy. So we always leave the back door unlocked."

"What? Why?"

"Otherwise that would be the obvious way to break in, my dear, and a broken door alone would cost hundreds and hundreds of dollars to put right, never mind the time and inconvenience – and who knows what they'd steal or damage once they'd gained entrance? The way it stands now, someone can simply open the door and come straight in, and once you're in the kitchen the very first thing you see is that box. Hard to resist, don't you think?"

I was smiling, charmed by the idea. "And does it work?"

"No idea," Brian said. "I have never once risen from my slumbers – nor returned from promenading during the day – to discover the envelope gone. The whole thing was Randall's idea, to be honest. I generally find it's best to let the old fool have his way. Except when it comes the proper method for making a nice, silky Hollandaise, of course, with regard to which he is… so *very* wrong."

A couple of days later I got back into my rental car and set off to wherever I went next (a vague trawl through the Carolinas, I believe, though as my route was completely without form, and void, it all gets a bit mixed up in my mind now). I evidently brought Randall's idea back home with me to London, however – buried beneath the levels of conscious recall until I moved into this house.

In my previous flat it wouldn't have made a lot of sense, what with it being on the third floor. Quite soon after I moved into my house in Kentish Town, however, I saw a little wall-box in a local knick-knack store, and the idea popped back into my head as if it had been waiting patiently for attention all along.

I bought the box and picked a spot on the wall, about six feet up the corridor from my front door. I spent a happy evening rather painstakingly painting the words *LOOK INSIDE!* onto the lid. You'd have to be charitable to describe the result as artistic, but it was legible. When I'd hung the result on a nail, I felt foolish.

Not because I'd done it – I was still charmed by the notion – but at stealing the fruits of someone else's personality. This was Randall's idea, not mine. In the house he shared with Brian (the latter sheepishly colluding, out of love) it was a song of individuality, like the mandatory dill stirred into their cottage cheese. If I did the same thing, I was merely a copycat.

So I changed it a little. Instead of putting an envelope of cash in the box on the wall, I left a note there telling them to look...

In the bread bin, in the kitchen.

And I didn't make an offering of cash, either. I left a piece of jewellery instead. It wasn't a piece that meant the world to me, admittedly, but it wasn't without some emotional value. I'd found it in Brighton years before, paid more than I could afford at the time, and had real affection for it. I chose it for the offering on the grounds that a genuine sacrifice could not be made without cost. It was probably worth about a hundred quid, or at least that's what I imagined you could get for it, should you show it discreetly around one of the area's less reputable pubs.

Like Brian, I'd never yet woken or returned to find evidence that the note in the box in the hallway had been found.

Never, that is, until now.

I walked quickly back to the hallway. I stopped when I was a few feet from the box, and approached cautiously.

It looked the same as always, though to be honest I'd stopped noticing it some time ago. I looked inside.

The envelope there had been opened.

Of course it had. It had to have been. Without reading the message I'd written on the card – almost verbatim the same as the one Randall had concocted – the person wouldn't have known to look inside the bread bin, and find what was there, and leave me the note.

Suddenly all the strength seemed to go from my legs, and I tottered into the living room and sat down on the sofa just in time.

* * *

The house was still empty, of course. I'd already established that, and what I'd just discovered made no difference to that fact. There was nothing to be frightened about. Nothing in the present situation, anyway.

But... yes there was.

I'd been right after all. Someone *had* been in the house. They'd prowled around, found the box in the hallway and the note and then the jewellery in the bread bin. Left a note, and then gone.

What should I do? Call the police?

Well, obviously I should. Someone had been in the house and taken something. Though it *was* something I'd invited them to have, of course.

Unless...

I did another quick tour of the house and couldn't find anything else missing. My iPad and iLaptop were all where they should be, along with my near-worthless television and DVD player. So was my other jewellery, the stuff I didn't store in the bread bin. I even dug out my under-used cheque book from the bedside drawer and established no cheques were missing from the middle (a cunning ruse I'd read about in some magazine or other – steal a few from the middle, rather than the whole book, and nobody notices they're gone until it's too late). I'm not sure even thieves use cheques much any more, though, and apart from a few objects of purely sentimental value, there was nothing else worth nicking in the entire house. And none of it had been nicked anyway.

But someone still shouldn't have come into my place, even if their only score was a piece of jewellery I'd effectively offered to them.

I grabbed my phone and went back into the kitchen to retrieve the note from the counter, ready to have it to hand when the police arrived. Did one dial 999 in these non-urgent circumstances, or were you supposed to look up the number of the local station? I had no idea.

I hesitated, and put the phone down.

* * *

The next day at work was hectic and slightly bizarre, as the woman who shares my office appeared to undergo a teeny tiny mental breakdown in the late morning, and stormed out, never to return. I'd always thought she was a bit bonkers and so I wasn't totally surprised, though I was impressed by how much chaos she left in her wake.

My boss took the event admirably in his stride. He looked dispiritedly at the mess she'd made, told me to leave it for now, but asked if I'd mind answering her calls until she either came back or he could hire a replacement. This meant I was busy as hell all afternoon, but I prefer it that way. The working day slips by far more quickly when you don't have time to think, and I'd already spent more than enough time arseing about on the Internet during the morning.

I had time to think on the tube journey home, and of course what I mainly thought about was what had happened the night before.

I hadn't called the police, in the end. It was late and I was tired, and although the event had freaked me out a little, I couldn't face dealing with them.

Also... I just thought *Well, that's the end of it*. The police wouldn't be able to find the thief (who wasn't even technically a thief, of course; I suppose "intruder" is all I could legitimately say he'd been), and so it'd end up in a dusty log in the local police station and they'd give me a crime number which I could use in dealing with the insurance company if I chose to try to claim something back for the piece of jewellery.

Before I'd gone to sleep I'd tidied the event away in my mind, electing not to think any more about it, and I reinforced this on the tube and throughout the five-minute walk in the freezing rain from the station – during which, wanton hedonist that I am, I also stopped at the corner store to buy a frozen ready-meal to zap in the microwave for my tea. Plus a small tub of ice cream. And some biscuits. All in all, my evening was shaping up very well.

This time, however, it was obvious that something was wrong the minute I stepped through the door.

One of the advantages of living by yourself is that you get to be in sole charge of certain decisions. The central heating, for example. My father is a total miser when it comes to gas bills, and my parents' house is so cold in winter that it's just as well my mother *does* have an Aga, so she and I can go huddle around it when Dad's not looking. Living by myself means no man gets a say in how warmly I spend my evenings. I have the heating set to come on mid-afternoon, so the place is nice and toasty when I get home. As soon as you close the door behind you, you're enveloped.

Not tonight, however. The heating was on, as I could tell from touching my hand against the radiator in the hallway, but the house was chilly.

I went into the living room. The windows were all shut.

Through one of them, I could see why the house wasn't as warm as it should be.

The back door was wide open.

It had been both closed and locked when I left for work that morning.

I *thought* so, anyway. I knew it had been closed, at least, but I hadn't actually checked that it had been locked. Hadn't even checked the key was in its normal place, stuck there in its lock.

I remembered my thought of the day before, that an intruder would be likely to leave a means of escape open if he was on the premises, and found my eyes drifting warily upward, to the living room ceiling and the floors beyond.

What if he was still here this time?

I got out my phone. I dialled 999, but did not press the call button.

"Is somebody here?" I called up the stairs, backing into the hallway and toward the front door. "If so, you should know that I'm calling the police. Right now."

There was no sound from above. I knew that if there was someone in the house and he chose to get violent, I could be a bloody and broken mess in the corner of the living room before the local cops got halfway here through the traffic on Kentish Town Road.

I opened the front door a little, and walked back to the bottom of the stairs. "The front door's open," I said. "I'm going to get out of your way. I'll... go in the kitchen, so I won't see you."

Was this a good idea? Or a really stupid one?

Stupid, I decided.

"Or," I said, "here's another plan. *I'm* going to leave. I'm going to go back out of the house and stand around the corner. I won't look this way. Shut the door to let me know you've gone."

And that's what I did. I went out of the front door, closing it behind me, my finger still hovering over the call button on my phone. I walked quickly to the corner.

I waited ten minutes. I didn't see anybody come out of the house. The front, anyway.

I walked back. I let myself back in, cautiously.

The back door was now closed.

I ran quickly up to the next floor, making as much noise as possible, and found it empty. Then I went right to the top, including poking my head into the tiny attic room. Nobody anywhere. No sign of anything disturbed.

When I made it back down to the kitchen, I realised the back door wasn't actually shut. The intruder had pulled it to when he left, but hadn't closed it properly.

I pushed it open and stepped out into the garden, on impulse, even though I knew he could still be out there.

To the side of my kitchen there's a tiny concrete patio. Beyond that, my "lawn" – a scrappy patch of grass that would be about ten feet square if it was actually a square. In fact it's a kind of parallelogram, barely six feet wide at the far end. Because of the high hedges that surround it, the grass rarely gets much light even in summer, and it's ragged and muddy in the winter.

Soggy enough this evening, I thought, that you should be able to see the foot marks of a departing intruder, indents from shoes or boots.

There were none.

Something else caught my eye, though, and I stepped gingerly onto the grass to have a closer look.

The garden gets its shape from the fact the left-hand wall slopes radically toward the back, and it's this that's made of stone and features the faded old plaque. The plaque's low down, as if to be at child-height, not very large and made of the same basic stone as the rest of the wall. I'd been in the house for nine months before I'd ever realised it was there. All it says is—

[...] GARDEN
ST. JOHN'S COLLEGE

—the first word so weather-worn and chipped that it's unreadable. The wall must pre-date the buildings that now overshadow it by several hundred years, this scrap of it left by early Victorian developers because it happened to more-or-less coincide with the layout of the minuscule back gardens they were affording these somewhat perfunctory workingmen's cottages.

Something was lying on the grass, close to the point in the wall where the plaque is.

It was my piece of jewellery.

* * *

Half an hour later I was in the living room with a cup of tea. The brooch was on the coffee table in front of me. The house was nice and warm now that the back door had been shut for a while.

It was my brooch, without doubt. It had a distinctive triangular design, capped at each point with a dot of some green, semi-precious stone. When I'd found it in the antique store years before, I hadn't been convinced it was even an antique. The shape was so minimalist – literally a triangle, albeit one of unequal sides and with a slight curve to all the lines – that it had looked pretty modern to my admittedly untutored eye.

It looked different now. When I'd got it back to the flat I was living in at the time, I'd intended to have a go at cleaning it. I realised I rather liked the tarnish, however, and decided to leave it be. Over the years since, it had become darker and darker, and when I'd put it in the bread bin months and months ago, the metal had been a very dark grey indeed.

Now it shone. The silver – and there was no longer any doubt that was what it was made of, which meant I'd probably got more of a bargain than I'd realised – was so shiny it seemed almost white.

It didn't merely look clean – it looked fresh-minted.

Whatever process had brought this about had revealed something else, too. There were designs all over it. Etched very lightly into the silver was an incredibly fine and detailed series of lines and curves and interlocking Celtic shapes. At first glance it seemed chaotic, but the more I looked – and I'd been sitting there for quite a while now – the more I sensed there was a pattern that I hadn't yet been able to establish. It looked beautiful, and otherworldly, and extremely old.

The problem was I was pretty convinced that the pattern hadn't been there before.

Yes, it had been tarnished when I got it, as discussed – but in the early stages of oxidation you'll often find that any engravings (or imperfections) in metal are *more*, rather than less, obvious. It's easier to spot hallmarks, for example. You'll *glimpse* a pattern, at least, especially when looking at something as closely as you do when you're considering blowing hard-earned cash on it. I hadn't seen any such thing.

So what was it doing there now?

I belatedly realised I hadn't done anything about my shopping from the corner store, dropped in the middle of the room when I'd seen the back door hanging open. I hurried over and grabbed the bag. The tub of ice cream was glistening in that way that says it's well on the way to melting, courtesy of my generous central heating policy. I carried it to the kitchen, still worrying at the problem of the design on the brooch, and stowed the contents in the freezer of my poxy little fridge.

When I straightened from doing this, my eyes were directly in line with the bread bin. Something made me reach out and open it.

The same smell of old bread greeted me again, though it seemed stronger this time, which made no sense.

There was a piece of paper in there, too.

I knew it couldn't be the one I'd found the night before, as I'd put that in the drawer of the bureau in the living room (an old and cheerless piece of crap that belonged to my grandmother).

I picked the paper up and read it.

I hope you like what I have made on it

I didn't need to compare the handwriting on it to the other paper. It was clearly the same.

There was another line of writing, an inch further down the page. Why hadn't I spotted that right away? Because it was much fainter. Not as if faded, however – in fact the opposite.

As I watched, feeling the hairs rise on the back of my neck, the writing, at first so faint it was barely visible, gradually strengthened until it was as distinct as the line above.

It said:

I have designs upon you, too

No, I didn't call the police.

I could have. Probably should have. I could have told them that both lines of the message had been visible when I found the piece of paper. I didn't have to tell them it had been left in my bread bin. I didn't have to say that I was convinced someone had somehow etched a faint and intricate design on an old piece of jewellery, so that it looked as though it had always been there.

The problem was, if I wasn't truthful about these things I wouldn't be conveying the reality of the situation. They'd assume some local miscreant was making a habit of breaking in, and I already knew that wasn't what was going on. I'd known this, or at least suspected it – and now I must finally start to be honest – since the beginning. Since I told my fib.

It was a small fib, but significant.

When I came home the night I had dinner with my boss, and first had the intuition that someone had been in my house, and checked the back door, it was unlocked. That's what I told you, anyhow.

But it wasn't true.

The back door was *locked*.

It was locked, from the inside. So were all the windows, on all the floors. So had the front door been, too, until I unlocked it on my way in. Nobody could have got into the house from outside to find my note in the box in the hallway and then the brooch in the kitchen.

Whoever did these things had already been inside.

I don't know for how long. Perhaps always. That's what I've come to suspect. At least since the house was built, upon land that had once been a garden meadow on a little hill, near woodland and a pretty stream now trammelled far underground.

Before the day went pear-shaped – after my co-worker went sweeping out of the office and saddled me with all her work – I'd spent an hour covertly using the Internet, doing some digging I probably should have done long before. I'd always assumed that the missing word on the stone plaque on the wall in my garden was *MEMORIAL* – the sign put there to cordon off a patch of garden where people came to remember those now dead.

I could find no reference to such a thing in the area, even though the records for this part of London are pretty good, and I'd never understood why the plaque was positioned so low, as if for the eyes of people well below normal height.

I did find a single mention of an "Offering Garden". An uncited reference on a rather amateur-looking local history site, claiming that the old stretch of open countryside belonging to St. John's College had featured an example of the long-forgotten practice of securely walling off a portion of any meadow or hillside or forest that had a reputation for being home or playground to wood-nixies or elementals, co-inhabitants of our world that could not be seen. The idea being, apparently, that any such creatures would remain within such walls. Forever.

The people who eventually developed the area, several hundred years later, would not have known this. The practices and the beliefs supporting it had long ago died out. They could not have been expected to notice, or to care, that the weathering on the plaque was uneven, almost as if someone had chipped away at the first word in order to obscure the wall's original purpose.

Just before my ex-colleague had her meltdown and I had to stop looking, I finally tracked down a website with a very old map of this part of Kentish Town. It had been badly reproduced and was hard to make out, but seemed to show a small, boundaried portion within a fifty-acre parcel belonging to a Cambridge college. The circumscribed area was not named or labelled, but by super-imposing it upon a modern-day ordnance survey map of my street, I was able to establish both that the plaque must have been placed on the *inside* of the wall, and that the area it had encompassed had not been large.

Just big enough to include my house.

* * *

I eventually microwaved my dinner and ate it in front of the television, turning it up loud. The frozen curry tasted a lot better than I expected. The ice cream was really good, too, and I finished the entire pack of biscuits. My appetite seemed huge, despite an odd tickle of nervousness in the pit of my stomach.

I had a bath. As I dried myself afterwards I noticed some very fine lines on the skin of my shoulders, not quite random, and when I went up to bed I discovered the room smelled faintly of new bread.

Not quite of bread, in fact. Though the odour was reminiscent of a fresh-baked loaf, now it was divorced from the bread bin in the kitchen I realised it was actually closer to the smell of healthy grass, warmed by a summer sun. Warm grass or recently opened flowers, perhaps. Something vital, but secret.

Something very old.

I saw that the cover on my bed had been folded back. Neatly, as if in hopeful invitation. A piece of paper lay in the area that had been revealed:

Soon, my pretty

—was all it said at first.

As I watched, however, another line revealed itself. It was delivered to me slowly, as if brought to life by the moonlight coming in through the window.

All I need is a little more blood

It was then that I heard the first faint creaks, like small feet on very old floorboards, coming from the little attic room above.

Though it turns out he's not so small.

If you know what I mean.

LITTLE RED

JANE YOLEN AND ADAM STEMPLE

Seven years of bad luck. That's what I think as I drag the piece of broken mirror over my forearm. Just to the right of a long blue vein, tracing the thin scars that came before.

There's no pain. That's all on the inside. It won't come out, no matter how much I bleed. No pain. But for a moment...

Relief.

For a moment.

Until Mr. L calls me again. "Hey, you, Little Red. Come here."

Calls *me*. Not any of the other girls. Maybe it's because he likes my stubby red hair. Likes to twist his stubby old man fingers in it. And I can't tell him no.

"You want to go back home?" he asks. "Back to your grandmother's? Back to the old sewing lady?" He's read my file. He knows what I will say.

"No. Even you are better than that." Then I don't say anything else. I just go away for a bit in my mind and leave him my body.

The forest is dark but I know the way. I have been here before. There is a path soon, pebbly and worn, but my fingers and toes are like needles and pins. If I stay here, stray here too long, will I become one of them forever?

* * *

It's morning now, and I'm back, looking for something sharp. Orderlies have cleaned up the mirror; I think Mr. L found the piece I hid under the mattress. It doesn't matter – I can always find something. Paper clips stolen from the office, plastic silverware cracked just right, even a ragged fingernail can break the skin if you have the courage.

Alby faces the wall and traces imaginary coastlines on the white cement. She is dark and elfin, her hair shorn brutally close to her scalp except for one long tress that hangs behind her left ear. "Why do you wind him up like that?"

"Wind up who?" My voice is rough with disuse. Is it the next morning? Or have days passed? "And how?"

"Mr. L. The things you say to him…" Shuddering, Alby looks more wet terrier than girl. "If you'd just walk the line, I'm sure he'd leave you alone."

Having no memory of speaking to Mr. L at all, I just shrug. "Walk the line. Walk the path. What's the difference?"

"Promise?"

"Okay."

"Yeah, play the game, let them think you're getting better." Alby straightens up, picturing home, I figure. She's got one to go back to. Wooden fence. Two-car garage. Mom and Dad and a bowl full of breakfast cereal. No Grandma making lemonade on a cold Sunday evening. No needles. No pins.

It's my turn to shudder. "I don't want to get better. They might send me home."

Alby stares at me. She has no answer to that. I turn to the bed. Start picking at the mattress, wondering if there are still springs inside these old things. Alby faces the wall, her finger already winding a new path through the cracks. We all pass the time in our own way.

* * *

We get a new therapist the next day. We're always getting new ones. They stay a few weeks, a few months, and then they're gone.

This one wants us to write in journals. She gives us these beautifully bound books – cloth covers with flowers and bunnies and unicorns and things – to put our ugly secrets in.

"Mine has Rainbow Brite." Alby is either excited or disgusted, I can't tell which.

Joelle says, "They should be snot-colored. They should be brown like…" She means shit. She never uses the word, though.

"I want you to start thinking beautiful thoughts, Joelle," the therapist says. She has all our names memorized already. I think: *This one will only last two weeks. Long enough for us to ruin the covers. Long enough for Joelle to rub her brown stuff on the pages.*

I put my hand on my own journal. It has these pretty little flowers all over. I will write down my thoughts. But they won't be beautiful.

CUTTER

scissors
fillet knife
a broken piece of glass
I can't press hard enough
to do more than scratch the surface
and blood isn't red
until it touches the air

Okay, so it doesn't rhyme and I can't use it as a song, but it's still true.

"What did you write, Red?" Alby asks.

Joelle has already left for the bathroom. I don't look forward to the smell from her book.

"Beautiful thoughts." I cover the poem with my hand. It *is* beautiful, I decide. Dark and beautiful, like I am when I dream.

"Little Red." Mr. L stands in the doorway. "Excuse me, Ms. Augustine. I need to see that one."

He points at me. I go away.

* * *

Four-footed and thick-furred, I stalk through a shadowy forest. My prey is just ahead of me – I can hear his ragged breathing, smell his terror-sweat. Long pink tongue to one side, I leap forward, speeding now. I burst through a flowering thorn bush and catch sight of him: Mr L., naked and covered in gray hair. I can smell his fear. Then I am on him, and my sharp teeth rip into his flesh. Bones crack and I taste marrow, sweet counterpoint to his salty blood.

* * *

I wake in the infirmary, arms and legs purple with fresh bruises.

"Jesus, Red," Alby says. "He really worked you over this time, didn't he?"

"I guess." I don't remember. Seems likely, though.

"Looks like you got him one, too."

"Oh, yeah?" I can hardly move, though I turn my head toward the sound of her voice.

Alby grins her pixie smile. "Yeah. Got a big bandage on his neck, he does."

I lick my lips. Imagine I can taste blood. "Probably cut himself shaving."

Her smile fading, Alby says, "Whatever you say, Red."

I try to roll over, turn away from her, but something holds me down: leather straps at my ankles and wrists. One across my waist.

"Five-point locked leather," Alby says, with some reverence. "You were really going crazy when they brought you in. Foaming at the mouth, even."

I lay my head back down on the small hard pillow. Close my eyes. Maybe I can get back to my dream.

* * *

Mr. L visits me in the dark room with the leather straps. He has no bandage on his neck, but there are scratches there. I know why. I have his skin under my fingernails. In my teeth.

"Little Rojo," he says, almost lovingly, "you must learn control."

I try to laugh but all that comes out is a choking cough. He wanders slowly behind me, his fingers trailing through my red hair, my cap of blood.

"You must learn to walk the path." In front of me again, he glances up, at the television camera, the one that always watches. Puts his back to it.

"And will you be my teacher?" I say before spitting at him.

He looks down at me. Smiles. "If you let me." Then he pats my cheek. Before he can touch me again, I go away.

* * *

The forest is cold that night and I stand on a forked road. One is the path of needles, one the path of pins. I don't know which is which. Both are paths of pain.

I take the left.

I don't know how far I travel – what is distance to me? I am a night's walk from my den, a single leap from my next meal – but I am growing weary when the trap closes on my leg.

Sharp teeth and iron, it burns as it cuts. A howl escapes my throat and I am thrown out of myself.

I see Mr. L standing over the strapped body of a girl. I can't see his hands. But I can feel them.

He looks up as I howl again, his face caught between pleasure and pain. I tumble through the thick walls and out into the cool night sky, into the dark forest, into my fur body.

I tear at my ankle with teeth made for the task. Painful seconds later, I leave my forepaw in the trap and limp back down the path.

* * *

It is days later. Weeks. Nighttime. Moon shining in my tiny window. They couldn't keep me tied down forever. The law doesn't allow it.

I am crouched in the corner of my room, ruined tube of toothpaste in my hands. I have figured out how to tear it, unwind it, form it into a razor edge. I hold it over my arm, scars glowing white in the moonlight, blue vein pulsing, showing me where to cut.

But I don't. Don't cut.

Instead I let the pain rise within me. I know one quick slash can end it. Can bring relief. But I don't move. I let the pain come and I embrace it, feel it wash over me, through me. I let it come – and then, I go away.

* * *

I am in the forest, but I am not four-footed. I am not thick-furred. I have no hope of tasting blood or smelling the sweet scent of terrified prey.

I am me: scrawny and battered, short tufts of ragged red

hair sprouting from my too large head. Green eyes big. A gap between my top front teeth wide enough to escape through.

I stand in the middle of the road. No forks tonight, it runs straight and true like the surgeon's knife. Behind me, tall trees loom. I take two tentative steps and realize I am naked. Embarrassed, I glance around. I am alone.

Before long I see a white clapboard cottage ahead of me. Smoke trails from a red brick chimney. Gray paving stones lead up to the front door. I recognize the house. It is more threatening than the dark forest with its tall trees. Grandma lives here.

I turn to run, but behind me I hear a howling, long, low, and mournful. I know the sound – wolves. Hunting wolves. I must hurry inside.

The door swings open silently. The first room is unlit as I step in. I pull the door closed behind me. Call into the darkness, "Grandma?"

"Is that you, Red?" Her voice is lower than I remember.

"Yes, Grandma." My voice shakes. My hands shake.

"Come into the bedroom. I can't hear you from here."

"I don't know the way, Grandma."

I hear her take a deep breath, thick with smoke, rattling with disease. "Follow my voice. You'll remember how."

And suddenly, I do remember. Three steps forward, nine steps left. Reach out with your right hand. Push the thin door open.

"I am here, Grandma."

Outside, there are disappointed yips as the wolves reach the front door and the end of my trail.

"Come closer, Red. I can't see you from here."

"Yes, Grandma." I step into blackness and there she is, lying in the bed. She is bigger than I remember, or maybe I am smaller. The quilt puffs around her strangely, as if she has muscles in new places. A spot of drool dangles from her bottom lip.

I look down at my empty hands. My nakedness. "I haven't brought you anything, Grandma."

She smiles, showing bright pointed teeth. "You have brought yourself, Red. Come closer, I can't touch you from here."

"Yes, Grandma." I take one step forward and stop.

The wolf pack snuffles around the outside of the house, searching for a way in.

Grandma sits up. Her skin hangs loosely on her, like a housedress a size too large. Tufts of fur poke out of her ears, rim her eyes.

"No, Grandma. You'll hurt me."

She shakes her head, and her face waggles loosely from side to side. "I never hurt you, Red." She scrubs at her eye with a hairy knuckle, then scoots forward, crouching on the bed, poised to spring. Her haunches are thick and powerful. "Sometimes the wolf wears my skin. It is he that hurts you." Her nose is long now.

"No, Grandma." I stare into her dark green eyes. "No, Grandma. It's you."

She leaps then, her Grandma skin sloughing off as she flies for my throat. I turn and run, run through the thin door, run nine steps right and three steps back, push open the front door, hear her teeth snap behind me, severing tendons, bringing me down. I collapse onto the paving stones.

Howling and growling, a hundred wolves stream over and around me. Their padded feet are light on my body. They smell musty and wild. They take down Grandma in an instant, and I can hear her screams and the snapping of her brittle old bones.

I think I will die next, bleeding out onto the gray stone. But leathery skin grows over my ankle wound, thick gray fur. My nose grows cold and long and I smell Grandma's blood. Howling my rage and hunger, I leap to my four clawed feet. Soon, I am feasting on fresh meat with my brothers and sisters.

* * *

I wake, not surprised to be tied down again. Seven points this time, maybe more, I can't even move my head.

"Jesus, Red, you killed him this time." It is Alby, drifting into view above me.

"Go away, Alby. You aren't even real."

She nods without speaking and fades away. I go to sleep. I don't dream.

* * *

Next morning they let me sit up. I ask for my journal. They don't want to give me a pen.

"You could hurt yourself," they say. "Cut yourself."

They don't understand.

"Then why don't *you* write down what I say," I tell them.

They laugh and leave me alone. Once again tied down. But I know what I want to write. It's all in my head.

GRANDMOTHER
What big ears you have,
What big teeth,
Big as scissors,
To cut out my heart
Pins and needles,
Needles and pins,
Where one life ends,
Another begins.

NEW WINE

ANGELA SLATTER

"If you leave that dish on the table instead of rinsing it and putting it in the dishwasher, I will make you miserable for a week."

Valerie's voice floats back to him from the entry hall of the too-big house. She's gone to collect the mail; there's the click of her heels on the parquet floors, coming closer.

"But it's my birthday!" Alek, having just risen, bag over his shoulder, is two and a half steps away from the kitchen table (where they eat in preference to the formal dining room).

"I don't care," she sings back.

He turns around, grabs the cereal bowl, and does what he should have done in the first place. He makes noise while he does it so she'll hear.

"Yes, Valerie." *How the hell does she do that?* Two years, almost, and he still hasn't figured it out. Every damned time. Maybe it's because she observes him at close quarters; Alek wonders sometimes if she pays extra attention to one child because she once failed to do so to another.

Alek likes his tutor, he really does. Although that's a weirdly small word for what she does: keeping him on top of his studies, managing the occasional day staff at the house (cleaners, gardener, repairmen), feeding them both, generally ensuring he stays out of trouble. And that was how his father, Reid, pitched the job to her: *Tutor my boy*. But the surrogate mom stuff? That kind of took them both by surprise, Alek thinks, but maybe they're good for each other. Everyone in Mercy's Brook knows what happened with Valerie's daughter, but that's the reason Valerie came into Alek's life and some days he finds it hard to feel bad about it.

Valerie in her sunflower summer dress appears in the kitchen doorway as Alek is closing the dishwasher; he waves his hands *ta-dah!*

"Lordy, don't you deserve a parade?" She smiles to take out the sting, and it's the brightest thing. Alek remembers his father Reid saying that most of the guys in their high school class had a crush on her, Reid included – almost all unrequited. From what Alek's seen of the stares from middle-aged men when he helps her do the groceries that hasn't changed much, and a lot of his own college friends aren't immune to her either, no matter that she's old enough to be their mom.

"Late lecture tonight?" she asks.

"Yeah."

He likes that she thinks he's smart. *Knows* he's smart. He even likes that she understands how lazy he can be. Plus Valerie's got that sixth sense for when he's slacking off. She just crosses her arms and stares at him with those hazel eyes until he pulls his head out of his ass and does the work. She's smart too, so smart it kind of scares him a little. Okay, a lot, but he likes having her around. Her sense of humor is so dry sometimes it almost chokes him. She knows him and seems to like him anyway. Sometimes he thinks he's lazy for attention or it's just to make sure his dad keeps her around longer. Truth is, Alek more or less stays on the straight and narrow when she's there because he doesn't want to disappoint her, not totally, and Alek's dad – who travels a lot, birthdays and Christmases missed more often than not – is fine with that. Ultimately the costs of a live-in tutor are nothing compared to boot camp, rehab, and lawyers' fees.

As he passes by he kisses her on the cheek, which he sometimes does, and gruffly says, "Bye."

The walls of the hallway leading to the front door are hung with a variety of antique mirrors. Alek's spent much of his life hating the things because looking in them was the most alone he ever felt. There were days he wasn't sure he was even there. In the past there had been days when he thought he could see through himself, through the reflection. But since Valerie'd come to stay, he's felt solid. He can live with the mirrors. Alek doesn't want to go back to looking through himself again. Valerie *sees* him; she gives him weight.

"Chocolate cake?" she calls after him.

"Extra frosting?" He grins but doesn't turn around. It's his birthday, but with his father away – Reid's always away with his IT business – and a big party planned for the weekend, it'll be just them tonight.

"Of course."

* * *

Valerie supposes that having had a daughter, once, makes it easier to care about the boy, which sometimes strikes her as strange because when Lily disappeared Valerie stopped caring about anyone for a long time. Especially when she realized all those well-meaning, fuck-all-doing cops who patted her shoulder and told her they'd do their best, just went back to eat their way through a truck-load of donuts – Sheriff Tully going through more than all the others. Her ex-husband was just as useless, losing himself in booze rather than baked goods.

Briefly she flips through the bundle of mail. There's a bunch of bills. A rectangle of pink addressed to Alek, and redolent of perfume that no doubt has some starlet's name attached to it and turns into a cat's piss stench after five minutes on the skin. The plain white envelope is the only one addressed to her, and in a very distinctive hand that makes her sigh. She feels the weight of the house: two floors above this one, all those empty bedrooms, unused bathrooms, a dust-filled attic; ground floor is the kitchen, library, dining rooms, three studies, and Reid's seldom-used home office; and below, in the basement, an extensive garage big enough for six vehicles, and a high-tech wine cellar, its old wine in old bottles protected by a keypad and code. Valerie's got no interest in booze.

Valerie drops the mail on the pine tabletop and sets about making a fresh pot of coffee. She eyes all the ingredients for the birthday cake, laid out beside the knife block – nothing more she needs to get – then opens the dishwasher that Alek failed to properly close. After restacking the contents, she shuts the door once more with the worn patience of a crucified saint, and returns to the task of coffee.

Alek's a sweet kid, mostly.

Not really a kid, she supposes; he's eighteen but seems younger. Some kids grow up faster when they're neglected, but she guesses it was *only* emotional neglect in Alek's case: all his other needs were met so that maybe kept him a bit childish, needy. Valerie knew his mother in high school – it wasn't like they were friends; they didn't hang out then or when they had their kids – but she was needy too, Laura Lane that was. Whatever void she thought marriage to Reid "Red" Howard might fill apparently remained empty and one day, when Alek was nine, Laura packed her bags and was gone, leaving the boy bereft. Then there was a series of housekeepers and private tutors who didn't stay long; it wasn't like Alek was especially bad, but his need for attention and reassurance were *constant* and if that wasn't met… well, Reid had told her that as a kid Alek would make a lot of noise; as a young teen his silence was positively apocalyptic. No one lasted, their nerves shredded one way or another; no one until Valerie.

Alek's father could have sent him to university anywhere, even Ivy League, but had kept him at home to attend the small one with no real reputation in the next town over. There's nothing wrong with it, per se, but not so much to recommend Addison U either (oh, it's got "University" in its title, but it's really just a college). There's a pretty campus, solid syllabi, decent teachers, no big scandals so far, small class sizes, and a relatively low-level drug problem. Kids who go there do so mainly on one-year transfer programs to Syracuse or Cornell or Princeton. Of course, more than one girl from a disadvantaged background attends there on the Laura Lane-Howard Scholarships Reid set up in the wake of his wife's leaving.

Alek doesn't seem to mind. Reid handed down the black Mercedes C-300 Coupe for him to drive, and he doesn't need to over-extend himself to achieve at Addison. He doesn't seem to want to go anywhere else; the boy's without ambition.

An easy ride is fine if your life doesn't change, Valerie thinks. But life *does* change, as she knows all too well. It changes when you're not looking, or even when you are looking but you've got your hands full with other stuff. At some point Alek's going to find life kicking his ass to the curb with a vengeance. Deprived of a mother's love, with an absentee father, the kid's so desperate for affection and attention that he applies girls to his ego like they're nicotine patches.

But he's not a bad kid, she thinks, for all that. He's just coping the way he knows how, following a need the only way he thinks he can. She suspects he doesn't like that echo of emptiness most folk experience in their lives. Some recognize it, embrace it; some ignore it, flee from it. Some days Valerie thinks she hears the sad chimes of his hollowness dueting with hers, just when she thinks she's got it beat. Truth is, the boy's an anchor for her and she hadn't realized how badly she needed one.

She pours a cup of coffee, breathes the aroma deeply as it fills the kitchen in a way that seems too big to come from such a small receptacle. It's magic, she thinks: the smell of it, the ritual of making, the effect it has on the senses. Strange that something so bitter can make you so content. She sits down and sorts the letters into piles. She opens the bills first; they'll get paid with the credit card Reid gave her. She pushes the pink envelope to the corner of the table for Alek to find when he gets home later tonight.

Valerie eyes the pink rectangle, wondering idly about the latest. She's always kind of amazed when the boy looks at her like she's some sort of witch every time she says, "What's this one's name?" Like he's some great man of mystery. *Lord, sweetheart*, she thinks, *for a smart boy you are dumb.* She could tell him he's predictable, and only the names change. She could tell him she sets her watch by him. But she doesn't.

When she first moved into the Howard Estate, Valerie would sometimes meet the girl for coffee and whatever cake grief required after the inevitable happened: Alek lost interest in the she-of-the-moment. Valerie'd listen to the crying and/ or ranting; she'd nod then tell the girl how life was likely to be. There's no great harm in Alek, she'd say, but he's a heedless boy. You don't want a heedless boy; they never notice what you need, or if they do they probably won't give it to you unless they can see an advantage in it for themselves. And heedless boys become heedless men, unless they get taught hard lessons early on.

Not all men, Valerie'd say, but enough of them to make life fucking difficult.

"You make your choice," she'd tell them. "Do you want to be the one to teach him those hard lessons? Coz I can tell you now, he'll listen but he'll start thinking of you as his mother, and trust me: no man wants to sleep with his mother. Those that do are not the ones *you* want to sleep with. Or do you want a man who's already had his lessons taught him by someone else?"

She'd never had one of those girls decide she wanted to be the one to teach Alek his lessons, although one did accuse Valerie of being an enabler. When she'd finished laughing, Valerie said, "What's enabling about encouraging a girl to walk away? If I tell you to stay and fight, to bang your head against a wall trying to force someone to love you, what the fuck kind of favor am I doing you? Enabling is sending a battalion of girls back over and over again like cannon fodder because they think they're going to win. You keep going back then what's he going to learn about consequence? Enough women walk away, maybe he'll wake up to himself."

She'd shaken her head and finished with, "One day you might have kids and you need to remember that you're the one who teaches your son how much shit a woman will put up with."

Eventually, though, she got exhausted by the stream of girls and told Alek to stop bringing them home until he found one he thought he wanted to marry. Really though, she knew somewhere deep down that fighting to force anyone to make better decisions was a lost cause.

Valerie likes to think that her daughter wouldn't have needed that sort of advice. Valerie likes to think her daughter would have been too smart to put up with that kind of juvenile shit. Valerie likes to imagine her life in Mercy's Brook if Lily hadn't gone, although "likes" probably isn't the right word. It's more like mental cutting. She doesn't pull her own hair, tear at her cuticles; she doesn't drink or smoke or do drugs; no, Valerie's self-harm is imagining better days that'll never ever come.

Lily would have graduated high school; she'd have gone on to university in New York or Boston. She'd have decided on being a doctor, lawyer, architect: she had all the choices in the world. Maybe she'd have come home to Mercy's Brook; maybe she'd have settled elsewhere and Valerie would have gone to visit. Maybe Chase would have come too; maybe Chase wouldn't have started drinking if their daughter hadn't disappeared. Maybe Valerie wouldn't have started an affair with the man who ran the drugstore. Maybe if they'd had some answers about Lily's fate the other stuff wouldn't have happened.

Or maybe it all would have happened anyway.

Valerie rubs a hand over her face and yawns. She's not sleeping well; the dreams have come in force. They always do around this time. Even if she didn't look at a calendar, she'd still know the date was on the horizon for the physical and psychic effects its forward march caused. It's not helped this year by the sense of helplessness that's crept over her. Every avenue seems to have closed down, not a clue left behind as to what happened to Lily.

Sighing, she reaches for the sole envelope with her name on it. She examines again the familiar old-fashioned handwriting, a style learned under threat of a ruler to the knuckles. Valerie's about to slide a long nail under the edge of the flap and begin the delicate process of working it open when the doorbell rings.

* * *

Alek lied about the late lecture, and he's surprised he got away with it. Normally Valerie knows his schedule like the back of her hand, but she's been tired lately and when she's tired, she gets distracted. Alek turns left instead of right, heads around the outskirts of Mercy's Brook instead of through the middle so there's less chance of being seen.

Valerie nicknames his various girlfriends after weather phenomena with a weary boredom. Hurricane Suzie. The French Tempest. Cyclone Elaine. He asks her every time how she knows he's got a new one and she just gives him *the* look, which is part of why he lied about tonight.

As Alek pulls up out front of Carrie's place, the butterflies begin their dance in his tummy. It's a big house, but there are more bodies rolling around inside this one than his: both parents, three sisters, four brothers, and a grandmother. A proper family lives here. A proper family who, according to Carrie, are all out today. The house isn't as big as the one he came from – not as much money here as Reid has to throw about – but Carrie's not one of the scholarship students either. She lives ten minutes out of town, twenty minutes from his home, and situated well off the main road, so he doesn't worry about anyone seeing him here. It's early days yet, and one thing he's learning is not to advertise his latest infatuation too soon, and not just because Valerie will make fun of him.

"This is a small town, Alek. It's kind of stuck in time, a very particular time with a set of very particular expectations," she'd said a few weeks ago at dinner. "You start seeing a girl, taking her out in public – and sweet Jesus, I am not telling you to sneak around like you're ashamed – but out in front of everyone? Meeting their parents, for the love of God? Once it's in the open, child, you don't get to enjoy anything in private. Everyone's watching, and every girl with dreams that revolve around a white dress and a charge card she doesn't have to make payments on is looking at you like you're the prized hog at the fair."

"Hog? Well, as long as it's the prized one…"

They'd laughed, but then she'd gotten serious again. "Ask yourself how much you're going to have to apologize for, Alek Howard. Think before you do something dumb, that's all I'm asking."

Now, he's sitting in the driver's seat. In his backpack is a box of chocolates, Fair Trade and expensive, the kind Carrie likes; buying them seemed like a good idea at the time, but now… he's not sure about taking them in. Is it too much or too little, or should he just turn up empty-handed and see what happens?

It's only been a week, jeez. He used to think he was being generous – if his father had taught him nothing else it was generosity – but Alek's wondering if it sends the wrong signal. *Creates too many expectations, too soon.* Valerie's voice is in his head nowadays. Shit, he can't even give a girl a box of chocolates without second-guessing himself.

How much are you going to have to apologize for?

The front door to the house opens and there's Carrie hanging in the doorway, all that long dark hair, wide-set dark eyes, slow smile, and tanned skin.

Alek grabs the backpack. He'll see how things pan out.

* * *

"Mornin', Valerie."

Sheriff Obadiah Tully is a barrel on short, skinny legs. His uniforms are specially made, but even personalized tailoring isn't a silver bullet, not with his eccentricities of form. Valerie thinks it unfair that Tully shouldn't have to worry about being beach-body ready; she'd love for him to be afflicted with just a small degree of the self-doubt that comes with being female. But nope, he just hitches his utility belt where it hangs under the awning of his gut with a peacock flourish.

"Sheriff. What brings you to my door?"

"Well, not exactly *your* door is it, Valerie?" Tully's never quite got over his pique at that.

As Tully's investigation into Lily's disappearance went nowhere, Valerie's complaints got louder and louder, while her husband got drunker and drunker. Tully got vengeful. Obadiah took it upon himself to sometimes tail her when she drove home late at night, or follow her up and down the aisles at the supermarket, making sure she knew he was there. He'd convinced both the State Police and the FBI that Lily Wynne had run away from home; under his telling, the honors student became a hellion with a turning of the tongue.

Then Chase Wynne emptied their bank accounts and left Mercy's Brook.

Then the bookstore where Valerie worked closed and she was out of a job.

Then the house had to be sold and things looked pretty grim.

That was when Reid Howard stepped in — almost a year to the day after Lily's vanishing — and offered her a job and a home and a child, of sorts. Tully wasn't brave enough to keep tormenting her after that, so it made Valerie wonder just what the hell Shitheel Tully was doing here now.

"Is there something I can help you with, Obadiah? Or are you just here to exchange pleasantries?"

"I just thought you might like to know that Lucius Anderson passed."

"Passed what? Wind? *Passed*: that is the stupidest term I've ever heard." Valerie's blowing smoke to cover the effect of the news, but unease and not a little sadness are making her stomach churn. She swallows, thinking of the last time she spoke with Lucius – well, argued with him. She thinks of the envelope on the kitchen table, the distinctive handwriting. "What happened?"

"Home invasion," says Tully. He pushes the hat back on his forehead, showing the receding gray hairline and the indentations where the band is too tight.

"Home invasion? Around here?" Her disbelief is clear, and it's not like the Sheriff should expect anything else, but still he draws himself up, a bantam rooster puffing his chest like he's about to do battle.

"You know there are meth labs back in the woods. There are folk passing through our little town who're happy to do ill. You should know that better than anyone, Valerie Wynne."

"What would some meth-chef want in Lucius Anderson's *home*? He didn't keep anything there, not when he had an entire drugstore filled with medicines."

"Well, maybe some *meth-chef* wouldn't know that?"

"Isn't it something you should be figuring out?"

"You know, I'm only here as a kindness, seeing as how he meant something to you. Or maybe he didn't."

"Whatever passed between me and Lucius is none of your business." Valerie's hand on the doorframe is shaking, and she can feel cold sweat breaking out under her arms, down in the small of her back. She clears her throat, thinks of the letter inside again. "Look. I'm sorry, Obadiah, I don't want to pick a fight with you. I'm just… shocked. I'm shocked, is all."

He shuffles back a few steps as if surprised by her conciliation, then nods. He narrows his eyes and asks in an offhanded manner, "You hadn't spoken to him recently? Lucius? He didn't mention anything to you?"

And Valerie sees where this has been leading. "Like if he was afraid of anyone? Or he'd seen someone hanging around outside at odd hours? Like that?"

"Yeah, like that."

She shakes her head. "Obadiah, you know things didn't end well between me and Lucius." And truly they had not for he'd thought she would fall into a marriage with him after Chase left. "I'm the last person he'd confide in." But she thinks of seeing him in the supermarket last week, how he looked like he wanted to say something but then turned away. She shrugs, makes a peace offering of her hand, which Tully takes in surprise. She hopes she hasn't laid it on too thick. "Will you keep me informed? I did care for him, no matter what happened."

She closes the door before he's at his car. She doesn't hear if the engine starts or not, if he leaves the estate. She's got other things on her mind.

Valerie'd never thought Tully had anything to do with Lily's disappearance; she'd never thought he might be covering up for someone; she just thought him incompetent and spiteful, and she'd never kept that opinion to herself. Now, she leans against the door, feels the wood solid at her back as a wave of nausea washes over her.

In her dreams, Lily calls for her, Lily in her black, sequined prom dress and the pretty red high heels, Lily with her dark hair swept up in a stylish chignon because the girl always had her very own tastes. Lily who disappeared the day before her prom on her way home from the shoe store on Main Street where she'd gone to get those gel pads to stop her feet slipping out of those red silk shoes.

In reality, Lily'd never got a chance to wear that dress or shoes for real, so the memory Valerie has is of the test run at home when she and Lily experimented with makeup and hair. When Lily perfected her stride in those high heels, pacing along the hallway upstairs until she got the sway just right.

But still, that's the Lily who haunts Valerie's dreams, although sometimes it's Valerie's own face she sees in place of her daughter's.

Back in the kitchen Valerie sits at the table before her knees give way. In front of her are the now-cold coffee and that envelope. Lucius Anderson had told her one afternoon as they lay side by side, naked and sweat-covered, that he'd been taught penmanship by his strict grandfather, that other kids laughed at him because no one else made their letters just-so.

Valerie thinks Lucius must have mailed the letter just before he was killed. She wonders if Obadiah Tully suspected something of the sort. She tears open the envelope, slides the single white sheet of paper out and unfolds it.

In the same elaborate handwriting are the words "Security camera, Anderson's Drugstore", then: "I'm sorry". That's all, just those words in the middle of the page and she draws a blank as to the meaning. Then her brain kicks along and she turns the thing over; the breath falls out of her.

In black and white print, ink jet because her sweating fingers smudge the edge of the image: there's a familiar black Mercedes C-300 Coupe heading down Main Street. The date stamp is the same day Lily Wynne disappeared, and the time shows a good hour after everything closed and the strip was deserted because folk had homes to get to and meals to prepare.

And Valerie leans closer and closer because the photo's been taken on an angle that means she can see straight through the windscreen, can see clearly the driver's head and the passenger's.

It could mean nothing, she tells herself, and that car might not have had anything to do with Lily's disappearance. It *would* mean nothing, she tells herself, if she didn't know the vehicle and driver all too well. If it wasn't Lily in the passenger seat, laughing. Valerie throws up all over the kitchen table.

* * *

John Wick is on the screen, deadpanning his way through a myriad of killings. Carrie's in Alek's lap, their soundtrack is a series of gunshots, of the gasps of dying men until from elsewhere in the house there's the sound of a door closing, then voices, a female and children. He's very gentle as he moves Carrie onto the sofa next to him, then shuffles a few inches to his left, adjusting himself slightly. On the coffee table is a half-empty box of chocolates, the kind she likes, that Carrie'd presented to him as a birthday present.

Carrie pouts, but laughs, reaches for another chocolate. She smells like vanilla. It's nice. *This is nice*, thinks Alek.

"Don't worry: Mom will be supervising homework for a while yet." The girl settles into the corner of the sofa, kneads her toes against his thigh. "Hey, when did your dad get back?"

"He's not home."

"No," she says. "I saw him this morning."

"You must have made a mistake." Alek sits up straighter.

"I was out jogging on the Mason Road. He slowed down and waved at me." She purses her lips. "You know, I do *know* your dad when I see him."

Carrie smiles around her snippy tone, and Alek feels a tingling down his spine, not fast, but creeping, like there's a spider with eight cold feet trying not to be noticed.

Reid had paid attention to Alek's girlfriends in the past and some he'd taken as easily as picking an apple. He didn't do it for a relationship – none of them lasted longer than a single night, dinner and bed – Reid did it because he could. Alek thought about Annie and Ellie, Elaine and Sukie, scholarship girls he'd met at Addison U. All smart and ambitious, but disadvantaged in one way or another, orphans or fostered, poor, from the small towns in the more remote parts of the state. The towns that had boomed in the early days but through which even the Greyhounds now roared without stopping.

Sometimes his father was one of the reasons Alek didn't stick with a girl, but he'd never told Valerie *that* because how pathetic was it? Having your dad steal your girlfriends? Besides, Valerie and Reid, they'd been friends at school, and if Alek told Valerie something that made her not want to hang around any longer, then where would he be? It's not just the threat of having to feed himself, it's the idea of no voice but his own, no face but his own in that big house. Valerie had made him feel not so alone; she saw something in him that was worthwhile, and he saw himself reflected better in her than the hallway mirrors.

His mobile vibrates in his pocket, and he plucks it out to read the text.

"I better go," he says to Carrie's surprised displeasure. Alek has to admit his interest in her has lessened in a very short space of time. He'd seen the look on Carrie's face when she mentioned his father, noticed the way she'd blushed and smiled, was flattered at unwarranted attention from a silver fox, and a rich silver fox at that.

"Why?" Carrie pouts.

"Valerie needs me at home."

"Well." And her mouth twists, turns sour where it had been so sweet and full mere minutes ago. "Wouldn't want to let Valerie down."

"No," he says, rising. And because it's the truth, he doesn't blush or feel ashamed. "I wouldn't."

* * *

247

New wine in old bottles...

The keypad is blinking slowly at her, an arrogant stare. She doesn't know the code. Six digits. If she inputs the wrong numbers, what happens? An alarm goes off somewhere? The private security firm will call the house and she'll answer, tell them it was an accident. Still and all, better no one knows she's snooping.

At first she'd thought about the garage — it was only natural, given sight of the Mercedes — but she'd been in there before. She's been in all the rooms of the house; it holds no secrets for her except for one spot, one spot about which she'd had no curiosity. *This one room.*

She puts her face against the dull silver of the door, feels it cool as death on her skin, sees her own reflection as a strange blurred shadow. Valerie presses her ear to the metal and listens as hard as she can, although she's not sure what she might hear. Whether it's with hope or fear, she doesn't know, but she still does it.

Nothing. There's nothing.

Valerie thinks about how she's never questioned this room's purpose. She thinks about how smart he was as he gave her the tour of the house the day she moved in. She recalls him walking her down the stairs to the basement, and along the stone corridor; he'd made sure they stopped outside the door, pointed it out. He'd even poked a finger at the keypad like an uncoordinated child, making *beep-boop* noises. He smiled.

"Wine cellar. It's very high-tech for all the investment

bottles. Not your average vino. No new wine in these old bottles," he'd said and laughed − Valerie remembered him telling it like an old joke, explaining that his own father had used it to refer to children. Explaining it hadn't made it any funnier. "I can give you the code, if you like? Do you want to have a look?"

She'd shaken her head. Valerie had no interest in booze, not given Chase's drinking habits, and Reid Howard had known that.

"Not even a little curious? Don't even want a peek?" he teased. They'd laughed, then moved on.

"I don't drink, Reid," she'd reminded him and seen that strange satisfaction on his face.

"Sorry. I forgot about Chase." Even though there'd been an element of *sorry, not sorry* about it, she'd shrugged it off; the room made no impression on her memory. There's a fully stocked bar upstairs, more wine and spirits than anyone, including a teenage boy and his friends, could get through. No need for Alek to come down here. The cellar was out of sight, out of mind for both of them.

Valerie pushes away from the door and looks at the green lights flashing in their usual sequence again.

Six numbers.

New wine in old bottles.

She puts her hand out, almost touches the keypad. She hesitates, her fingertips hovering so close, so close. What if she's wrong?

What would happen?

But if she doesn't try. If she waits until he comes home, she'll never be able to hide what she suspects. If she doesn't find out now, she might not be able to control herself when he finally returns.

Valerie touches the numbers that make up Alek's birthday.

The keypad blinks angry red at her, makes a low, flat sound of disapproval. Too much to hope for, she supposes. Too easy. Her hands shake, her fingers go cold with disappointment. Then... it occurs that there's one more number she might try.

Valerie picks out the numbers of tomorrow's date, the anniversary of Lily's disappearance.

The seconds after the last number are the longest she's ever lived. The keypad beeps, the lock clicks. Valerie pushes the silver door open and steps through.

No blood, no bones bleached by either sun or moon.

What did she expect?

Not this.

It's a huge room, white-painted and filled with pedestals.

There's a short flight of stainless steel stairs that take her from the landing just inside the door down to the floor of the cellar. Valerie steps up to the first pedestal: it's waist-high and made of thick green glass. And on it, just like on all the other pedestals, is a pair of pretty, high-heeled shoes. All around, shoes for a variety of special occasions. She leans forward, looks more closely at the nearest ones: pink shoes, prom shoes, diamantes on the straps, as well as specks of dried blood.

Valerie moves on to the next display: black stilettos, red Louboutin soles, dull brown splotches adhering to the ebony leather.

Next: purple patent, no designer label, cheap and nasty and stained.

A pair of light green Jimmy Choos.

All the colors of the rainbow, all styles, from all manner of economic strata and different fashion eras.

It's a while before she finds Lily's.

It takes all of her self-control not to rush around, making increasingly high-pitched noises, desperately seeking the red silk shoes. She knows if she lets herself do that she'll lose all semblance of control; she'll just sit on the floor rocking and weeping, and she'll stay there until Doomsday.

She's so intent on concentrating on *just the next pair* that she's stunned to discover them in front of her. Lily's lovely prom shoes. In patches, the red silk is darker where blood has soaked in.

And that is all her daughter has been reduced to: this pair of ruined footwear. There's nothing else in the whole place, no other doors or rooms, no hint as to where the rest of her child might be.

Just the shoes.

How many pairs? A hundred, perhaps?

No bodies.

Just the shoes.

Row upon row.

Valerie reaches out. These are all she's got, probably all she'll ever have of her baby ever again. They are surprisingly sturdy, the stiletto heels tough, no matter how delicate they look.

"Don't touch." The tone is sharp, so commanding that Valerie hesitates, is almost tempted to obey. "It's a rare collection, as I told you before, Valerie."

"Fuck you," she says and wraps a hand around the right shoe. She curls it into her chest, cradling it. Then she turns to face him.

Reid Howard is handsome, though not especially tall – a head shorter than Valerie, not much difference between him and Obadiah Tully, frankly – and dressed far more casually than his usual tailored business suit: dark jeans, t-shirt, Timberlands. Alek's got his features but not his red hair. Reid doesn't have a beard, he's clean-shaven, and his eyes are a clear green. He's as popular with women as his son is – God knows Valerie almost fell for it herself once before coming to her senses – he's got no reason to hurt girls, but Valerie guesses he just likes it.

But she senses she needs more time, she needs to stall, so she asks, "Why? Why would you take her? You barely knew her, she was nothing to you. Why take her? Why take my child then bring me to look after *yours*?"

His grin as he walks down the steps, heavy boots punctuating the silence, tells her *Because I could*. The smile slips between her ribs, lodges like a knife in her heart. "I do like you, Valerie, never doubt that. But your baby looked just like you did in high school, just like when you said *no* to me, and *yes* to that

252

idiot, Chase. Then Lucius – fucking Lucius! I'm a patient man, but I'm not very forgiving." His smile widens. "And why wouldn't Lily accept a lift home from her momma's old friend?" He shrugs. "You being here kept you under my eye, stopped fricking Tully complaining about you – Lord you have irritated him over the years. The bonus was you looked after my idiot son. He behaves himself; I'm not distracted from either business or pleasure." He raises his hands, palms up. "I took one child away, but I gave you another. You're very fond of Alek. In a way, it all evens out, yes?"

It takes a moment before shock wrings a shriek of "No!" from Valerie; her fingers tighten convulsively on the shoe.

"No?" He feigns surprise. "Ah well. How did you get in?"

"New wine in old bottles. At first I thought it was Alek, but you meant *my* new wine." Part of her mind is astonished to be having this conversation so coolly. But she's got to keep a clear head, if she wants to survive. Reid's produced a knife, the biggest from the block in the kitchen, which he taps against the glass of the pedestals as he passes, the sound a strange singing.

"Ah." He smiles wryly. "I shouldn't have underestimated you. Too clever by half, you, too clever to get into my bed. Still, everyone makes mistakes: not too clever to marry Chase or fuck Anderson though."

"Lucius? Did you…?"

"Tully said he was wavering. You'd pissed him off by leaving – you do piss men off, Valerie, it is one of your defining traits –

and I'd bailed him out, he was hemorrhaging money on some bad investments, so it was as much venal as vengeful. Oh, he didn't know what had happened to your Lily – don't think that of him. He believed I'd dropped her on the way home and she'd met her fate elsewhere, but his conscience was starting to get to him, and he was starting to wonder why it needed to be kept from you. When he was angry at you he was happy to play along."

"Everyone makes mistakes," she can't help but say. He snorts.

"Should have chosen me, Valerie, or at least for a little while."

"Why are you home? Now?" He never bothered to come home for his son's birthday, but…

"The anniversary, Valerie – *our* anniversary. I love watching you every year on the day Lily disappeared. You're strangely radiant with grief, it's quite bewitching. I wouldn't miss that for the world."

Valerie begins backing away as he comes closer. "What about Alek?"

"What about him? I'll tell him you left. I'll tell him you got tired of him, just like his mother did, that you were disappointed in him. He's used to that. He won't pursue it. Kid never sticks at anything, you know that better than anyone."

"He's not like he was. You wouldn't know, you're never home. You don't know your own son." A burst of hysterical laughter catches in her throat at the morbid domesticity of the argument, two parents in a tug-of-war over a child. "He's not the boy you made anymore; he's not *your* new wine."

"Granted you've helped him settle down, it keeps him out of trouble, but even if you hadn't made this ill-considered incursion into my space your time was coming to an end. I worry he'll develop too much of a conscience if you're around much longer and that's an inconvenient thing. Best you be gone, let him think himself deserted once again." He tilts his head, pondering. "Do you think you're so fierce about protecting him because you failed Lily?"

She swallows, doesn't answer that, instead says, "Where…"

"What?"

"Where's his mother?"

Reid points to the far end of the cellar; Valerie can make out a worn pair of white sandals with wedge heels. Long out of fashion.

"Laura didn't go willingly. She did love her boy."

"Dad?"

Both of them whirl to find Alek on the landing at the entrance to the cellar, in answer to Valerie's text to come home, sent because she couldn't think of anyone else she needed by her. His hands are held up in a gesture of surrender. Behind him, Obadiah Tully stands – clearly Valerie's act was unconvincing – his service weapon pointed at the boy's back.

* * *

Alek is slow as he takes the stairs, not just because of the gun barrel that periodically pokes him in the ribs. He's heard everything

255

Reid and Valerie had to say, and seen his own reflection in the steel of the door, as if his father's words have remade him into something shadowy. Destabilized. His stare moves from his father to his tutor, to the pedestals and shoes, the ceiling, the floor, the walls. He's still processing everything he heard before Tully appeared and gestured for him to enter the cellar.

Tully's footsteps have stopped, but Alek keeps going for some paces. He looks over his shoulder at the Sheriff. Tully's face is a picture. He's clearly never been down here, just like Alek, only his expression is one of realizing just how deep a hole he's stepped into. Alek guesses Obadiah's been happy enough to take Reid's money to smooth things over, inconvenient investigations and the like, but he didn't really appreciate what Reid was doing. Alek had no idea himself and now he wonders on which side of the line Tully will fall.

He stops by a pedestal, takes in the cheap purple patents; they're eye-catching, not something he's likely to forget even with no particular interest in footwear. His head tilts to the side and he reaches out to touch them. "Annie's." His gaze moves on, he points at a pair of knock-off Prada pumps in electric blue. "Ellie's."

Somewhere in the cellar, Alek thinks, Elaine and Sukie's shoes also await. All the Howard Scholarship girls, the girls Alek didn't see again. He didn't bother with them after they'd seen his father, he'd wiped them away to salve his hurt boy's pride. Abandoned them. He tries to swallow but it's hard, like there's a rock in his throat.

"Dad," he says again, noting the kitchen knife Reid's carrying. Alek feels sick. Sick and sad and pained. He says it again, as if it's the only thought that's in his brain. "Dad."

"Alek. Terrible timing, my boy, as always." Reid shakes his head.

"What you gonna do with them, Reid?" When Tully's voice comes, it's clear he's made his choice; any hopes Alek had that the Sheriff might have chosen to help are swiftly gone. In the hole, Obadiah's going to keep digging. Holes, Alek wants to remind him, don't work like that.

"Well, my lovely Valerie here is going to meet with an accident – you don't need to be around for that and probably best if he isn't either. Obadiah, take Alek to the kitchen and sit with him until I'm done."

"You can't be serious, Reid. Kid's not going to keep his mouth shut."

"He's my son and he'll do what I tell him to." Reid raises his knife, not in threat but more as a lecturer would a pointer or a cane: *Attend to this, Tully, if you know what's good for you.*

Alek, standing between his father and the Sheriff, notices what the grown men have forgotten: Valerie. Reid's got his back to her, Tully's attention is on Reid with the sort of tunnel vision that's rendered him one of the worst investigators Mercy's Brook has ever had the misfortune to employ. But Alek can see her from the corner of his eye – clear as a perfect reflection – and he's careful not to draw their gaze to her as she inches closer to Reid. Her footsteps are light, so light, but still there's a whisper of her approach and his father seems set to turn.

Alek repeats, "Dad?"

Reid looks at him with irritation as Valerie unfurls the hand from her chest and raises the red shoe. Alek sees her rush forward, and he pivots, drops his shoulder and charges at Tully, who doesn't even get a shot off, but tips straight back, his head striking the rise of the bottom steps. Obadiah's eyes stay open, his stare uncomprehending.

Alek sits up, rubbing his shoulder. He hears the noise his father makes but it takes him a few moments to gather himself and look.

Valerie stands over Reid Howard, who's on his knees, swaying, a red stiletto heel buried in the top of his head. He looks as surprised as Tully, although more outraged. Then he loses his grip on life and gravity takes over; slowly he flops face-forward onto the polished concrete.

* * *

As far as Mercy's Brook is concerned, Obadiah Tully died a hero, saving Valerie and Alek from Reid Howard's psychotic episode, before his own untimely demise. No bodies have been found in the grounds of the estate, and the Mayor is happy with that since he considers a graveyard of girls might be bad for the town's morale and future economic prospects. *Least said, soonest mended and all that,* he says to Valerie and Alek, meaning, *Keep your mouths shut and no one looks at your actions too closely.* The hastily appointed new Sheriff keeps telling Valerie that they might never find anything more than the shoe collection.

Valerie keeps the red stilettos in a box in her cupboard. If she could, she would get rid of the memory of that day, but it's like a golden key with blood on it that she can't rub off. Some nights she re-dreams the moment in the cellar with its collection of pretty, bloody shoes; she dreams Alek is much smaller, younger, that he says "Daddy", and Reid takes the boy's hand in a way he never did in life.

Some nights, too, she dreams that he turns into his father. She dreams that the apple hasn't fallen that far from the tree, that he might have no choice in any of it, that the switch will flick whether either of them wants it to or not. But she also knows he made his choice about who he wanted to be.

Lily doesn't come to her in dreams anymore, though, and she can't quite work out if it's a gift or a curse.

HAZA AND GHANI

LILITH SAINTCROW

Our father was a woodcutter and that Year of the Dog was an ill-luck one, for not only did Mama die as cold winter ebbed but the temple lottery fell upon us as well. Late at night, my brother and I lay awake in the attic listening to Father sob, for a son is the only wealth a woodcutter knows. *Now, now,* his new wife crooned, wrapping her sinuous body around his work-hardened one. *You can always make more children. And little Ghani, she can make more children too.*

I did not know quite what she meant, then, but Haza's face turned to a stubborn stump's as he listened and he slipped out the narrow hole under the thatched eaves that night, coming back only when dawn began to pull mist through the warp and weft of trees. When the priests came to take him, he went with bulging pockets but without a backward glance, his queue tightly braided and freshly oiled. The rope of red-black hair would be cut off at the temple steps, of course, but I had made it as pretty as possible, my thin fingers in his hair and my belly growling.

A girl eats last.

That night Father's new wife built up the fire after dinner, and brushed her long black hair. She beckoned me close, but I refused even though Father gave me a clout on the ear and snarled at me to mind, which he had never done when Mama was alive.

But when a woodcutter finds a new wife of supple spine, long hair, and unblinking eyes in the forest, it is already too late. That evening I pretended to sip from the wooden cup she held for me, with its sickening smell of anise clotting in my nose and making me drowsy. I went to bed in the attic when she told me to, and when I heard my father making grunting noises and the wooden bed squeaking downstairs I slipped through the same hole Haza had, with a tiny bundle wrapped in rough fray-cloth upon my back.

I also lit a precious, filched candle-end with a stolen flint, settling the tiny gleam very near the attic thatching; when I reached the far end of the valley and looked back through the trees there was a rosy glimmer in the night. The pale stones Haza had dropped led me along the path the priests had taken, and though the dark was deep the moon shone upon them and I did not lose my way.

* * *

Haza must have quickly run out of pale stones, but I did not need them once I reached the slash-road through the forest. I followed that ribbon all night and through the next day as the

262

forest receded and settlements rose on either side. Eventually the temple of the Flayed God floated into sight, a stacked white triangle cut into a mountainside over a great bowl full of smoke and noise.

I had never seen a city before, but I had seen plenty of anthills, and decided it was similar.

It was round, flounce-skirted Kali the kitchen-queen who saw me in the bustle and scramble of the Great Market, kicking the shins of an older urchin who attempted to steal my tiny, pathetic bundle. I had not eaten in three days, but I was used to that, and it was her approach that caused the boy's friends to scatter. The cut on my forehead – they had thrown stones to help their leader – bled into my eyes, so it was through a scrim of salt-stinging crimson I saw the round, black-haired beldam with her frayed multicolored skirts and iron hoop earrings, her horn-hard feet as bare as mine and her hands rough-blistered by the work of cooking. Kali held my chin and examined me, a funny floating feeling filling my skull, and she *tch-tch*'d at my dusty, dirty hands.

Still, she must have seen something in my still-unformed joints, for she snapped at me to hold fast to her skirt, setting off at a brisk pace.

So it was I learned the way from the Great Market to the servant's door piercing the temple's wall-girdle, and so it was I descended into the smoky underhell of the kitchens, where Kali set me to chopping a gigantic pile of roots and other vegetables.

It did not occur to me to question or complain.

Not then.

* * *

All that spring the new trainees practiced in the temple's broad stone avenues. Most dropped from exhaustion or refused to go further after a particularly brutal session. Their hair was allowed to grow back in a skull-stripe; they would perform rites and services but never be admitted into the inner sanctum.

Those who did not falter were feasted and shaved each evening. The art of the Flayed God's monks is sharp and direct, punches that shatter bone and kicks that splinter metal.

In the kitchens, though, there is the Flower Style. It is a dance of lifting, bending, chopping, running; Kali declared I had aptitude. I did not even mind the savage stretching of a child's ligaments and tendons; the queen of the kitchens, though round-hipped and of generous belly, was also a bending reed when she wished to be. If I ever found a movement too difficult she would perform it with an ease that beggared my ineptitude. I held myself lucky she did not clout me over the ear as our father had.

Even the Abbot himself was said to hold Kali in some regard, for it was she who prepared the bitter-spice sacred drink in its vessels of beaten silver for the new-moon and other rites, especially the Great Awakening when the God frees his skin and dances without it.

I saw the Abbot only once during that time, a bulky man in sumptuous, flowing, but unbleached robes – for the Flayed God is humble, and likes to hollow out the proud – whose pate glisten-gleamed as he passed along ranks of sweating temple trainees shouting the cadence of *strike, parry, kick, ia!*

One of them was Haza, and the Abbot stopped to admire my brother, stripped to the waist and gleaming with sweat, scarlet-faced with peeling sunburn, and moving with the same thoughtless grace our father did when he danced with axe, block, and saw to wrest wood from forest depths.

Watching from the shadow of the fruit-garden, where Kali sent me to gather the fallen and overripe nourishment for sleek black temple pigs, I felt the sun's warmth turn cold for a moment. It was whispered in the kitchens that the Abbot's eyes had grown filmy.

But that could not be, for the Flayed God required his servants whole.

* * *

He came to the back door often, Old Vril, with his quick dark eyes and his copper-shod staff. The copper was green with decay, and his teeth were yellowed, drunken soldiers leaning upon each other for comfort. His rags were foul, but he did not smell of rot and the body's simmering, only of dry dust and funerary spice.

Perhaps that was why I risked Kali's wrath to give him scraps wrapped in large glossy leaves; the queen of the kitchens wished the beggars to wait in the courtyard given to their purpose, with the perpetually fouled fountain and the young monks going among them to learn the medicinal and healing arts. I did not like that courtyard, for it was full of moans and cries, and the way the beggars fell upon the food – both the coarse fare prepared out of the bounty of taxation for the Flayed God's chosen and the leavings of the great feasts – made me uneasy, especially once I had gained some little weight.

For Kali encouraged us to taste and sip. A good cook should know the texture of a dish at every stage, and that lesson has lingered all my life. What Kali did *not* encourage was feeding any of the beggars at the kitchen doors, and it was my ill luck that one of the other birds – for such we were called in the kitchens, plump, downy, and nestling under her skirts – saw me pass a leaf-wrapped chunk of spicy charred roast to Old Vril. He did not eye my bare arms and legs like the others did, even the ragged, hungry women.

It was Kali herself who wielded the thin, flexible switch as I stood with my hands clasping a stone atonement pillar carved with the Flayed God's many names, and she was not cruel. Still, I sobbed without restraint, sharply aware of her disappointment and afraid I would be sent back into the smoke-bowl of the city to fend for myself again.

That night, face-down on my pallet in the low dormitory attached to the dormant kitchen, I heard a scratching like a mouse, and pulled myself painfully upright, shuffling for the door as if I had to make nightsoil.

The path to the soilhouse was overgrown to provide modesty, and Haza met me at the bend in deepest shadow, first hugging me, then thrusting a clumsily tied leaf-package into my hands. "I thought you would find the way," he said in an undertone, his shaven head glistening a little as moonlight dappled the broad waxy leaves overhead. "How is Father?"

"I left the night after you did." The packet was still warm; it smelled of roast and the meaty starchroot I had helped make that very evening while sniveling with pain. "He is probably happy, with *her*."

There was no need to tell him more, and in any case, he did not seem interested. "You've been in the kitchens?"

"Kali found me." I longed to tell him of Flower Style, of the groaning of my tendons, how it was different than the monks' directness. But there was a rustling, and we drew back into the bushes on either side of the path like the forest creatures we once had been, waiting as a senior in a saffron robe wandered past with a lantern, scratching luxuriously at his crotch and yawning.

When he had vanished into the soilhouse we emerged again, breathing in tandem, and I reached for Haza's hand. "You are well?"

His face was shadowed, but there was a line between his eyebrows I knew. His fingers were chill and damp. "We eat well."

Did I not know as much? "Better than home."

"This is home, now." He freed his hand from mine, not ungently. His queue was cut; he was supposed to have no family but his fellow monks. "We cannot let them know, Ghani."

As if I was stupid. But I did not mind. We were together again, and a boy always wants the last word.

On my way back into the dormitory, I stopped by a particular long-leaved bush tucked near the temple's protective wall. I plucked some few leaves and bruised them inside another, different leaf, dropping the palmful upon the thin pallet of the snoring girl who had betrayed me as I passed, and in the morning she had a spreading, virulent rash from sticky sap.

* * *

That summer there were no rains, and the dust grew thick. The governor of the province came with a long train and made offerings inside the gleaming stone pyramid, incense rising in clouds and cymbals shatter-clanging through day and night to keep the sun awake, feasting afterwards spreading its largesse to the steadily increasing number of beggars choking their fouled courtyard. Old Vril's eyes burned with fever and his skin was scorching; he settled in a vine-shaded corner and watched. His staff's copper shoe developed lacy holes, green rot nibbling at metal, and his gaze followed me when I braved that cauldron of suppuration, begging, and soft hopeless cries to bring him scraps.

I could not do so often, for Kali had examined our hands again after the Frog Festival, and those of us who had special signs in their palms began to learn the fermenting, drying, grinding, and brewing of the round, ribbed fruits sacred to the Flayed God. Dexterity is needed, a fineness of touch even through calluses, and the cupped palm of a cook must be married to long fingers and several other subtle signs. Now, of course, I can tell at a glance who has the hands for it, but then I was a child, and knew only that Kali found something she was looking for in me.

Indeed, she was the only one who ever had.

It was in the deepest days of drought that the rumor began. At first it was only exchanged in looks between senior monks, but like fire, suspicion spreads in dry times. After the Frog Festival and the visit from the governor there was another temple lottery, and many boys were shaved upon the temple steps and brought into the stony girdle.

During the Water Jar Festival the Abbot dropped his staff, its godbird feathers fluttering, and when he bent to retrieve that most sacred item he reached for empty space. One of the senior monks had to rescue its flutter-length, and the rumor was proved before a crowd of worshippers and notables.

I was frothing the spice-bitter holy drink under Kali's watchful eye as whispers raced through the kitchen. A mere girl cannot taste the drink, but I could smell very well when it became ready and see the froth change. Kali tapped my head with a bone scraping-spoon, to remind me not to falter – if the stirring pauses, the drink will not blend properly.

The Abbot dropped his staff. The Abbot could not grasp it. *The Abbot is blind.*

It was strange, I thought as I stirred. The Flayed God's high priest cannot be infirm. He must be whole as the God before his sacrifice. But I put the question aside, for a mere kitchen-bird does not meddle in those matters.

Or so I thought then, especially since Kali's expression grew set and she laid about with that long-handled spoon when she caught other kitchen-birds with guilty faces and wagging tongues. The girl who had tattled on me was clouted twice, and I bent to my work to give the kitchen-goddess no time to catch me thinking. Later that evening something foul was fished from the temple well, and brackish water turned the day's cooking fetid.

The next day, another lottery was announced. This one, though, was for the junior monks like my brother.

The entire temple watched one gasp-hot morn as the young ones mounted the steps one at a time, reaching into the basket with a hole in its lid and drawing forth a smooth, dark stone. They were black and glossy, those sacred eggs, each one brought from burning mountains belonging especially to the mother of all gods, She whose name is not spoken, who wears serpents in her ears and provides warmth to the dead if they have lived a righteous life.

Again and again they drew forth black eggs, and I drowsed in lace-pierced shade on the fringe of the courtyard. Nobody else seemed to have any trouble staying awake, but I had been up all night stirring and afternoon would hold more of the same. Much of the sacred drink was required for the monks in this season, to bring them clarity.

At least it did not reek of anise, like Father's new wife. And at least Kali's training made the pain only a distant ache.

I must have closed my eyes; I woke to a susurration that was the sigh of the crowd. My chin jerked up, my eyes flew open, and I saw Haza before the basket, his sunburned, shaven head gleaming, the set of his shoulders expressing shock.

In his palm was a single, satin-smooth, pale stone.

* * *

They put him in seclusion, in the long cloister full of stone-walled cells. His young body was shaved daily by the most solemn of the Abbot's attendants, but his head was left to grow its fur again. The best we could cook passed to his cell first, where he was supposed to spend the days meditating. But my brother, used to roaming the forests or spending his days with strike and kick, hardly touched the platters before they went in turn to the Abbot's table.

Kali was called upon for more tempting dishes, rarer flavors, sweeter fruits. I could have told her Haza preferred thick porridge with savory leaves, with perhaps some fat from last night's dinner if it had been a good autumn and Mama had not taken to coughing. I could have told her the squirrels in the forest, turgid for the beginning of winter and roasted in brookside clay, was a dish my brother could never resist.

But I did not. I mixed the sacred drink, learning its foam and its froth as I absorbed the Flower Style and other kitchen-arts. When you are a blank sheet, everything leaves a mark.

When a night came that I wasn't deadly exhausted and the passage to the soilhouse was deserted, I slipped from my pallet and stole through the temple's familiar wilderness, dodging drowsy door-guard monks and climbing hand over hand along a balcony much more solid and easily navigable than bending, cracking branches.

Everything is easier when you nibble all day in the kitchens, a mouse in a block of starch. The only danger is growing too sleek-heavy, but the Flower Style provides for that. We soften but do not grow truly corpulent, we who stir and chop and bake.

"Haza," I whispered through the grating in the middle of the heavy door. "Haza, it's me."

After a short while there was another rustle, and Haza's fingers, bathed and scented, came through the holes. "Ghani?"

"You must eat." I pressed my lips to his knuckles. His own mouth, breath redolent of expensive spice, touched mine; he rubbed his chin – softer, with oil worked into the skin, no trace of stubble yet – against my fingertips. "Everyone is worried."

"I can't stand it," he whispered back. "It's a cage."

"It's only for a short while," I soothed. "Then you'll be abbot. I'll cook for you every night."

"I can't stand it," he repeated. "You have to get me out."

"Where would we go?" I did not bother to recite the punishment for a monk fleeing his fate. Boiling in oil was good to make savory puffballs, but not so good for a young man. "How would we live?"

"The forest. I'll cut wood."

I shook my head at his child's stubbornness, though I was his younger sister. "Just a little while, Haza. Then you'll be the Flayed God's chosen one. It won't be so bad."

"You don't understand." But he subsided. Always, he was the first to flame and likewise cool, my brother. "I'm worried about you. Are *you* eating?"

Now he asked. "Of course. I mix the drink." I could not say its name, being a mere girl, but he could.

"_____." He named the drink with a sigh. There was a gleam of his dark eyes at the grate. "He doesn't speak to me, Ghani. The God is mute."

"They say the drink *makes* him speak." I listened for the sound of the guard at the far end of the hall. That fat monk's breathing had not changed, and I decided I could stay a few more moments. "Or lets you listen. Shall I bring you some?"

"Maybe." He didn't say what we both knew – that if I was caught, it wouldn't be just a whipping, for either of us.

But what else could I do?

* * *

I was still a child, and foolish. Kali noticed my measurements were for more than the beaten-silver cups required. She let me skim a miser's portion into a flask when my enemy, the slipfingered tattling girl, added too much distillation to a glazed fowl and a jet of flame spurted high.

My enemy also screamed and dropped the pan, the idiot, for I had loosened the wood-slats upon the handle just enough for hot

273

metal to slide between them and bite her hand. The distraction succeeded better than I hoped, but that night on my way to the soilhouse the kitchen-goddess rose from a pool of deep shadow without even a frond-rustle and caught me by the throat.

Dragged into a patch of hot light from the moon's scabbed face, my neck under her fingers, she thrust her nose almost into my mouth, sniffing deeply. Then, squeezing as I kicked, blackflowers blooming at the edges of my vision, she studied me, her eyes like coals before the white ash covers them – dark, and hot enough to burn, two black-glass eggs.

"Little thief," she hissed softly, and all the bushes rustled uneasily. Sweating brought no relief in the drought, but many trees attempted it, weeping resins to be scraped carefully free and used for flavor, for incense – and for other things. "But I see, it is not for you."

I twisted and tried again to strike. Her fingers relaxed, and I drew in oven-hot air through my bruised breathpipe.

"The little quickfinger has a beloved. Which one is he? A young monk, I hope; the old ones are too selfish." She cackled, but softly, and gave me a rough but good-natured shake. "If you had not the hands, birdling, I would put you in the ovens. No man is worth this."

I opened my mouth to say he was my brother, and remembered myself just in time. She stripped the flask from my chest-wrapping and shook her head.

"At least you are not overly stupid." She *tch-tch*'d her tongue, and dragged me to the well. I thought she meant to throw me in, but she merely dumped the sacred drink in, tossed the flask after it, and shoved me towards the soilhouse. "Cry in there, if you must. Tomorrow it's back to mixing." Her brow clouded just as the moon did, and hot thunder roiled in the distance.

Some thought it was a sign the Flayed God was pleased, and would bring the rains. But the dry lightning did not strike the earth, and there was no relief.

* * *

There was to be a feast at the dark of the moon, and Kali made me her pet. Even my enemy did not begrudge that high position, because it meant fetching, chopping, grinding at the furious pace of the kitchen-queen herself. My pallet was moved to the doorway of her cubicle in case she called during the night, and I had to hold the lantern in the soilhouse while she pissed at midnight, when lightning played over the far-off forest. Despite all that, I managed to visit Haza twice before the great secret, sacred feast.

I brought him a flask both times, but it was not the sacred drink. It was its cousin, without the pungent froth and the additives that make it holy. But my brother, not yet senior enough to know the taste of the sacred drink, thanked me in a quiet, begging voice like our father's the night he brought his new supple-spined wife home.

"I dreamed last night," he said the second time. "I think it was the God. He told me to be brave. Isn't that good?"

My head was sweetmush for the elderly who cannot chew, exhaustion making the world a painted wall of bright shallow colors. "You *are* brave," I whispered back, and passed through the leaf-wrapped meat I had done my best to prepare in clay like we used to.

It was fowl scraps, not squirrel, but I do not think he noticed.

* * *

Three nights later was the dark of the moon. The feast was indeed solemn, but the kitchen became a mountain with fire in its bowels and all the birds, undercooks, scrubbers, and slicers jostling egg-rocks in its throat. Several kitchen-birds fainted in the inferno, were dragged outside and splashed with brackish water before being treated to vigorous rubbing and thin yeasty sourdrink to get them upon their feet again. One undercook, enthusiastic, sliced half his finger into a basket of rolled fritters in oil, and his piercing howl was swallowed in the din.

There was no longer a girl named Ghani. There was only the food dancing under fingertips, the flame coiling around my wrists, the painted world-wall spinning like a bright round toy I had seen in a pedlar's basket once and cried for, knowing we were too poor to afford it but yearning still.

I collapsed as the last round of savory flowers left the kitchen's second doors, but by then most of Kali's large-eyed kitchen brood had as well, and we were carried into our dormitory for sleep or death, we knew not which. Perhaps it was Kali herself who tucked me into her own narrow, sweet-smelling bed with its musk-tinge of old woman.

I do know Kali slept in the kitchens that night, her round chin propped upon one hand and her other dimpled fist still wrapped around a cleaver, as whoever could endure it carried on the laborious scrubbing of bowl, dish, pot, pan, stick, spoon, tongs. I know because I woke at the moment the entire seething temple-anthill sighed to itself, a mass of its inhabitants sliding into slumber after collective gorging.

That night, upon the dark of the moon, I could move as I pleased. I wish it had been Haza's voice that roused me, a silver thread pulled through my ears, but it was not.

Instead, what pulled me from unconsciousness was the smacking of a copper-bottom staff in the beggar's courtyard, where the emaciated lay in the sun to die in increasing numbers each afternoon no matter how many feasts the monks shared with those less fortunate.

* * *

My brother's cell was empty. Torchlight dappled the far end of the stone hall, and I passed dream-slowly through shadows painted by dying sputters. A faltering, fading chain of light passed me from one flicker of darkness to the next, a black rosette blooming behind me as they sighed and dozed off into their final rest.

Each little darkness held a faint click, as of a pebble dropped. The inner courtyards were high and almost cool, stone stubbornly resisting the sun's showering heat. I saw the chambers of the god-mysteries, the shimmer of halls that should have held even on this holy night a minimum of chanting brothers on sweetgrass-stuffed cushions repeating the sacred name – an exercise for the invisible parts of a monk that temple style does not train – but were eerily empty. The scriptorium where chisel and brush, stone and woven fiber, colorful pebble and dyes ground from kitchen herb were arranged to tell sacred histories was merely another kind of kitchen.

It was in the very inmost of courtyards I found the monks, and at first I thought I was watching a great carcass lifted in the stone butchering-room while the knives were readied. It was hung by the heels, but the shape was wrong.

I knew then, but I did not want to know. Instead I stared, every hair long or short on my own body attempting to rise.

The Abbot was not sleeping. His bony limbs, painted, streaked, and splattered red-black, were draped in long strips sewn roughly together with tendon, an inelegant coat. The flap of the scalp bounced, with a healthy short black stubble that said it had grown from one full moon past another to the dark face of the night's great lamp.

"*I am HE! I am HE!*" the old Abbot yelled drunkenly, and those among his senior attendants who were not feast-sotted took up the cry, the name of the Flayed God. The dry-dust drought was all through me, and lightning crackled far away over the forest's many green breasts.

The film over the Abbot's eyes was gone.

I did not cower. I did not tremble at the misuse of the Flayed God's name. I was not struck mad, or dumb, or blinded myself; the blasphemy did not move me. It was my brother's body I stared at, each joint and curve glistening.

Spread over the inmost altar of the great temple, his blood still steamed.

* * *

Some few monks fled that night. Exhausted temple servants were simply glad of the quiet. Much brackish laundry water was drawn from our failing well for the next few days, monks hurrying to and fro with frowning faces and strange, terrified gleams to their gazes. The laundry was full of strange things, but the feast *had* been large. A tray was taken to Haza's cell as usual, and returned untouched, which was not unusual.

When I woke in the hottest part of afternoon, dried mud had crumbled between my toes. It was not the dust of the courtyards or the yellow fine grit of garden dirt. It was thick, and red, like the sluggish shrunken river cradling the city. The dry air, however, erased it of its glue.

And who looked at a kitchen-bird's bare feet, or even an undercook's, as I was from that morning? Those of us who had endured were promoted, each given a paring-knife to be kept in our belts, and allowed to wear our hair in braids.

Kali's temper grew somber, and she brought a clutch of new birdlings from the market's seething. Town and city held many starving castoffs that dry, hungry year.

279

For, though the crops were in peril and the forest had turned brittle, the next celebration was the Dry Moon Feast in a scant few handful of days. It was to be the time Haza was brought out of seclusion and installed as the new Abbot... unless there was a miracle.

And rumor now whispered that the Abbot could *see*.

* * *

A paring knife, its bright blade thinned by repeated sharpening. A tinge of red river mud upon the doorstep of an unused butchering room. A bolt of rich soft cloth filched from a storeroom. A small sickle-shaped sharpness, cutting deep to separate muscle from bone, a cut I had seen repeated so often with bigger knives.

A bundle lowered into a well, and a market-fetcher bribed to bring a further measure of thick river clay.

A thinning to Kali's lips as she listened to the gossip. A glance at her undercooks, hunching their shoulders and bending double to their work. A salting. A seasoning.

A special dish for a feast.

* * *

Two or three of the kitchen staff vanished, perhaps wiser in reading rumor than the others. There were rumblings like the breath of distant dry lightning, a slight uncomfortable pressure when gazes met.

Or perhaps those who left between the two feasts merely

had family in the fields, where a nervous, thirsty famine stalked. The rains still had not come, though the clouds massed over forest, temple, city, and the broken plains beyond. Or perhaps they had kin in the market where goods were becoming scarcer and a new temple lottery announced, this time for goods instead of sons.

A messenger came from the governor of the province and was shown a refectory of somber, sparse-eating monks before a serene, beaming Abbot. The messenger, godbird feathers fluttering uneasily on his headdress, left crease-browed before a meal could be made in his honor, barely pausing to scatter the requisite handful of coins in the beggars' courtyard. The beggars had little use for the money, though some from whom the last scraps had not yet been pressed scrabbled for the gleams.

The Dry Moon Feast leapt for us, but the governor coming to witness its holiness was delayed. A fire had reached across his route, the forest swallowed by a beast of flame.

* * *

When the full moon rose at sunset feastday, it was a dull glaring eye through smoke. I left the kitchen and came across Old Vril in scant shade near the herb-garden wall, gazing intently at me just as he did in my thin nervous dreams.

"Listen, old uncle." I thrust a few leaf-wrapped scraps into his hands. "Do not eat the leavings tonight. This instead, do you understand?"

He grinned, the simple fool with patchwork yellow teeth, and bobbed his head as if he did not. I longed to shake him, or kick him.

"Nothing else," I said impatiently. The longer I tarried instead of returning at a run with pungent leaves and long thin flexible spears of woody spice, the more chance of being seen. "Just this."

He bobbed again, and smacked his staff on the courtyard stone. I almost ran away, and it was during that hot afternoon that several of the kitchen staff first began to clutch their stomachs and moan, for the well-water had a foul taste and the river-water carried uphill in jars did, too.

The malady avoided Kali as all else did, yet the round-faced kitchen-queen was snappish, striding through the chaos, sending great plates staggering out the door. And I?

I mixed the sacred spice-drink as Kali taught me. I poured it into the beaten-silver cups. I was Kali's pet undercook and had a hand in everything for the Moon Feast: the smallest roast clay-robed as the peasants cooked it and so, tender-succulent; the vegetables; the flatbread; the piled yellow grain. Loud was the merriment that night in the temple of the Flayed God. The wine was called for often, and the sacred drink in cups of beaten silver upon great round gleaming trays.

The Abbot, relieved and renewed, drank deepest of all.

* * *

At dawn I lifted my bundle – just as small as when I left the forest, though a little less shoddy – to my back. I slipped from the undercooks' dormitory with the quiet of one trained in the Flower Style, and edged through the small postern by the closed great doors, a monk who had bemoaned guard duty last night drowsing empty-bellied but safe in the tiny gatehouse.

Outside the temple walls, I drew in a deep, smoke-freighted breath. But there was a chiming sound, and there was Old Vril, his teeth not so drunken-leaning and a new copper boot clasping the bottom of his staff. Beside him, Kali shook her round black head, clicking her tongue as if I was late returning from the soilhouse or clumsy with my paring-knife.

"Ah, there she is." Old Vril spun his staff upon its new copper toe, and the ragged feathers – once from godbirds, but now draggled and smoke-tinged – fluttered. "Quick of finger and sharp of eye. Little one, little one, what will you do now?"

My throat had gone dry under Kali's glare. "All I can do is cook," I managed.

Old Vril laughed, a dry whistling sound, and his staff tip-tapped closer. He pressed something round and hard into my sweating left palm, and Kali made another impatient sound, beckoning. She pushed a fold of her flounced skirt into my free hand. "Hold tight," she snapped as the beggar turned away, his form stretching like softened glue-starch in broth. "I travel quickly, little bird."

In the distance, the city gates opened for the governor's men, brazen horns given breath not their own. The thing in my left hand was a pale, smooth, egg-shaped stone, seen through a wavering of saltwater as my eyes filled.

Far away in the forest, the drought broke with a crashing of thunder.

* * *

Steam-smoke rose from the forest, flames beaten into tatters by rising wind and falling water. The governor of the province, arriving late to the festival, found the great white temple of the Flayed God eerily silent. There were no beggars in the courtyard with its often-fouled fountain, its spire now bone-dry. The kitchen was deserted, the great fires low embers or cold ashes. Even the head cook, a round black-haired beldam much whispered of in the Great Market, was gone.

Most of the servants and kitchen-birds had fled by noon, the sun a red eye and queer yellow-green light filling the temple, and when the governor's men broke open the holy doors to the great refectory they found monks frozen in attitudes of feasting, platters piled with choice delicacies strangely avoided by banks and wedges of gem-bright flies. The Abbot, in his pale but unbleached robes, sat at the great table, eyes wide open and staring, stone-stiff, stone-still.

Those who stole bits of the roasts, the grains, the piled, drought-scorched fruits were safe. Those porters and undercooks who stole sips of fragrant wine or, in one case, an entire merrymaking jug intended for their betters, were likewise safe. But soft perfumed flesh roasted in river clay can mix strangely with spiced alcohol, and both can mix with odd resins added to a frothing, spicy, bitter drink. Some of those mixtures may petrify flesh while keeping mind, soul, and breath – though only a trickle of each – trapped within a body's congealing borders.

The governor and his men will burn those inert bodies, not knowing what might be clawing for release from their cooling, recalcitrant meat, and Haza will be avenged. And I?

Oh, I am not worried.

As the kitchen-goddess says, there is always work for a cook.

HATED

CHRISTOPHER FOWLER

The first inkling Michael Everett Townsend had that something was wrong was when his wife slapped him hard around the face.

She had never slapped his face before. Michael hadn't been expecting the blow. He was carrying a glass of milk, and it shot out of his hand, spattering them both. The glass was cheap and just bounced on the rug, but he jumped back in shock and stepped on it, cracking the thing into shards, one of which pierced his bare foot. Gasping in pain, he dropped down on the edge of the bed just as the blood began to pour freely from his wounded sole. Instead of the sympathy he expected to receive, however, his wife gave a scream of rage and a mighty shove, and tipped him onto the floor. Then she began looking for a knife.

Michael's wife really loved him.

But then, everyone did. Michael was the most popular man in the entire apartment building. The security guard gave him preferential treatment because, unlike the other tenants, he never complained about the heating, which was always too hot or non-existent. Betty, Michael's next-door neighbour, adored him because he had once scared a drugged-up burglar from the hallway at two in the morning, because he professed an admiration for the people of North Yorkshire where she had grown up, and because he had shown her how to replace the washers in her bathroom taps. Mitzi and Karen, the two blonde Australian flight attendants on the floor below, liked him because he was cute and a gentleman, because he paid them the respect they were denied in the air and because they were attuned to potential romantic material, married or otherwise.

But it wasn't just the apartment building. The staff at work loved Michael and showed it, which was unusual, because in London-based companies very few people are willing to reveal their personal loyalties in any direction. The Asian couple who ran the deli at the corner doted on him, because he always asked after their handicapped son, and managed to pronounce the boy's name correctly. And dozens of other people whose lives crossed Michael's felt a little bit richer for knowing him. He was a popular guy. And if he was honest with himself, he knew it.

Michael had been aware of his popularity since the age of five, winning over creepy aunts and tobacco-stained uncles with an easy smile. An only child in a quiet middle-class family, he had grown up in sun-dappled suburbia, lavished with love. His parents still worshipped him, calling once a week to catch up with his latest exploits. He had been a golden child who remained golden in adulthood.

Golden. That was the perfect word.

Blond haired, blue eyed, broad shouldered, thirty-two, and married to an intelligent, talented, attractive woman. When Michael spoke others listened, nodding sagely as they considered his point. They wanted to call him by a nickname that would imply intimate friendship, Micky or Mike. What they liked about him was hard for them to define; perhaps they enjoyed basking in the reflection of his success. Perhaps he made them feel more confident in their own abilities.

The truth was simpler than that. Michael was at ease in his world. Even his most casual conversations made sound sense. In a life that was filled with uncertainties he was a totally reliable factor, a bedrock, a touchstone. And others sensed it. Everyone knew that they were in the presence of a winner.

Until the night of the accident, that is.

* * *

It really wasn't Michael's fault. The rain was beating so heavily that the windscreen wipers couldn't clear it on the fastest setting. It was a little after 11 pm, and he was driving slowly and carefully back from the office, where he had been working late. He was thinking about Marla curled up in bed, waiting to hear his key in the lock. He had just coasted the Mercedes through the water chute that a few hours ago had been the road leading to Muswell Hill Broadway when a bicycle materialised from the downpour. On it sat a heavy-set figure in a yellow slicker – but not for long. The figure slammed into the bonnet of the car, then rolled off heavily and fell to the ground. Michael stamped his boot down on the brake, caused the car to fishtail up against the kerb in a spray of dirty water.

He jumped out of the vehicle and ran to the prostrate figure.

"Jeesus *focking* Christ!" The cyclist was in his late forties, possibly South American, very pissed off. Michael tried to help him to his feet but was shoved away. "Don' touch me, man, just don' *focking* touch me!" He turned back to his bicycle and pulled it upright. The thing had no lights, no brakes, nothing. And the guy sounded drunk or stoned. Michael was feeling less guilty by the second.

"Look, I'm really sorry I hit you, but you just appeared in front of me. It's lucky I wasn't going any faster."

"Yeah, right – lucky me." The handlebars of the bike were twisted, and it didn't look like they could be straightened out without spanners. He hurled the bicycle onto the verge in disgust.

"I can give you a ride," offered Michael. The driver door of the Mercedes was still open. The leather upholstery was getting wet.

"I don' want no *focking* ride in a rich man's car, asshole!" shouted the cyclist, pushing him away.

"Look, I'm trying to be civilised about this," said Michael, who was always civilised. "You had no lights on, you came straight through a stop sign without even slowing down, what on earth was I supposed to do?"

"I could sue your ass off is what *I* could do." The cyclist stared angrily as he gingerly felt his neck and shoulder. "I don' know that nothin' is broken here."

"You've probably pulled a muscle," said Michael, trying to be helpful.

"What, are you a doctor?" The reply was aggressive, the glare relentless.

It was a no-win situation. Time to get away from this crazy person and go back to the car, dry off the seats and head for home. Michael started to back away.

"I've offered you a lift, but if you're going to be——"

"Don' put yoursel' out. I live right over there." The cyclist pointed across the block. "Just give me your address. Write it down so I can contact you."

Michael hesitated. He didn't like the idea of giving his address to a stranger. "Why would you need to call me?" he asked.

"*Jeesus*, why do you think? It turns out I got a dislocated shoulder or something, I gonna get a claim in on you, make you pay to get it fixed. You just better pray they don' find nothin' wrong with me, man."

Reluctantly, Michael pulled a business card from his wallet and passed it across. Moments later he was heading back to the car and checking his watch. The whole business had lasted less than a couple of minutes. Behind the wheel once more, he watched the yellow slicker drift away into the rain mist and thought about the accident.

It was unusual for him to be placed in any kind of confrontational situation and not come out a winner. His likeability could defuse the most volatile of personalities. As he turned the key in the ignition, he wondered if there would be any repercussions. Suppose this chap had actually broken something and didn't know it yet? How did he stand, insurance-wise? He was thinking of himself, but hell, it had been the other party's fault. Michael was nice but no saint. His comfortable life made few allowances for upsets, and breaks in the smooth running of his routine irritated the hell out of him.

* * *

"Darling, you're all wet. What have you been doing?" Marla reached up and hugged him, her bed-warm body against his damp jacket.

"There was a bit of an accident. I hit a cyclist. Had to get out of the car." He gently disentangled himself and began removing his clothes.

She pulled the sheet around her. "How awful. What happened?"

"He wasn't looking where he was going. I could have killed him. Luckily, he didn't seem hurt, but—"

The telephone rang. Marla shared his look of surprise. Their friends all knew that they had a seven-year-old son in the next room and never called the house late. Michael pulled the instrument toward him by the cord and raised the receiver. A wail of bizarre music squealed from the earpiece.

"Hello, who is this?"

"This the guy you *hit* tonight, brother."

"How did you get my ho—"

"My shoulder's dislocated. Bad news for you. Real bad karma."

The guy couldn't have seen a doctor already, even if he'd gone straight to casualty.

"Are you sure? I mean, how—"

"Sure I'm sure, you think you're dealing with a fockin' idiot? Patty, she says it's all bust up. Which means I can't work. An' you have to pay me compensation. S'gon be a *lot* of money, man."

"Now wait a minute…" Maybe this was some kind of scam, a professional con trick.

Marla was tapping his arm, mouthing, "Who is it?"

He slipped his hand over the mouthpiece. "The chap I hit tonight."

"You still there? You gonna pay me to get fixed up or what?"

"Look, if you think you have a case for extracting money from me, I think you're wrong." Michael's famous niceness was starting to slip. Who the hell did this guy think he was, finding his home number and calling so late at night? "But if you really have damaged yourself, it's your own fault for riding without lights and not watching the traffic."

"You don' know who you're dealing with," came the reply. "You just made the biggest mistake of your life."

"Are you threatening me?"

"I'm just saying that people like you need to be taught a fockin' lesson, treating guys like me as if we don' exist."

Michael stared at the receiver. This was bullshit. He was in the right; the other party was in the wrong. The law was on his side. And he cared, he had a social conscience. But the thought struck him, what if the accident had somehow been his fault after all?

"You still there? Tell me, Mr Townsend, what's your biggest fear? That your child get sick? That your wife get up and leave you?"

A chill prickled at Michael's neck. He didn't like this crazy man using his name, talking about his family. And how did he know he was even married? Was it that obvious, just by looking at the car?

"No, you scared o' something else even more, but you don't even know it. I see through people like you. Don' take much to break a man like you." There was contempt in the voice, as if the caller was reading his mind.

"Now listen," Michael snapped, "you have no right to threaten me, not when you endangered my life as well as your own. I could get the police——"

The voice on the line cut in. "When you come to find me – an' you will – it won' be with no damn police."

Suddenly the line went dead. Michael shrugged and replaced the handset.

"Well, what did he say?"

"Oh, he was just – abusive," he replied distractedly, watching the rain spangle over the streetlights.

"Do you have his number?"

"Hmm?"

"His number, do you have it in case there's a problem?"

Michael realised that he didn't even know the name of the man he'd hit.

* * *

He rose early, leaving his wife curled beneath the duvet. Surprisingly, even little Sean had slept on in the adjoining bedroom. Michael showered and donned a shirt, grabbed a piece of toast and poured himself a glass of milk. Then he climbed the stairs and gently woke his wife.

And she slapped his face.

The glass broke. The milk splashed. He stepped back and cut his foot, but the pain had already given way to hurt. Puzzled, he ran his fingers across his reddening cheek.

"What the hell – what are you looking for?"

She was frantically searching beneath the mattress, then pulled up short in confusion.

"You – shouldn't creep up on me like that." Marla slunk back beneath the covers, sleep-pressed hair folding over her eyes. She turned her back to him, embarrassed by the vivid dream that had leaked over into reality. Picking the glass from his foot, he watched a drop of crimson blood disperse in an alabaster puddle of milk like a spreading virus.

An Elastoplast took care of the wound. He rattled the glass fragments into a box, which he sealed and placed in the pedal bin beneath the sink, then listened as his son thumped downstairs.

"Sean? You want Crunchy-Crunch?" He cocked his head. No answer. Odd. The boy could always be drawn by mention of his favourite breakfast cereal. "Seanie?"

He looked around to find the boy glaring distrustfully at him through the bars. "Sean, what's the matter? Come down and pour your milk on."

The child shook his head slowly and solemnly, mumbling something to himself. He pulled his stripy sweatshirt over his chin and locked his arms around his knees. He stared through the bars, but he wouldn't descend any further.

"Come and have your breakfast, Sean. We can take some up to Mummy." Another muffled reply.

Michael set the dustpan aside and took a step toward his son. "I can't hear what you're saying."

"You're not my daddy," the boy screamed suddenly, scrambling back up the stairs to the safety of his bedroom.

* * *

Michael checked himself in the rear-view mirror. The same pleasant, confident face looked back, although the smile was a little less certain than usual. He drove through the avenue of sodden embankment trees heading into the city and wondered about the behaviour of his family. He didn't wonder for long; the three of them had managed to maintain a problem-free existence until now, cushioned perhaps by Marla's inherited wealth and his own easy-going attitude. If they got under each other's feet in town there was always the cottage in Norfolk, a convenient ivy-covered bolt hole that provided healing seclusion. But the memory of the slap lingered as clearly as if the hand print had remained on his face.

Michael parked the car in the underground garage and took the lift to the seventh floor where he worked for Aberfitch McKiernny, a law firm dealing primarily with property disputes. The receptionist glanced up as he passed but failed to grant him her usual morning smile. The switchboard operators glared sullenly in his wake. Even the postboy seemed to be ignoring him. Why was everyone in such a bad mood today?

Michelle was already waiting by his door. She was the most efficient secretary he had ever employed. Power dressed in tight black raw cotton, her pale hair knotted carefully at her neck, she impatiently tapped a pair of plastic folders against the palm of her hand while she waited for him to remove his coat.

"You were supposed to take these home with you last night," she explained, passing them over.

"I didn't get around to them. The Trowerbridge case took up all my time. I'll try to run them later this morning."

She reached over and took the folders back. "I don't think that will do any good. Your 'opinion' was needed yesterday; no one will want it today."

She stressed the words strangely, as if she no longer held much respect for him. Michael seated himself behind his desk and studied her. What was going on here? Michelle had always been his biggest fan, his greatest supporter. It was obvious to everyone that she was more than a little in love with him, and he played on the knowledge mercilessly. But today her tone had changed. There was a testiness in her voice, as if she had seen inside him and no longer desired what she saw.

"Michelle, are you okay?"

She folded her arms across her chest, pure frost. "Fine. Why?"

"I don't know, you sound so—"

"You'd better get into Leo's office. He's been calling for you. He sounds pretty angry about something."

Leo Tarrant, fifty-seven, the calm centre of the firm, was at peace because he knew he was retiring in a year, and no longer let anything in the world worry him. But this morning he wasn't like that. His usually slick grey mane was ruffled about his head. His face was sclerotic and mottled with suppressed rage. He tipped back his chair and flicked rhythmically at the sides of a gold cigarette case, reminder of his past habit, now a talisman of his strengthened heart.

"You've let me down badly with this Trowerbridge business," he admitted. "I thought I'd get an early result by placing it in your hands. Instead it now looks as if they'll have to go to court after all."

Michael shifted uncomfortably in his seat. He simply couldn't comprehend Leo's attitude. Trowerbridge Developments had been sued by one of its tenants for failing to maintain a property. The company, aware that it had little chance of winning the case, had requested the negotiation of an out-of-court settlement by its longstanding legal representatives. Michael had done everything within his power to ensure that this would happen. After all, the clients were friends of his. They saw each other socially. Their kids even played together.

"I don't know what you're talking about, Leo," Michael confessed. "I completed my end of the deal in plenty of time to prevent the planned court action from going ahead."

"That's exactly the opposite of what I've heard," said his boss, clicking away at the clasp of the cigarette box. "According to the client's own progress report you've been holding back the negotiations and leaning so far in favour of the tenants that there's precious little time left for Trowerbridge to cut himself a deal. Neither he nor his son can see any way of making a satisfactory settlement. And there's something else."

Michael was dumbfounded. He couldn't have worked any harder for these people. If this was their way of showing gratitude…

"Have you ever received any financial inducements from the Trowerbridge family? Negative-equity absorbers, anything like that?"

The old man was accusing him of taking a bribe? He could scarcely believe his ears.

"No, of course not," he spluttered furiously. "I'm amazed that you could even consider—"

"Calm down, I'm not saying you did. It's something that the corporation suggested I look into. Think back over your relationship with Trowerbridge during the past few months, would you? You'd better make damned sure that there's nothing in your recent dealings with them that could damage your standing with this firm. Now let's go over these complaints in detail." He produced a slim red file and carefully unfolded it.

For the next hour and a half Michael was interrogated about his handling of the impending lawsuit. Although he left Leo's office more or less vindicated, he knew from the look on the old man's face that something irretrievable had been lost; a level of trust had been removed. The layer of good faith that had always existed between himself and his superiors had been torn away like the stripes from a dishonoured soldier's tunic. It wasn't just a matter of rebuilding Leo's confidence in him. He wanted to know why his abilities had been so quickly doubted. Clearly the Trowerbridge family, father and son, had lied, and Leo had believed them. But why should they do that? What had they to gain beyond an undesired delay to the lawsuit? It made no sense.

He considered the problem for the rest of the morning, during which time his secretary proved barely capable of common civility. She appeared briefly throughout the day to dump dockets on his desk, and at one point when he glanced up at her looked as if she was about to file a harassment suit against him. Michael felt the ground shifting fast beneath him. As he was leaving the building that evening, the doorman grumpily revealed that his parking space had been switched to a smaller, more awkward stall further away from the main doors.

* * *

Marla already sounded bored with the topic of conversation. They had washed up the dinner things together. Now she had turned back to the sink and was wiping down surfaces unnecessarily; the cleaning lady was due first thing tomorrow. Eventually aware that he had asked her a question, she sighed and faced him. "I just don't know, Michael. These things happen. There's no point in getting paranoid. Nobody's out to get you."

"Well, it certainly feels like they are," he complained, digging a bottle of Scotch from the cupboard and pouring himself a generous measure.

His wife made a face: disbelief, dissatisfaction, he couldn't read which. "You know," she said slowly, "maybe you're just experiencing the real world for a change."

"What the hell is that supposed to mean?"

She gestured vaguely about her. "You know what you're like. You've always had this kind of – aura of perfection surrounding you. People go out of their way to make things easy for you. Perhaps they're not doing it this once, and you've simply noticed for the first time."

He drained the glass and set it down on the kitchen table. "Marla, that's ridiculous and you know it."

"Is it? You glide through life in a golden haze expecting people to move out of your way just because you're you." She fell silent for a moment, then turned back to the sink. "It was something I noticed about you the day we met. A quality very few men ever possess. It's something you normally only find in very pretty girls, and then just for a couple of years. Doors automatically open. No one has ever found me special like that, only you. The rest of us trail in your wake. Well, maybe it's our turn in the sun for a while."

It seemed to Michael that he was being presented with a day of revelations, that he was somehow seeing himself clearly for the first time, from above, perhaps, or from a distance.

He rose and moved to his wife's side, gently placing his hands upon her hips. "I can't understand why you've never talked to me about this before," he said softly, "why you couldn't have been more honest with me."

"What's the point when you're not prepared to be honest about yourself?" she asked, coolly removing his hands. "If you want complete candour, then I'll tell you. I really don't think I can bear you touching me any more."

The room fell silent and remained so. Sean would not come down to kiss him goodnight and hid behind his mother's skirt until she took him up to bed.

* * *

He didn't think the situation could get any worse, but it did.

Marla would not talk about her refusal to allow his touch. At night she kept to the far side of the bed and took to sleeping in a T-shirt and pants. In the mornings she was up and dressed before him. She had usually washed and fed her son by the time he arose, so that the pair of them presented his sleepy form with a smart united front.

302

Although she refused to be drawn on the subject of their halted sex life, she conceded that no one else was stealing her affection from him. It was simply something that had finally, and perhaps inevitably, occurred. Frozen out of his own home, he increased his hours in the office.

But there the situation was just as bad. The Trowerbridge case had been lost and everyone now regarded him with suspicion, as if he'd been caught stealing office supplies and let off with a warning. Sometimes members of staff insulted him just out of earshot. At the very least, they ignored him. Michael became aware that parties and dinners were being arranged behind his back and that he had become the butt of cheap, stupid jokes. Much of the time no one seemed to notice him at all. If he joined a group at the coffee machine and struck up a conversation, they would glance over his shoulder, noting something or someone that interested them more. If he tried to make a social arrangement they cried off with transparently feeble excuses, not even bothering to convince him of their unavailability.

Petty grievances, of a kind that had never occurred before, began to accumulate. He was given the dullest briefs to work on. Someone left a bottle of Listerine on his desk in response to an office perception that he suffered from halitosis. Even the parking attendant had the temerity to suggest that he attend more carefully to his personal hygiene.

At last, at the end of his tether, he asked his secretary to enter his office and to close the door behind her.

"I want you to be honest with me, Michelle," he said carefully, seating himself and bidding her do the same. "I find everyone's attitude towards me has changed drastically in the last two weeks, and I'm at a loss to understand why."

"You want the honest truth?" asked Michelle, pointedly examining her cuticles.

"Please," pleaded Michael, ready to absorb her reply and analyse it at length.

"Well, it's the way you treat people, like they're satellites around your planet. I used to find it exciting, very masculine. I rather fancied you, all that rugged decisiveness. Others did too. Now I wonder how I could have been so blind." She shifted uncomfortably. "Can I go now?"

"Certainly not!" He snorted, wondered, shook his head in bewilderment. "Explain what you mean. What do the others say about me?"

Michelle stared up at the ceiling and blew the air from her cheeks. "Oh, I think you know. That you're self-centred, boring, pushy, less clever than you think you are. You're just not a very likeable man any more."

"And you can sit there and say this to my face?" he asked.

"I've already applied for a transfer," she answered, rising.

Michael realised then that if he went out and bought a dog it would probably run off, just to be away from him. Seated on a wet bench in the bedraggled little park beneath the office, watching as the pigeons strutted toward his shoes and then veered away, he became seized with the idea that someone had placed a curse on him. Not your usual get-boils-and-die curse, but something subtler. There was only one wild card to consider, one suspect, and that was Mr Whatever-his-name-was on the bike, the Latin chap he'd knocked over. The more Michael considered it, the clearer it became that his troubles had truly begun after that angry night-time phone call. He remembered the voice on the line: "What's your biggest fear…? Don' take much to break a man like you… When you come to find me – an' you will…" It all began to make sense. Could there be a rational explanation for what was happening to him? Was the guy some kind of shaman in touch with the supernatural, a malevolent hypnotist, or just someone with the power of suggestion? Wasn't that how voodoo worked? He was determined to take positive action.

It was dark by the time he finally got out of the office. Nosing the car back toward the intersection where the accident had occurred, he remembered the cyclist's response to his offer of a lift. "I just live over there."

"*Over there*" proved to be a prefabricated two-storey block of council flats. With no other way of locating his tormentor, he began ringing doorbells and facing irate residents, most of whom were in the middle of eating dinner. One of them even swore and spat at him, but by now he was used to that kind of behaviour. Trudging along the cracked, flooded balconies like a demented rent collector, he suddenly recalled a name mentioned in the phone call – Patty. Hadn't she checked out the cyclist's damaged shoulder? At least it was something specific, a person he could ask to see.

After being abused in four more doorways, he was nearing the end of the first floor with only a few apartments remaining when a young Asian man with dragons tattooed on his arms pointed to the flat at the end of the corridor.

"She's married to a Mexican guy who plays weird music all night," he complained.

Leaning against the garbage chute was the bicycle that he had hit, now repaired.

"That's the one," said Michael, thanking him and setting off. He stood before the door and read the printed card wedged next to the broken bell.

"You're back sooner than I expected," said Ramon del Tierro, faith healer, opening the door at his knock and ushering him in. "I didn't think you'd come to me for at least another week."

The hallway was in darkness. Mariachi music was playing in one of the bedrooms. The flat was slightly perfumed, as though someone had been burning incense earlier. Ramon was slighter and smaller than he remembered, pallid and unhealthy looking. His left eye was milky, blinded. He led the way to a small, smartly decorated lounge and waved him to a seat. Michael didn't want to sit. He no longer considered the situation absurd. He just wanted an answer, and an end to the hatred.

"You did this to me, didn't you?" The tightness in his voice made him realise how much anger he was holding back.

"Did what? Tell me what I did." Ramon shrugged, faking puzzlement.

"You made me – made everyone detest me."

"Hey, how could I do that? You soun' like a crazy man. You want to know how my shoulder is? Thank you for askin', it's gonna be okay." He turned away. "I'm gonna make some coffee. You wan' some?"

"I want you to tell me *what you did*, damn it!" Michael shouted, grabbing a scrawny arm.

Ramon glared fiercely and remained silent until he released his grip. Then he softly spoke.

"I have a gift, Mr Townsend. A crazy, pointless gift. If it had been second sight or somethin' I might have made some money from it, but no. When I come into contact with strangers I can see what makes them happy or sad. Sometimes I can sense what they fear or who they love. It depends on who I touch. Sometimes I don' feel nothin' at all. But I felt it with you. An' I made you see how life can be when you don't have the one thing you value most. In your case, it's your popularity. I took away your charm. You're no longer a likeable guy. I just didn't think it would screw you up as bad as this. I guess you must love yourself a whole lot more than you love anyone else."

Michael ran a hand across his face, suddenly tired. "Why did you pick on me?"

"Because I can, and because you deserved it. Now, what you gonna do about that? Go cryin' to the police, tell them nobody likes you?"

Fury was rising within Michael, bubbling to the surface in a malignant mist. "What do you want?"

"I don' want nothing from you, Mr Townsend. You got nothin' I want."

"You sabotaged my job."

Ramon shook his head. "No sir, I did not. Anythin' that's happening to you is happening 'cause people just don't like you no more."

"Then you can make it end."

The healer considered this for a moment, scratching at his chin with a thumbnail. "I guess I could, but I don't want to. See, it's better for you to relearn yourself from scratch. Won't be easy the way you are now, but just makin' the effort would turn you into a better person." Michael knew that if he moved too close he would lash out at Ramon. His temper was slow to rise but formidable to witness. Now he clenched his fists and advanced on the little Mexican. "You get this fucking thing off me straight away, you filthy little spic, or I will beat you unconscious and burn this shit hole down with you in it, do you understand?"

"Now you're showin' your true colours, Mr Townsend." Ramon took a step back, wary but not nervous. "A soul like yours takes an awful lot of fixin'. Tell me what it is you want."

"I want you to make everyone love me again," he said, suddenly embarrassed by the realisation of his needs.

"That I can do."

"How soon?"

"In a few seconds, with just a touch. But you won't like it. Consider the other way, I beg you. Relearn. Begin again with the personality you have now. It will be more difficult, but the rewards will be much greater."

"I can't do that. I need this to happen tonight."

"Then it will have to be the hard way. Come closer to me."

Michael walked into Ramon's outstretched arms. Before he had time to realise what was happening, he felt the thin-bladed knife that Ramon had pulled from his pocket bite between the ribs traversing his heart. The fiery razor edge sliced through the beating muscle, piercing a ventricle and ending his life in a single crimson moment.

* * *

So many people turned up at St Peter's Church that they ran out of parking spaces and had to leave their cars on the grass verges lining the road. The funeral service boasted eulogies from the senior partners of Aberfitch McKiernny, from friends and relatives, from his colleagues and from his adoring wife. Everyone who went to the burial of Michael Everett Townsend volubly agreed; the man being laid to rest here was truly loved by everyone.

THE MERRIE DANCERS

ALISON LITTLEWOOD

It was after nightfall when I first saw my new neighbour, though I didn't know when she had decided to go out into the garden. I'd been busy unpacking boxes and telling myself I should be grateful for what I had, and it was dark when I went to draw the curtains across the window. She was in a wheelchair, nothing but a hunched, shadowy shape against the shrubbery. I might not have seen her if it wasn't for the movement of her feet, kicking continually at the blanket covering her legs. I thought of Parkinson's, of restless leg syndrome, other illnesses I couldn't name and knew little of. Had she been taken ill just now, or was it of long duration? Did she need my help?

I felt bad that I didn't know. I'd never met her before, though Mum had lived in this house for some years. I'd left home as soon as I was eighteen, anxious to experience all that London had to offer, and only came back when she got ill. I'd chosen to look after her, though I hadn't wanted it, and by the time I reached her it was already too late. Now I was here, it was as if I couldn't leave again – couldn't be so ungrateful as to abandon her a second time, even though she was already gone.

The old lady next door tilted back her head to stare up at the stars, shielding her eyes as if they were too bright, and I just made out the smile that touched her lips. It seemed suddenly terribly romantic. She was old, infirm, perhaps couldn't even walk, and yet there she was taking in the night air and dreaming, while I was twenty-four and acting as if my life was already over.

I didn't go to check on her after all. I didn't see her again that night, didn't watch to see that she'd gone inside, closed the doors behind her, that she was safe. I slept right through to the next morning, stretched the stiffness from my limbs, brushed my teeth and dressed before I opened the curtains to see her sitting there, still in the place she had been.

I couldn't breathe. Was she stuck there, unable to get inside by herself? Had she fallen asleep – or something worse than that? She was old and alone and she had needed help; help that, once again, I had failed to give.

Thinking of heart attacks and strokes and other terrors of the elderly, I rushed downstairs and into my own back garden. Our two houses were the only ones set at the top of a leafy lane, separated from each other and the softly rolling hills around us by knee-high fencing. I stepped over it and rushed towards her, calling to see if she was all right, and she turned towards me, her look of astonishment stopping me dead.

"Goodness," she said. "Have you seen a ghostie, lass?"

My alarm turned to apologies. I explained my concern and introduced myself, and she told me she was Annis Scollay, that she had just this moment stepped outside again – *wheeled*, I thought but didn't say. Her legs still kicked against their blanket, a grey tartan, and the thought came again that she had some kind of illness, a muscular palsy over which she had no control. I tried not to look, though now and again a sharper kick drew my gaze.

"I did come out for a wee while last night," she said. "I hoped to see the merrie dancers. It was on the news they might be seen this far south, but I didn't see anything at all. Did you happen to see them, Sophie?"

I said I had not, though I remembered the news item she referred to – I should have thought of it before. If I hadn't been so set on finding a place for everything, I might have tried to see the Northern Lights myself, though despite the newscaster's assurance it had seemed unlikely they would grace the skies of Lincolnshire. They were meant for wilder climes, more northerly parts of the world.

"It's still oorlich, though," she said, shivering as if to explain her meaning. "We had that part of it, at least." She fumbled under her blanket, pulling another one free; it looked as soft as mohair. She passed it to me and I shook my head – I'd come out here to help her, not the other way around – but she said, "That shade of brown, it's called a murat. One of the finest you've ever felt about your neck."

A strange curiosity came over me and I took it, wrapping it around my shoulders, and felt comforted at once. I snuggled into its warmth.

313

"My father reared the sheep gave that blanket," she said. "Shetland sheep, on the isles. That one's from my favourite. Bonxie, I called her, after the Great Skua chicks that lived on the sea cliffs. She was one of the best; the kindly sheep we called them, the ones that gave such wool."

I couldn't resist rubbing it against my cheek, almost thinking I could smell not the lanolin of sheep but the briny scent of the ocean.

"That's right," she said, as if I'd spoken. "There were ponies too, of course, our neighbours had them, and I'd go there whenever I could. I'd put on their halters and lead them about like dogs, for they were no bigger."

"You grew up on the Shetland Islands?" My eyes widened. They seemed as unknowable to me as a place in a story. I wasn't certain I could have pointed to them on a map.

"On Foula," she said, clearly loving to speak of it. "The most westerly of them all, and separate from the rest – divided from them by a nasty reef, the Shaalds, though I always thought of them as the hungry rocks. The loneliest island in Britain." She said this last with a touch of pride.

Caught up in her words, I only said, "I thought I detected an accent," though the truth was that at times I could and at others I barely heard it. It seemed to come and go, like something she half-remembered.

"Aye, it's still in me, when I think of it," she said. "Mostly it's gone. I lost a lot of things when I left. Found some too. That's what happens, I suppose."

She glanced at me as if she saw right through me and I thought of the way I'd inherited the house, had been given everything. It had been at once too easy and too hard. I had lost my mother; I had done nothing to help her. I hadn't earned such a home, hadn't *given* enough. But I was helping now, wasn't I? Old people liked to chat about their lives, their memories. Annis certainly seemed to relish the chance to talk to someone, and my mother might have liked to know that I listened – so I asked Annis to tell me all about her life on Foula.

I wasn't sure she heard. She was staring into the garden, focused on a little twig that was still twitching as if a bird had just flown; then she looked away as if it was nothing after all. Her gaze softened, as though she saw only distant places, other times.

"I saw a trow when I was thirteen years old," she said. "Is that the sort of tale you like, hen?"

I smiled and nodded, wondering what on earth a trow was – a fish? A bird? – trying not to feel like a child at bedtime, listening to stories at her mother's knee.

"The aurora shone that night," she said. "The dancers were merry then, perhaps a little too merry, so in a way it was all their fault, for if they weren't shining the path would have been too dark to go out. It was approaching winter, and the nights were longer than any you'd imagine, though it was between the weathers; we had gales before and gales after, but that night it was still.

"I'd only been to the Turvelsons'. They had the next croft

to ours, and my mother had sent me to borrow a little butter. She was baking biscuits for the wee ones' birthdays, but it was me who had to go."

Her accent seemed to deepen as she remembered. She pronounced mother as *modir*.

"It hadn't taken long, and the parcel was greasy in my pocket. It's lucky our neighbours were close by. Fewer than forty souls lived on Foula even then, all of us on the easterly plain. Most of the Isles are empty, did you know that? And none can count them. There are said to be a hundred islands and skerries, but no one really knows, and some are said to appear and disappear at the bidding of the selkies."

I smiled at her whimsicality, but now that she had begun she seemed barely conscious of my presence.

"The sky to the north was all aglow," she said. "Every few steps the path shone green at my feet and I saw everything – and nothing, for the shimmering in the sky made the hills darker than ever. The trows are hill-dwellers, did you know that? I looked at the great mound of Hamnafeld, which drops on the other side sheer into the ocean. On its top, that's where they say the door is: the Lum of Liorafeld, an opening that goes straight down to their homes underground. Some have let lines down to try and find the bottom, but no one ever can. Those who seek it rarely even find the door.

"That's what my grandmother told me, and that's what I was thinking of. Perhaps that's why it happened – they were drawn to my thoughts, or perhaps it was only the butter, or they liked the pretty lights. Whatever the reason, I felt their eyes on me.

"That feeling you have sometimes, of being watched – it doesn't happen often on Foula. There are more ponies than people and more sheep than ponies and more birds than the rest put together, and never a stranger, especially not in winter. Still, I knew it when it came, that feeling, crawling all over me like dirty fingers.

"I turned about and there he was: a shape where none should be. He stood halfway between their home and mine, as if he'd just then stepped out of the peat bog. One moment he was clear, outlined in the flicker, and the next I could barely make him out. But tall he was, and grey; I thought his clothes were grey and his skin too, his raggedy beard and tatty hair, all of him, and I knew he was looking at me, though I couldn't rightly see his eyes.

"I don't know what I would have done, screamed or run or nothing at all, but thanks be, he started walking away. He didn't walk like ordinary folk, though. He walked like a trow, and that is, backwards – he never so much as glanced behind him to see his way. At least, I don't think he did. He came and went in the light, but I felt him still watching me, and I shivered, because I knew then I'd seen one of the folk. Some say the trows are like Norwegian trolls, others the English fairies, but I think they're something in-between.

"The fear took me then and I ran all the way home. When I let myself in at the door, my mother called out for the butter; my little brother and sister looked up from their game; and

Gran took one look at me and shrieked fit to wake all the angels in heaven.

"Well, there was uproar then. 'What is it? What is it?' My mother cried, and I could scarce speak for trembling, but Gran only held my face to the lamplight, tilting it this way and that way.

"'What did you see?' she spat, and I was so frightened I thought to lie, but I knew she'd see it on me. She saw many things, my Gran; too many, perhaps. So I told her.

"She crowed as if she'd caught a fish. 'I knew it!' she said. 'It's left its mark on you!'

"Well, my brother grinned and my sister laughed, but my mother only sighed and went back to the oat-biscuits, taking the butter with her. Me, I went to the mirror. I stared and stared into it, trying to see whatever Gran had seen. *Left its mark on you*, she'd said, but no matter how I tried, then or after, I never could see a trace of it."

Annis stirred in her wheelchair, blinking as if she didn't entirely know where she was. I became conscious of her feet constantly shifting against the blankets, the sound seeming suddenly loud. I realised it had been there all the time she spoke, almost like whispering, or perhaps like waves breaking on the shore. Now I realised she was waiting for me to respond and yet I didn't have the first idea what to say.

"There's more to it, of course," she said. "I should tell you of the year I turned sixteen – of Yule, and of the thing that happened to the twins – my brother and sister."

318

Her whole body twitched in her seat and she gave an especially hard kick. The tartan blanket fell aside and I caught a glimpse, not of some wide-fitting brogues or house-slippers or any such thing, but the most exquisite bright red shoes. She caught her breath, pulling at the blanket to cover them once more.

"I'll tell you of those too," she said, "but not now."

I must have stepped closer without meaning to, thinking to help her I supposed, for she reached out and grasped my hand in one bony claw, crushing my fingers.

"I'll go inside," she said. "I've said enough, I think."

She cast glances to the left and right before waving me towards my own garden, ignoring my goodbyes and offers of help as she pulled at the wheels of her chair. I'm not sure I was really seeing her any longer. I could still picture those shoes, the brightness of them, the perfect red of them: their pointed toes, the tiny, almost invisible stitching, the suppleness of the leather. I realised I hadn't said a word about her story. It wasn't until I got inside that I found her soft woollen blanket was still draped about my shoulders.

* * *

As I got on with the task of settling into my mother's house, Annis's tale began to seem more and more outlandish. I didn't know what to think of it, or of her for telling it. Her words were surely make-believe, or at least little more than a mingling of her past and the tales she must have heard in childhood.

Still, I kept returning to the blanket where I'd left it on the table, picking it up and touching it to my cheek. Was that scent still there – the harsh, raw wind, carried across the Atlantic? But when I closed my eyes it was those shoes I saw, such pretty shoes for one so old, and I wondered how it must feel to wear them. Was that why she was always fidgeting, as if she longed to dance? Or did her feet simply follow in the wake of her wandering thoughts?

I shook away the idea and decided I would look in on her again. It seemed like fate, then, when I looked out of the window and saw her emerging into her garden, into a day that was still struggling to become bright.

After last time there seemed little point in standing on ceremony and so I went into my own garden and waved as I stepped over the fence. I made to hand over the lovely blanket but she gestured for me to hold on to it, so I wrapped it about me and nestled into it once again.

"My grandmother had a lot of superstitions," she began, as if I'd never been away. "She always said the trows would punish a lass for forgetting to place a little resting peat on a waning flame. They like the fire, you see. They also like to wash their bairns on a Saturday and she would bid me leave out the water for them. If I neglected to do it, or if I did it well, before she'd even thought of it, why, she put it all down to the night I saw the peedie man.

"She wouldn't let me forget, and anyway, I could not. I thought of him often: standing out there under the dancing sky, watching and watching for me. I don't know if I still carried the mark Gran had spoken of. I didn't like to think of it, much less ask – but the longing of it was on me, that's what she always said, and it sent a shiver through me every time, as if I was still out there in the cold and the dark.

"But it's Yule when the trows really wander above the ground. They come out seven days earlier, on Tul-ya's e'en, and so it was the year I turned sixteen. Gran had me stick knives into the hams to stop the trows getting them, and it was me had to do the blessing on the little ones.

"I did it myself first: washed, then dipped hands and feet into the water while my mother dropped the coals in, so the trows couldn't steal away the power in them. Then it came time for me to bless the twins, but they were older then, eleven years old, and they didn't want me; they pulled faces and splashed till I was drenched, and so I told them they could take their chances.

"Truth be told, I was sick of them then. I had to cook for them, make sure their silly matching faces were scrubbed, comb their matching hair. I had to fetch this, tidy that, while they put out their matching tongues at me behind our mother's back. Besides, that was the year of the red shoes, and after I saw them, I could think of nothing else."

I realised that her feet were restless still, shifting and rustling under their blanket. I'd almost forgotten their movement, had neglected, somehow, to notice.

"Oh, but I was wild for those shoes. I saw them in a fancy shop on the mainland, right in the window they were and covered in ribbons, and I couldn't talk of anything else. Besides, the dance was coming, and I felt I had to wear them. If I only had those shoes, Alex Galdie might dance with me. If I only had those shoes, I'd never ask for anything else again. Have you ever wished for something like that, Sophie – needed it so badly it's like a knot inside of you that won't come loose?"

She paused and I cast my mind back, but it was her shoes that came to mind, the lovely red of them, their softness, their perfect form, and I thought of dancing – of flying through the air as if I'd never fall to earth again. I blinked away the thought, but she hadn't noticed my reverie.

"I saved and saved," she said. "I dropped one penny after another into a jar to help buy them, though it was never enough. I begged; I wept. I did everything I was asked to do, washing the bairn's mucky clothes before I was told, sweeping the hearth, anything my mother asked of me. And in the end she gave a great sigh and said I must be witched – *in the hill* was how she put it, meaning in the trow's power – but she said they would be mine.

"Maybe she thought me cursed even then, you see, but I didn't see it that way. Why should a girl only be dutiful all her days? Why must she think only of work and home and bairns and nothing more? It was a great wide world outside the door – right across the ocean. Every time I looked out I thought of it, and every time the young men looked at me I heard fierce music playing, felt the dance already in my feet."

322

I could almost see it; that, or a memory. When she went on, I had to drag myself back from the vision.

"On Foula, Auld Yule is still celebrated in January, as it was in the Julian calendar, though all the rest of the world changed that in 1752. We hung onto things long past anyone else, perhaps because there was so little to go around. And so the dancing was set for the sixth. After that, the grey neighbours would go back inside the hill, their holidays over, but before then they'd dance all they could – and so would I.

"There was rarely any snow on Foula. You may not believe that, since it's as far north as Cape Farewell in Greenland, but Atlantic currents keep the climate mild; it only feels so cold because of the wind chasing in from the sea. But it snowed that night – the night of the dancing. A good skim of white, and the wind made it bitter, every flake like a knife driving into your skin. And the way they flew all about, it was hard to see your hand before your face.

"The sea was alive as we made our way to Norderhus, near the harbour. I heard its song, deep and fierce. The Atlantic and the North Sea were at war, the sea black, the sky above pale as death. That wasn't the lights, though; the only merrie dancers were all within. I could hear the fiddles on the wind, loud one moment, the next quiet and quick. I wasn't yet wearing my red shoes, was carrying those under my oil-coat so they wouldn't get wet. There was my mother, grandmother and me; the twins were judged too young, and I wasn't sorry for that.

"Everyone was in the ben, the inner room, and in there, it was roasting. I left my boots with all the rest and slipped on my lovely shoes and the music was in them at once, fast and free and telling of new places, and almost as soon as I set foot in the room I was off – clasped by the hand by Alex Galdie, as close as you like, and he didn't tear his eyes from mine a moment while we spun and we twirled. There was a light in his face when he smiled at me, and if I wasn't witched before, I was witched then. I saw my mother watching and my grandmother both, and I didn't care a bit. My shoes carried me off, and I was happy to go.

"I never once thought of home, or duties, or the land I was born in or the trows and their ways – not even their love of the dance. That tune ended and another began, wilder than the first, and Alex never let me go. He danced with me again, whirling me by the waist, and my feet went faster and faster till I laughed with joy.

"Trows love the fiddle, did you know that? It's said they stole away the Fiddler of Yell for years and years, though he thought only a night had passed while he played for them. And it seemed they were not the only ones, for after a while I noticed from the tail of my eye the door opened and the twins glided in, all quiet-like, their eyes wide and their faces two matching smiles. Sneaked by they did, not speaking to anyone before they joined the dance. I saw them now and again as our paths crossed, touching hands, whirling away. Little knowing looks they gave me, and never a word. I remember thinking they must have longed for it just as I had, and I couldn't blame them for that. I'd not sat down for a moment, never wanted to again.

"They danced beautifully. Not a hink nor a kink in it, and them so young.

"It was around midnight when my mother grabbed me by the hand and said we must be off. I looked about for the twins and couldn't see them anywhere, so I asked her where they were, fidgeting all the while because the music played on and Alex waited and I could not bear to stand still.

"She shook her head. I thought the music had stopped her ears and so I shouted louder, but she couldn't fathom the question. All the time the twins had danced, you see, something had stopped her from seeing; she'd never even noticed they were there at all. And then Gran said they couldn't have come, not all alone, because when she stepped out of the door she'd made sure to lock it behind her.

"Well, there was an uproar then. The dance stopped quick enough and everyone put on their oilskins and sou'westers and went out to look.

"The snow hadn't stopped falling, but the sky was dark again, deeper and blacker by contrast with the lights that danced across it. The merrie dancers had come after all, just as if they were mocking us.

"The bairns were not at the croft, of course. That was quiet, the door standing wide and the snow drifting in across the clean floor. Their beds were empty.

"We found the twins at the edge of the peat bog, just where I'd seen the peedie man. They were dead. They were lying in the snow, their eyes open to the sky, and snowflakes drifted into them, not melting. They'd been there all night, you see. They never had been dancing and never would – it was the trows that had come, stealing their likenesses so they could join in with the human revels.

"I don't know if the trows had to steal their breath before they took on their shape, or if it was an accident they died. I didn't know if those little bodies were really the twins at all – or if my real brother and sister were stolen away under the hill and those were nothing but the empty skins the trows had put on for the night, just like they were puppets.

"I wonder sometimes if the twins are dancing even now, under great Hamnafeld. I wonder if that's why my feet will never be still – because my dancing is an echo of theirs. When at last my shoes give me peace, maybe I'll know my brother and sister are dead. But then, years pass differently under the hill. They might be children yet – or far older than I am, my brother with a beard reaching to his feet, my sister with the light of ages in her eyes.

"My mother wailed and my grandmother wept, and I couldn't comfort them. I remember I looked down into my brother's eyes, and my sister's, at the snowflakes falling into them, and I thought of the way I'd saved for those red shoes, one shiny coin after another falling into a jar. It was me who'd failed to bless the twins. It was me who'd tired of them, me who'd wished so hard to be free of them. And I *was* free – except for the way my shoes kept on twitching and shifting, not done with their dancing yet, restless as sin, reminding me of what I'd done.

"Did the grey folk grant me a wish that night when I was thirteen, do you think? Or did they curse me for always – or was it both together? For I'll tell you this: sometimes, having your dearest wish put into your hands is the biggest curse of all."

Annis stopped speaking but she didn't look at me, just went on staring into the past, and I was glad of it because I didn't know what to say. Did she really imagine her feet fidgeted the way they did because her shoes wouldn't stop dancing? That was something out of a fairy story, one I had read myself when I was young. The girl in "The Red Shoes" was also punished for thinking too much of her finery; her new shoes forced her to dance and dance until she was exhausted and a kindly woodcutter saved her by chopping off her feet with an axe. Was that the root of Annis's tale? Perhaps she didn't have a physical illness at all. Perhaps her legs wouldn't be still because she was punishing herself for some accident that happened to her siblings, and her ailment – her curse – was psychosomatic. But why did she not simply take off the shoes? I gazed at her in dismay, realising that perhaps I couldn't help her at all, that maybe she needed more than I knew how to give. I had no idea if she was mad, but I didn't think she could be altogether sane.

"Oh, it wasn't like the auld story at all." Slowly, Annis lifted her head and looked at me, and I fought the urge to squirm.

Once again, she made me feel that she saw into me, that she saw everything.

"You think you know it, but it wasn't the same. Andersen's tale came out of a softer land, and it was naught like mine. There's no woodcutter in my story, nor any wood; there were never any trees grew on Foula. It was a peat-cutter I'd set my heart upon, and he never did chop off my feet. He didn't carry me over the threshold or tie my dancing feet to the kitchen table so I could gut the fish for his dinner. What kind of a man would do that? No: Alex Galdie decided he didn't want me after all. He married a girl from Hametoon and settled on the island. It was me who left, on the very next boat I could. What else could I do? I couldn't go home again. I'd got my freedom all right, but I carried the place away with me, and I'll tell you, I was right about those shoes – once I had them, I never truly wanted anything else again."

I still didn't know what to say, so I took the blanket from my neck and wrapped it about hers. As I did, she grasped my fingers, gently this time.

"You could help me," she said. "Would you help an old lady, dear?"

I told her that of course I would. I asked what it was she needed.

"I canna take them off," she said. "I've tried and tried. But I know that you could – if you were willing. If you knew the story of them and chose to take them anyway, to make them your own."

She kicked away the tartan covering her legs. Her feet kicked freely, her toes pointed, marking out the steps she couldn't take. For an instant, the shoes looked as if they were being worn by someone younger; someone being whirled in a young man's arms.

I focused again on her face, which was old and lined, her eyes watery. I reminded myself that hers was a mad, wild tale, with no sense in it. I didn't believe she'd worn those same shoes for so many years. I didn't believe that she couldn't stop dancing – but *she* did. I could free her from her unhappy delusion. I may have failed to help my mother, but now I could help her neighbour – her friend.

And Annis could rest at last. She could have peace. She could go where she wanted, even home, perhaps. An image rose before me: Annis going to join her brother and sister with the trows, walking away from me backwards, her steps steady at last, and never taking her gaze from my face.

Another feeling came over me then, one that had been waiting beneath: of longing, almost of greed. I told myself it would be doing her a favour to take them – and they really were lovely shoes. They were wasted on her. She was *old*. What was the use of her dancing?

I reached out and felt soft leather brush against my fingers. As I did so, a sound reached my ears: the swift, low music of a fiddle. And I remembered what it had been like, in the city, so few years ago: the close dark, infectious music throbbing from tall speakers, the touch of a young man's hand. I remembered how it had felt to dance, to be free, to never want my feet to be still. I knew I could be a part of that dance again – and the thought came to me that perhaps she was right: that if I let go, it would be for always. I might be joining the dance forever; I might never come home again.

It's only a story, I thought.

Yet still, I couldn't choose. I reached out and touched the red shoes and I listened to the rhythm of the dance, felt it beating in my blood. I could smell the sea, feel the cold ocean breeze in my hair. And I looked up, into Annis's eyes, and found I couldn't move a limb.

AGAIN

TIM LEBBON

It wasn't the first time Jodi had died, but it might have been the strangest.

The wild dogs were sniffling at her bleeding, broken body, nudging her with their wet noses, and each point of contact was a shock, so cold that it felt hot, their breath chilling her where blood pulsed from her many wounds. She felt a rough tongue lapping at the hollow of her elbow, and the sharp kiss of teeth. A promise of what would come soon. For some reason they seemed to be waiting until she was dead before they started eating her. That was a blessing. She must have done at least one good thing in this past life to merit such treatment.

Her breath was clotting in her throat. Pain cut in cooler and sharper than the knife that had been her undoing. It reached past the wounds, deep down to her bones, her centre, the deepest parts of her where memories of countless similar agonies resided. It was easily as terrible as any of them, but the pain was inconsequential. She put a distance between it and her. She would not remember the pain, and it served no purpose because soon – in minutes, possibly even seconds – she would be dead. Then the pain and everything else she had seen, experienced, and known in this life would be no more.

For a while, at least.

Then she would wake again somewhere, somewhen, and as someone else, and Jodi had become very good at not taking the sensations of dying agonies with her. There was a reason for that. A good, solid reason.

She didn't want to go mad.

"I saw fifteen bees yesterday," a voice said, and Jodi's crackling, wet breath held in her throat.

I didn't know she was still here.

"Eighteen the day before. Considering these fields, these woods, are filled with flowers at this time of year, there should have been hundreds. Or thousands."

I thought she'd just left her dogs behind to finish the job.

As if the hounds had heard her thoughts, she felt teeth beginning to gnaw at the slashed fingers of her right hand. Defensive wounds, they might be called. They'd done no good. It was the terrier, she guessed, though she couldn't lift her head to see. A beautiful blue sky was her view as a small dog started to eat her hand. She smelled blood and bluebells. Small flies buzzed around her head and landed on her face, and she felt every single one of them, as if the skin of her face had become super-sensitive.

I'll forget the pain.

Her shoulder jarred as the dog started tugging.

"I save as many bees as I can," the voice said, and Jodi remembered her then, the old woman with the pack of pet dogs, her clothes made from countless scraps held together with heavy pink stitching. She was well liked in the village, something of an oddity but a member of the village council, an advocate of dog waste bins and a new playground on the village green. Her name was Helen. She killed people for fun, and she'd told Jodi – a wanderer, a visitor to the village, and soon to die for the fifteenth or eighteenth time – not to take it personally.

"I always wonder when I save a bee from a bird bath or the surface of a pond in the woods, whether I've saved the world. Everything has a point of balance. The last cigarette that will kill you, the last deep breath of a city's polluted air that'll cause a cell in your body to mutate and start splitting at an unnatural rate. The last inch of a knife stab that'll shift you from life to death."

Just below my heart, Jodi thought. *I think that was the one.*

"The last bee I save, that will mean the world is no longer doomed, that a particular spread of flowers will be pollinated. I'm out to save the world. Daisy, don't eat the lady's hand until she's dead."

The terrier let go of Jodi's tattered hand, and her final breath might have sounded like a laugh.

The beautiful blue sky grew dark, and Jodi's last thought was, *I wish Eveline were here to see me through.*

* * *

She saw her from a distance, and as usual she held back, taking in the sight and seeing how much she'd changed. It always came as something of a shock.

Eveline was growing old. Still beautiful, still radiant and with a whole bearing that seemed to exude life and enthusiasm and love. Her hair was mostly grey, the skin around her eyes and mouth creased from smiling. She sipped a small coffee and looked around the café, phone face-down on the table before her. A good fifty per cent of the clientele were skimming their phones, thumbs stroking screens and clicking away their lives.

Jodi knew more than most that every second was precious. That was why she loved Eveline so much. Happy or sad, moving or still, she absorbed each life experience with relish.

The old woman's gaze passed across Jodi and moved on. Jodi smiled. Eveline paused and looked back, and that was all it took. Their eyes connected, and Eveline reflected her own smile. *It's always your eyes I see first,* she'd once told Jodi, maybe forty years before. *It's probably inexplicable, because they're never your eyes, not physically at least. But I always know you.*

Jodi raised her eyebrows and walked towards Eveline.

"Get you another?" she asked, nodding down at the empty coffee cup.

"My doctor's been telling me to cut down on the caffeine."

Jodi felt a jolt in her stomach. She didn't like the idea of her old friend being ill, let alone growing old. It felt so unfair.

"But fuck him," Eveline said. "Flat white, please. And a chocolate brownie."

While Jodi went to the counter she felt the older woman's eyes on her, sizing her up, drinking in who she had become.

"I never knew where you went," Eveline said when she returned to the table.

"I'm sorry." Jodi sat down, settling a tray containing their drinks and food. Eveline didn't take her eyes off her as she did so, as if afraid she would be dead and gone again in moments. And perhaps she would. Jodi had long ago ceased trying to sense her approaching deaths, because she knew there could be no escape.

"So where have you…?" Eveline asked. She'd never quite come to terms with Jodi's situation. Perhaps she didn't even quite believe, because it was ridiculous and unlikely and unnatural. She saw, she felt, she understood, but allowing her intelligent mind to fully accept Jodi's nature was one step too close to madness.

"A woman in the village killed me," Jodi said. "Helen seemed a nice old thing, and everyone liked her, but she had this… predilection. I was gone for longer this time, but then…" She glanced down at her new body, the new woman she had become. "Guatemala. A car crash. She was flung from the wreck and hit a tree, died instantly. And I popped in."

"Popped," Eveline said. She sipped at her coffee. It was too hot, so she held it to her mouth and blew gently, as if eager to fog the sight before her.

"Her family was kind, and good, but I didn't stay. I've been travelling ever since. Up through South America, Mexico, the

'States. I spent some time in Alaska." Jodi smiled. "Once, I slipped and twisted my ankle and spent a night out in the snow, and I thought that was it for this time. But a couple of men and their dogs found me."

"And it took you this long to come and find me?" There was no accusation in Eveline's tone, and no sadness either. Their relationship was, perhaps, the strangest in the world between two people. How could it not be? In the beginning, Jodi had expected to find others like her, to run across them on the fringes of society, to recognise them as Eveline recognised her each and every time, just by the look in their eyes. But she'd found no one, and no one had found her. Two lives ago she had stopped looking. One life ago, she'd mentioned the idea to Eveline and she'd laughed. *You're watching too much TV*, she'd said.

"It always seems to be…" Jodi said.

"I know the patterns," Eveline said. "You find me, we spend some time, and then…"

"But I can't *not* spend time with you," Jodi said. "You're the only one who understands."

Eveline laughed. "And I don't understand at all." She lifted her coffee, then put it down again. "Come on. I've got something to show you."

They left the coffee shop together, hand in hand. They could have been mother and daughter, or lovers.

* * *

"You found him," Jodi said.

"I found tales about him," Eveline replied. "The wonders of the internet."

Jodi wasn't sure she even wanted to know. She'd never gone looking herself, and even later, when she was sure he must be dead and it was only her left echoing down through the years, death to life, death to life again, she'd had no inclination to research him. In her mind he'd just been a random beast, a sickly, evil man who'd wronged her and who had died soon after.

"You want to see?" Eveline asked. They were in her house, a small, comfortable cottage on the outskirts of Crickhowell in South Wales. It was beautifully furnished with homemade decorations, and the kitchen was a pleasant mess of vegetable baskets from her back-garden crop, jars filled with pickles and chutneys, and a tray of early season fruit. Jodi had witnessed her growing and ageing, coming into and leaving her life several times over the space of the past few decades. It wasn't fair, she knew, but the love between them was too strong for either to ignore. Eveline could have shunned her if she so desired. Jodi could have chosen not to return. Neither of them did.

The cottage was close to the river, and later they were going for a walk. Jodi had been here twice before in other lives. She still remembered the cool kiss of the river from when they'd gone swimming above the weir seventeen years and a lifetime ago.

"No," Jodi said. "I don't think I do want to see."

Eveline looked shocked, and then hurt. "I've spent so long…"

Jodi raised one corner of her mouth in an apologetic smile.

"If it's good for you to know about him, I'm glad. But I've spent a long time trying to forget."

"He cursed you to this life."

"These *lives*, you mean," Jodi quipped, but Eveline was not smiling.

"He died back in the thirties," Eveline said. "He was a renowned occultist. A cult leader. A bad, evil man, and there are plenty of testimonies about abuse and murder and—"

"I've done my best to forget."

"But maybe knowing more about him, delving deeper, might reveal a way for you to change things."

Jodi didn't respond to that. She looked around the room, eyes alighting on a rack of wine. "Fancy taking a couple of those bottles down to the river?"

Eveline sighed, then smiled gently, and as Jodi selected the wine, she busied herself in the kitchen putting together a picnic for two. It was still warm outside. By the time they reached the river the sun would be settling into the Welsh hills, and they'd be able to talk about all the things they had missed since they'd last seen each other.

Picking up a bottle and reading its label, seeing that it was bottled after her last death and rebirth, Jodi thought, *I don't want to change anything.*

* * *

Three years later, a rock shifted beneath Jodi's foot as she and Eveline were hiking in Snowdonia. Eveline was almost seventy years old but as fit as she'd ever been, and she put a lot of that down to Jodi. She wanted to keep up with her. The Guatemalan woman Jodi had fallen into was barely in her forties, and it gave Eveline something to strive for.

Jodi's ankle twisted and she fell, tumbling sideways and slipping down a steep slope for almost twenty feet. Striking a rock prevented her from falling any further. Unfortunately she struck it with her head, and she passed away in the mountain rescue helicopter called in to lift her to safety. Eveline was sitting beside her – the first time she had witnessed her passing – with Jodi still slipping in and out of consciousness, and although the sound of pounding rotors through the still-open doors prevented any talk, a look between them said it all.

I'll see you again.

I'll be watching for you.

Jodi's final thought as she slipped into a darkness from which this form of her would never recover was, *I only hope I still have time.*

* * *

In truth, she had never forgotten about the man who cursed her. He was always there when she was birthed again, in blood and pain, sometimes with screaming, sometimes into a body suffering extreme convulsions or terrible wounds. The memory of his voice, his face, his old man's petulance and anger at her rejecting his sickening advances, hung around Jodi as she became herself and someone else once again.

"You'll never die," he says.

"I wish you would," she replies.

"I'm a special man. A *wondrous* man. You could have been by my side, but you chose—"

"Exactly. I chose. Just not you."

"Then you will... never... die."

And he touches her, softly with one leathery fingertip, on her left cheek. She pushes his arm aside and steps back. He chuckles.

She leaves him and his place and his people, a sick community of weak-minded individuals – the biggest mistake of all her lives – and flees south towards London, reaching the city a few weeks later and losing herself in its chaotic, smog-laden atmosphere. She never expects to see him again, and for a while she doesn't. Not until she dies.

The horse and cart come out of nowhere and strikes her down. Darkness hauls her into its cold embrace. Nothingness. An absence. No experience, sensation or memory, and then she is lying in a hospital bed in a place and body she does not know.

You will never die, she hears, and she sees a memory of that wizened old man shadowed beside her, perpetuating the curse he has laid upon her. Then a family of surprised faces appears around her bed and she begins a second, confused life.

The confusion soon ends, and endings and beginnings become a part of her existence.

The old man was right in what he said. Down through the years, Jodi has striven to change his words from a curse to something else.

It still troubles her that he could have been amazing, but chose to be bad.

* * *

There seemed to be no rule dictating how soon after her death she would find herself alive once again. Sometimes it was almost instantaneous, other times she was gone for years. Sometimes she took a while to find her way back to Eveline, partly because of where she might have been reborn – the farthest from home had been Australia in the mid-seventies almost seven years after she died, the closest just a mile from where she had passed away three days before – but also because sometimes, the situation she was reborn into made an instant return difficult. Once, she was hauled back to life in the body of a recently deceased drug addict. Huddled in the fetid dampness of a stinking squat, surrounded by aimless, vacant souls who hadn't even known the woman in the body before her, she smashed into the burning agony of craving like a car hitting a wall. It took her breath away and gripped her in a filthy fist; that was the time when she had most regarded the old man's curse as true to its name.

This new resurrection might have been the strangest yet.

She felt pressure, coldness, an all-encompassing embrace, and something nudging insistently at her face. Opening her mouth to gasp in her first new breath, Jodi realised with a jolt that it would likely be her last. It was not quite dark, not quite still, and there was no air around her.

Something struck her shoulder, and when she turned to look – slowly, pushing herself against the water holding her deep – it nudged again at her face, shoving her head to one side, but gently, almost affectionately.

A sound reverberated through her head, like the distant buzzing of a phone. She felt across her body in a ridiculous gesture. *It might be Eveline, I'm back and maybe she's calling—*

She coughed water from her lungs, expelling as much as she could in one heaving expulsion, and with it went whatever dregs were left of her last breath.

Not mine, she thought. *Someone else's.*

The porpoise pushed against her again, then slid its nose beneath her left arm and pulled her towards the light.

Jodi looked up. The water's surface gleamed and waved, like a solid sheet of light dancing somewhere above her. It might have been six feet or sixty, and if it was the latter then this would be her shortest life yet.

Everything around her blurred. She did not panic, because moments before she had been nothing and now there was something, and she grasped onto the miracle of that.

More nudging from the porpoise, and the pressure of its nose beneath her arm was almost painful. Then she broke surface and everything hit her at once: the fresh air; the heat of the sun, blinding her already blurred eyes; the pain.

She coughed again, and again, and vomited sea water, and then rolled over and floated on her back. She was aware of the porpoise swimming around and beneath her, and she sent her thanks. Lulled by a gentle swell. Staring at the sky. Hearing the sound of waves gently shushing onto a nearby beach.

Did I jump, was I pushed, was I swimming, is there someone on the beach looking for me, was I happy to be alive or desperate to die?

For a few minutes she asked these questions but saw no urgency in discovering the answer. She was alive. For a while, that was all that mattered.

* * *

"At first I thought I was somewhere in the Bahamas. The sun was so warm, and there was the porpoise, and it seemed so... exotic. But then I finally reached the shore. There was a small pile of clothes folded neatly on the sand. Just a small beach, a hundred feet from side to side, with no one else there. I figured it was somewhere only the woman I'd once been knew about, and it made me sad. She'd wanted to go there to kill herself. Such a waste. So I dressed in her clothes, and climbed the steep cliff path, and as I started walking inland I saw a road sign and realised I was in Cornwall."

"Ahh," Eveline sighed. They'd been to Cornwall together for a weekend about forty years before, when Jodi lived in a tall, thin, one-armed woman's body. She'd not known the previous owner's story. She never tried to find out, because that would make breaking away from her life that much more difficult. And she always did break away. She could never pretend, to loved ones or children.

That, she always told Eveline, was the real curse. The

potential heartbreak her resurrection caused others. She did her best to move on quickly, but it was not always possible. Confused, sad faces haunted her sleep. Tears followed her from one life to the next.

"And as soon as I saw the date, I came straight back to you."

They were sitting in Eveline's cottage garden. It was not quite so well kept now, with overgrown borders, rose arches hanging heavy with beautiful fat blooms, shrubs that needed trimming. It had gone wild, and Eveline said she liked it that way. It buzzed with countless bees, and Jodi thought back to that time in the village with a small pet dog gnawing at her bloody hand and a mad woman talking her down into death. Birds frolicked in the apple tree. Butterflies fluttered here and there, rainbows dancing in the sun.

"I... might have found a way for you to... escape," Eveline said. It was the most Jodi had heard her say since she'd returned two days before. She was a very old woman now, pushing a century, and her body was slowly winding down. Not her mind, though. Her mind was still fresh, as if experiencing its own strange renewal at Jodi's reappearance.

"What do you mean?" Jodi asked. She shivered. The idea of escaping her existence had troubled her for a time, when it all first began. But for the past half-century she'd given it very little thought.

"I researched him," Eveline said. "All my life. All your lives. And there might be a way. All you have to do is go back to that place, his library's still there in the old mansion, look for—"

"No," Jodi said, and Eveline fell silent, breathing heavily as if she'd just returned from a long run. She settled back into the reclined chair, as if pleased she didn't have to go on. "Catch your breath," Jodi said.

"But I can... help you."

"You've always helped me. Always." A blackbird sang in the tree at the bottom of the garden, its varied song delighting the air. She remembered Eveline calling it the jazz of nature. "And I don't want to change. He thought he cursed me, and for a time he had. There are still moments when…" She shook her head, trying to blink away the sad faces and tears of family members she did not know.

Eveline reached out and squeezed her hand. She was not strong, but still it was tight.

"You want to lose me?" Eveline asked.

"I'll lose you anyway." Jodi felt tears on her cheeks. "But I've been the luckiest person alive, in every life, to have known you for so long. And I've beaten his curse. I've experienced so much that he never did. Just think of everything I've seen and done, all the experiences I've had, both good and bad. He missed all that. My lives have cancelled out his short, foul existence."

"But you keep dying. The pain, the suffering—"

"Are inevitable. Love isn't." She lifted Eveline's hand and kissed it, then they sat back together and watched the sun dappling down through leaves stirred by a breeze, and listened to bees going about their business.

"I wonder how many bees you need to save the world," Jodi said.

"Silly," Eveline said. And she laughed.

THE GIRL FROM THE HELL

MARGO LANAGAN

Rhododendron invades areas both vegetatively and via seed...
A single plant may eventually end up covering many metres of
ground with thickly interlaced, impenetrable branches...
*[S]eedlings cannot become established under the lightless canopy.**

Moonlit near-midnight. The house looks even more collapse-y. The yard is blocks and battlements of rubbish, frozen explosions of bedsprings, the cracked shed weeping newspapers, bottles and jars in a glinting fall from rain-sagged boxes, more old fridges and stoves than one old woman could ever have gone through.

Young Agnes stands catching her breath in the dappled shadow of this kind tree. The rage that propelled her here has slowed and chilled; all that running has put a fine edge on it. The cold air feels good on her face and hands. Her trousers and shirt-ends are icy, still heavy damp.

---

* "Rhododendron: a killer of the countryside"
  www.countrysideinfo.co.uk/rhododen.htm

She puts her sack on the ground and takes out the bag of ash and earth.

* * *

That other house, broad and clean and the gardens neatly kept, shrubberies moon-carved out front, vegetable garden a wintry straggle behind. The dog that will run right up to her now, all wriggling and friendly. Will lead her to the cupboard, huff and wag as she takes the bread and cheese. Will stand at her shoulder as she digs in the ash pit.

* * *

She blocks the ward at the gate and goes through. The old woman – her *grandmother*, what a shock – will be in the kitchen, scheming and stirring. Her busyness is an insect, high at the back of Agnes's brain.

Agnes begins on what's left of the path, by the warped veranda stairs. She lays the ash by feel, keeping the line unbroken. It is delicate work through the weeds between the rubbish and over the bed-springier piles, but she will do what's necessary. Her runners brush grass, her sleeve whispers along a stove-edge, the breeze breathes now and then at her ear. They all conspire with her. They're in on the secret.

Aah, sighs something else. *I thought I heard a mouse creeping.*

The cat is at its window. Its face is even more like a skull in the moonlight. Its one good eye looks down at her, wide and black.

You are lucky I am old and lazy.

It watches her pass, the ash and sometimes the earth trickling from her fingers.

You are lucky I care for nothing. And am amused by everything.

* * *

Its teeth catching her hand. The eye rolling up at her, the mouth a grin. Cat laughter, cat mutter. Cat bum-hole preceding her around the wreckscape of the garden, a crinkled pink star beneath an upheld tail.

* * *

The back garden is wilder, weedier. Herb-scents gust up from her passing. The old lady's feet shuffle and stop on the kitchen floorboards. Vessels clink and clank. The house itself is a pot, her spell-making bubbling at one edge. The ash is drawing a line around it, making it her last. Soon enough she'll wake up to that; soon enough she'll see what she's brought on herself.

* * *

That was when I realised, says Mum. *Walking up the creek and hitting the sleep. Walking down the other way, and there it was again. Swimming out, scrambling out over the plants, every which way. I could only ever go so far; then his mother faded me out.*

* * *

Halfway around, Agnes pauses to look up and to breathe. This will take everything she has – she mustn't hurry it.

The felted frizz of the old woman's hair moves a little left, then more to the right, like some small mangy beast on the windowsill. Yellow light from the bare kitchen bulb stains the piles pressing up under the window. Above the skillion roof, the pocked moon washes out the icy sky. Its strings and its fingers are in everything. They are what Agnes is gathering to make this happen.

* * *

Don't do anything crazy…

Mum's voice tailing off as she steps too far and hits the sleep.

But how could she tell Agnes all that and expect her to *stay*? To sit there in the hell with her, trapped and strangled?

Crazy is all there is. Crazy is the only sensible thing left to do.

* * *

Get back to it. Sometimes crazy has to be methodical, if it's to work. It takes silence, concentration, the right ingredients and the correct tangling and funnelling of the moon to set a boundary like this. The disaster must be built from the ground up. Agnes is feeling her way forward through the newness and the rightness, *keeping* it right, handful by soft cool handful, inch by dribbled inch.

When the ring completes, she feels the shiver in her spine, up the back of her head and over, tickling her eyebrows as she hurries out to the tree, to the bag. She takes out the silky dark plait, the rougher beard, unties the ends of the one, unknots the other. She spreads them on the flattened bag and mingles them, ties them again by one end. The wire must first be straightened, then curled into a cone. She drapes the hair over it with the bound ends at the top.

* * *

Mum's hair is like black water poured past her face and shoulders, down her back. In the sunlight, caught strands show all through the hell, wafting wherever she's scrambled or swum. *Cut it off*, she says, when Agnes brings home the scissors. *Cut it all off. It's just another trap, another binding.*

And then they can't burn or bury it, or cast it to the wind or water. It's too strange, too much Mum. There's a power in it, just as there's a power in Agnes, voiceless, unwoken.

Agnes puts it away with the scissors and the other treasures. Mum watches, stroking her new hair, which is short and soft all over like a bird's breast feathers.

* * *

She unscrews the jar of river water, takes up the bread and cheese from the good house. A crust of bread will do. She drops it in. A corner of cheese. She eats the rest quickly, for strength, when usually she lingers over it, brooding on its flavours, its cost, its possible meaning.

* * *

Hiding inside the clipped shrub, watching the woman walk out to the cupboard – her *grandmother*, another one! Who surely knows Agnes is here, the way she looks about, the way she calls her – *Kitten? Kitten?* Knows but doesn't know, as she leaves the food, goes back up the path, searching the night. Tomorrow she'll know. Tomorrow, Mum and Agnes will go straight up the front path, no sneaking.

Oh, and *Dad*, she thinks with a start. She'll have a dad then, too. She marvels at that idea, there among the leaves.

* * *

She takes her knife and the torn hell-piece, cuts it back to where it will hold its balance in the jar. Two of the spare leaves she weaves into the cone of hair and beard. All around her, through and beyond the tree's shade, the moon is shedding its stuff; a shaft of it is moving on her arm like a pain, and she must breathe, breathe, readying herself to go out in it again. She's so close. It's so soon. It's coming at her, fast and dramatic.

Up she stands, hair-cone in one hand, jar in the other. She walks in through the gate-gap, up the path. The house has been silenced by the ash, but as soon as she steps across the line she feels the pot bubbling, the old woman caught up in her rituals, the cat watching from the sill, through all the walls and the hoard packed between them.

She sets the jar down, takes from her pocket a plastic cigarette lighter, flicks it alight, fixes the catch open with a rubber band. Stands it carefully on the flattest veranda board, centred on the front door. Brings the cone down over it.

Immediate stink. The bunched hair at the top catches and flames briefly, writhes and disappears. The pain and stench catch in Agnes's throat. She recoils, speeds coughing around the house with the jar.

The cat regards her. The cat has always known. The cat has told her nothing, only waited for it all to come home to her. This cat is old, studded with tiny cancers and brindle besides. Its black eye and its white can see her equally well.

What a pong, it says. *She will smell that, any moment. The game will be up.*

Agnes crosses the line, steps up onto the side of the old copper. Steadying herself against the peeling-painted wall, on tiptoes she places the jar on the sill next to the cat, where it might fall either way. It's up to the cat to do what it says it doesn't. To care one way or another. To decide how much it owes the grandmother.

From the kitchen, an exclamation. Witch-attention, like lightning. The game is up.

Agnes jumps down. Just inside the line, she stops and looks back.

The cat yawns, its tongue a curled wet moonlit leaf. The jar gleams too, and the rhododendron spray. Framed together, they're clearly part of the same family of magic.

The grandmother's voice is belling spells down the hall. Agnes has something at her fingertips for that, at her lips, something to muffle and stifle. She is well acquainted with strangulation.

The skull-cat keeps watching. Footsteps in the hall.

But the hall is as cluttered as every other room in that house. It must be wound through, weaved through, clutches of leaning spoil pushed aside. The burning leaves and hair flare and wail from the front veranda. Witch fear smells like a fire that boys have peed on. It flows through the walls like a wind. Agnes whispers into the blast. The cat watches like a stone cat.

And just as the grandmother reaches the door, wrestles the lock, the cat's skinny paw comes leisurely out from under its chest, and knocks the jar from the sill.

Into the house.

Water and growth are at Agnes's knees. She throws herself over the line, out of the ring. Black shot with moon-flash, surging with stems that leaf and thicken and flower, the water rumbles upward, a rippling shining cylinder bounded by the good ash, the good earth. High above, it whooshes and washes and rattles the leaves.

Agnes crawls and runs around the wall of her creation, to the path where she has the tree and its shadow at her back, a friend nearby. Exhaustion is headed for her, riding in on the waves of the wonder before her. Inside it somewhere the old woman struggles and spells, but her incantations are garbling, breaking up, her limbs locked among the stems, the spell-water forcing down her throat towards her lungs.

* * *

The boat, the river, the moon moon moon. Leaping across and through the moon-water as he turns the boat for the something-thousandth time. Reaching round him like a hug, but with a knife, a knife with a shard of moon on it. Rocking with him as he rows, trapped in his rowing so he can't fight her off. Catching his beard, rocking back, cutting through. Hissing in his ear, *I'll put a stop to this!* Kissing his weathered cheek fiercely, still in her rage, unable to say it yet: *Father.* Leaping back, the water clawing her waist, dragging her legs. Fighting towards the shore—

* * *

The house falls silent. The wards snuff out. The water sags, the spell-hell branches lean with it, draining, dying. All the natural smells, of river and rhododendron, evaporate. Moon strings, star strings pour and dangle down. The house is slimy with magic, swampy with it within, a sodden aftermath. And then it is itself, dry, disintegrating. The wire cone stands bare on the veranda, the lighter flame inside it small, bright, loyal, among the leaf-ash and hair scraps. The door is part open, wedged by a stack of telephone books. Beyond it, nothing, no bubbling pot, no attention flickering. Stacked hoard, dead space.

* * *

You're joking! says Mum. *All these years, rowing back and forth? Her own son? And here I was thinking she only hexed me. That he was spared, and went on and had a family. Another family, I mean. He didn't know, did he, that he already had one. I didn't know, when she put me here.*

Tell it from the beginning, says Agnes. *I'm not following any of this.*

* * *

Agnes lowers herself to the veranda edge, emptied out, unstrung. Waits to know what to do next. If anything.

A mouth unsticking on a silent *miaow*. The rub of fur on splintery wood. A cat, young, brindled, winds itself away from the gatepost and up the path, pauses to sniff at the scuffed wet ash, lifts two black eyes to look at her.

I've never drowned before, it says. *It's quite good. Very little fuss.*

It steps up beside her, seats itself, tidies its tail around its toes.

And there they wait for the others, who will come, from rhododendron and from river. Who are yet to meet along the moonlit road. Who will walk up the hill to the house together, hand in hand.

CASTLE WAKING
Jane Yolen

There is a shudder through the castle foundation.
Hedge trembles, falls, felled by curse's end.
The hawk on the ground stirs, tragedy avoided,
feathers shaking as if in a strong wind.

The flies begin to buzz, like windup toys,
though they have not been invented yet.
Palace guards click heels, stand at attention.
There's no mention of a magic debt.

Cook's wooden spoon suddenly descends
on the shoulders of the pot boy's old errors.
The queen stretches prettily, the king roars a swear.
It seems as if moments, not centuries are here.

Only in the tower a stillness – unlikely as love –
enters the room. Afraid of a blunder,
it hesitates, looks around, takes a breath,
fills the space with wonder.

ABOUT THE AUTHORS

Jane Yolen, called "The Hans Christian Andersen of America" by *Newsweek* magazine, is the author of over 382 books ranging from children's books to poetry collections, novels, cookbooks, short story collections, graphic novels, non-fiction, and even a verse memoir of her immigrant family. She lives in both America's New England and St Andrews in Scotland. She writes a poem a day and sends them out to over a thousand subscribers. Find out more about Jane at janeyolen.com.

Christina Henry is the author of *The Girl in Red*, *The Mermaid*, *Lost Boy*, *Alice*, *Red Queen*, and the seven books in the urban fantasy *Black Wings* series. She enjoys running long distances, reading anything she can get her hands on and watching movies with samurai, zombies and/or subtitles in her spare time. She lives in Chicago with her husband and son. You can visit her on the web at christinahenry.net, facebook.com/authorChristinaHenry, twitter.com/C_Henry_Author, and goodreads.com/CHenryAuthor.

Neil Gaiman is the *New York Times*-bestselling author and creator of books, graphic novels, short stories, film and television for all ages, including *Norse Mythology*, *Neverwhere*, *Coraline*, *The Graveyard Book*, *The Ocean at the End of the Lane*, *The View from the Cheap Seats*, and the *Sandman* comic series. His fiction has received Newbery, Carnegie, Hugo, Nebula, World Fantasy, and Will Eisner awards. He was the writer and showrunner for the mini-series adaptation of *Good Omens*, based on the book he co-authored with Sir Terry Pratchett. In 2017, he became a Goodwill Ambassador for UNHCR, the UN Refugee Agency. Originally from England, he lives in the United States, where he is a professor at Bard College. Visit him at neilgaiman.com.

Catriona Ward was born in Washington, DC and grew up in the US, Kenya, Madagascar, Yemen, and Morocco. She read English at St Edmund Hall, Oxford and is a graduate of the Creative Writing MA at the University of East Anglia. Her debut, *Rawblood* (W&N, 2015) won Best Horror Novel at the 2016 British Fantasy Awards and was shortlisted for the Author's Club Best First Novel Award. Her second novel, *Little Eve* (W&N), won the Shirley Jackson Award and was shortlisted for a *Guardian* best book of 2018. She lives in London and Devon. You can follow Catriona on Twitter @Catrionaward.

Jen Williams is a fantasy author from London. A fan of dragons and pirates from a very young age, these days she writes character-driven epic fantasy with an eye on feminist themes and snappy dialogue. *The Copper Cat* trilogy was repeatedly nominated for the British Fantasy Award, and *The Ninth Rain*, the first volume of the *Winnowing Flame* trilogy, won Best Novel in 2018. When not frowning over notebooks she's also a bookseller and a copywriter, and she co-founded the monthly social group Super Relaxed Fantasy Club. Jen loves animation of all kinds, as well as overly complicated video games, and she lives in her favourite bit of London with her partner and their small ridiculous cat. Jen currently hangs out on Twitter under the handle @sennydreadful.

M.R. Carey is a BAFTA-nominated screenwriter, novelist and comic book writer. Born in Liverpool, he worked as a teacher for fifteen years before resigning to write full-time. He wrote the movie adaptation for his novel *The Girl With All the Gifts*. Produced in the UK by Warner Bros., the movie opened the Locarno festival in 2016 and subsequently went on international release. M.R. has worked extensively in the field of comic books, completing long and critically acclaimed runs on *Lucifer*, *Ultimate Fantastic Four*, and *X-Men*. His comic book series *The Unwritten* has featured repeatedly in the *New York Times*' graphic novel bestseller list. He is currently writing a series for Dynamite Entertainment featuring the sci-fi icon Barbarella. He is also the writer of the Felix Castor novels, and (along with his wife Linda and their daughter Louise) of two fantasy novels, *The City of Silk and Steel* and *The House of*

War and Witness, published in the UK by Victor Gollancz and in America by Chizine Press. His most recent novel, released in both the UK and USA in November 2018, is *Someone Like Me*, a psychological thriller with a supernatural edge. Follow Mike on Twitter @michaelcarey191.

James Brogden is a writer of horror and dark fantasy. A part-time Australian who grew up in Tasmania and the Cumbrian Borders, he has since escaped to suburbia and now lives with his wife and two daughters in the Midlands, where he teaches English. When not writing or teaching he can usually be found up a hill, poking around stone circles and burial mounds. He also owns more Lego than is strictly necessary. His short stories have appeared in various anthologies and periodicals ranging from *The Big Issue* to the BFS Award-winning Alchemy Press. *Hekla's Children*, *The Hollow Tree* and *The Plague Stones* were published by Titan Books, with his new novel *Bone Harvest* in May 2020. Blogging occurs infrequently at jamesbrogden.blogspot.co.uk, and tweeting at @skippybe.

Maura McHugh lives is Galway, Ireland and has written three collections: *Twisted Fairy Tales* and *Twisted Myths* – published in the USA – and *The Boughs Withered (When I Told Them My Dreams)* from NewCon Press, UK. She's written comic books for Dark Horse, IDW, and *2000 AD*, and is also a playwright, screenwriter, and critic. Her monograph on David Lynch's film *Twin Peaks: Fire Walk With Me* was nominated for a British Fantasy Award for Best Non-Fiction. Her website is splinister.com and she tweets as @splinister.

Karen Joy Fowler is the author of six novels, including *Sarah Canary*, which won the Commonwealth medal for best first novel by a Californian and *The Jane Austen Book Club*, a *New York Times* bestseller. Also three short story collections, two of which won the World Fantasy Award in their respective years. Her most recent novel, *We Are All Completely Beside Ourselves*, was published by Putnam in May 2013. She currently lives in Santa Cruz and is at work on a historical novel. Find out more about Karen at karenjoyfowler.com.

Christopher Golden is the *New York Times*-bestselling, Bram Stoker Award-winning author of such novels as *Ararat*, *The Pandora Room*, *Snowblind*, and *The Ocean Dark*. With Mike Mignola, he is the co-creator of two cult favorite comic book series, *Baltimore* and *Joe Golem: Occult Detective*. As an editor, he has worked on the short story anthologies *Seize the Night*, *Dark Cities*, and *The New Dead*, among others, and he has also written and co-written comic books, video games, screenplays, and a network television pilot. In 2015 he founded the popular Merrimack Valley Halloween Book Festival. He was born and raised in Massachusetts, where he still lives with his family. His work has been nominated for the British Fantasy Award, the Eisner Award, and multiple Shirley Jackson Awards. Please visit him at christophergolden.com.

Charlie Jane Anders' latest novel is *The City in the Middle of the Night*. She's also the author of *All the Birds in the Sky*, which won the Nebula, Crawford and Locus awards, and *Choir Boy*, which won a Lambda Literary Award. Plus a novella called *Rock Manning Goes For Broke* and a short story collection called *Six Months, Three Days, Five Others*. Her short fiction has appeared in Tor.com, *Boston Review*, *Tin House*, *Conjunctions*, *The Magazine of Fantasy and Science Fiction*, *Wired Magazine*, *Slate*, *Asimov's Science Fiction*, *Lightspeed*, *ZYZZYVA*, *Catamaran Literary Review*, *McSweeney's Internet Tendency*, and tons of anthologies. Her story "Six Months, Three Days" won a Hugo Award, and her story "Don't Press Charges And I Won't Sue" won a Theodore Sturgeon Award. Charlie Jane also organizes the monthly Writers With Drinks reading series, and co-hosts the podcast Our Opinions Are Correct with Annalee Newitz. Follow Charlie Jane on Twitter @charliejane.

Michael Marshall Smith is a novelist and screenwriter. Under this name he has published ninety short stories, and five novels – *Only Forward*, *Spares*, *One of Us* and *The Servants* – winning the Philip K. Dick, International Horror Guild, and August Derleth awards, along with the Prix Bob Morane in France. He has won the British Fantasy Award for Best Short Fiction four times, more than any other author. In 2017 he published *Hannah Green and her Unfeasibly Mundane Existence*. Writing as **Michael Marshall** he has written seven internationally-bestselling thrillers including *The Straw Men* series, *Intruders* – recently a BBC America series starring John Simm and Mira Sorvino – and *Killer Move*. His most recent novel under this name is *We Are Here*. Now additionally writing as **Michael Rutger**, in 2018 he published the adventure thriller *The Anomaly*. A sequel, *The Possession*, came out in 2019. He is currently about to start co-writing and exec producing *The Straw Men* for television. He is also Creative Consultant to The Blank Corporation, Neil Gaiman's production company. He lives in Santa Cruz, California, with his wife, son, and two cats. Find out more about Michael at michaelmarshallsmith. com, his eBooks at ememess.com, and follow him on Twitter @ememess and Instagram @ememess.

Adam Stemple (adamstemple.com) is an author, musician, web designer, and professional card player. He has written nine novels, including *Pay the Piper* (with Jane Yolen), winner of the 2006 Locus Award for Best Young Adult Book. Of his debut solo novel, *Singer of Souls*, Anne McCaffrey said, "One of the best first novels I have ever read."

Angela Slatter is the author of the Verity Fassbinder supernatural crime series (*Vigil, Corpselight* and *Restoration)* as well as nine short story collections, including *The Bitterwood Bible and Other Recountings* and *A Feast of Sorrows: Stories*. She has an MA and a PhD in Creative Writing. She's won a World Fantasy Award, a British Fantasy Award, a Ditmar Award, an Australian Shadows Award and six Aurealis Awards; her debut novel was nominated for the Dublin Literary Award. Her work has been translated into French, Chinese, Spanish, Japanese, Russian, and Bulgarian. Her novelette "Finnegan's Field" has been optioned for film. Angela's website is angelaslatter.com.

Lilith Saintcrow lives in Vancouver, Washington, with two children, two dogs, two cats, and a library for wayward texts. You can visit Lilith at lilithsaintcrow.com.

Christopher Fowler is the multi award-winning author of nearly fifty novels and story collections, including the Bryant & May mysteries. His novels include *Roofworld*, *Spanky*, *Psychoville*, *Calabash* and two volumes of memoirs, *Paperboy* (winner of the inaugural Green Carnation Prize) and *Film Freak*. In 2015 he won the CWA Dagger in the Library for his body of work. His most recent works include *The Book of Forgotten Authors* and *The Lonely Hour*. Find out more about Christopher at christopherfowler.co.uk.

Alison Littlewood's latest novel is *Mistletoe*, a winter ghost story. It follows *The Crow Garden*, a tale of obsession set amidst Victorian asylums and séance rooms. Her other books include *A Cold Season*, *Path of Needles*, *The Unquiet House* and *The Hidden People*. Alison's short stories have been picked for several Year's Best anthologies and she has won the Shirley Jackson Award for Short Fiction. Alison lives in Yorkshire,

England, in a house of creaking doors and crooked walls, with her partner Fergus, two hugely enthusiastic Dalmatians, and a growing collection of fountain pens. Visit her at alisonlittlewood.co.uk.

Tim Lebbon is a *New York Times*-bestselling writer from South Wales. He's had over forty novels published to date, as well as hundreds of novellas and short stories. His latest novel is *The Edge*, final book in the *Relics* trilogy. Other recent releases include *The Silence*, *The Family Man*, *The Rage War* trilogy, and *Blood of the Four* with Christopher Golden. He has won four British Fantasy Awards, a Bram Stoker Award, and a Scribe Award, and has been a finalist for World Fantasy, International Horror Guild, and Shirley Jackson awards. His work has appeared in many Year's Best anthologies, as well as Century's Best Horror. The movie of *The Silence*, starring Stanley Tucci and Kiernan Shipka, debuted on Netflix in April 2019, and *Pay the Ghost*, starring Nicolas Cage, was released Hallowe'en 2015. Several other projects are in development for TV and the big screen, including the original screenplays *Playtime* (with Stephen Volk) and *My Hunted House*. Find out more about Tim at his website timlebbon.net.

Margo Lanagan has published two dark fantasy novels (*Tender Morsels* and *The Brides of Rollrock Island*) and seven short story collections, most recently *Singing My Sister Down and Other Stories*, *Phantom Limbs* and *Stray Bats* from Small

Beer Press. She has collaborated with Scott Westerfeld and Deborah Biancotti on the *New York Times*-bestselling YA superheroes trilogy, *Zeroes*. Her work has won four World Fantasy, nine Aurealis, and five Ditmar awards, and has been shortlisted in the British Science Fiction Association and the British Fantasy Awards, and the Nebula, Hugo, Bram Stoker, Theodore Sturgeon, Shirley Jackson, International Horror Guild, and Seiun awards, and twice made the James Tiptree Jr Honor List. Her books and stories have been translated into nineteen languages. Margo lives in Sydney, Australia. You can follow Margo on Twitter @margolanagan.

ABOUT THE EDITORS

Marie O'Regan is an award-nominated author and editor, based in Derbyshire. She's the author of three collections: *Mirror Mere* (2006, Rainfall Books); *In Times of Want* (2016, Hersham Horror Books), and *The Last Ghost and Other Stories*, (2019, Luna Press), as well as a novella, *Bury Them Deep* (2017, Hersham Horror Books), and her short fiction has been published in genre magazines and anthologies in the UK, US, Canada, Italy, and Germany, including *Best British Horror 2014*, *Great British Horror: Dark Satanic Mills* (2017), and *The Mammoth Book of Halloween Stories* (2018). She was shortlisted for the British Fantasy Award for Best Short Story in 2006, and Best Anthology in 2010 (*Hellbound Hearts*) and 2012 (*Mammoth Book of Ghost Stories by Women*). She and her co-editor were also shortlisted for the 2019 Shirley Jackson Award for Best Anthology for *Wonderland* (Titan Books). Her genre journalism has appeared in magazines like *The Dark Side*, *Rue Morgue* and *Fortean Times*, and her interview book with prominent figures from the horror genre, *Voices in the Dark*, was released in 2011. An essay on "The Changeling" was published in PS Publishing's *Cinema Macabre*, edited by Mark Morris. She is co-editor of the bestselling *Hellbound Hearts*, *Mammoth Book of Body Horror*, *A Carnivàle of Horror – Dark Tales from the Fairground*, *Exit Wounds*, *Wonderland* and *Trickster's Treats #3*, plus the editor of bestselling *The Mammoth Book of Ghost Stories by Women* and *Phantoms*. She is Co-Chair of the UK Chapter of the Horror Writers' Association, and is also the Managing Editor of Absinthe Books, an imprint of PS Publishing. Marie is represented by Jamie Cowen of The Ampersand Agency.

Paul Kane is the award-winning, bestselling author and editor of over a hundred books – including the *Arrowhead* trilogy (gathered together in the sellout *Hooded Man* omnibus, revolving around a post-apocalyptic version of Robin Hood), *The Butterfly Man*, *Hellbound Hearts* and *Pain Cages* (an Amazon #1 bestseller). His non-fiction books include *The Hellraiser Films and Their Legacy* and *Voices in the Dark*, and his genre journalism has appeared in the likes of *SFX* and *Rue Morgue*. He has been a Guest at many conventions in the past, including Alt. Fiction five times, the first SFX Weekender, Thought Bubble, Derbyshire Literary Festival, HorrorCon, The Dublin Ghost Story Festival, IMATS Olympia, Celluloid Screams and Black Library Live, as well as being a panellist at FantasyCon and the World Fantasy Convention, and a fiction judge at the Sci-Fi London festival. A former British Fantasy Society Special Publications Editor, he is currently serving as Co-

Chair for the UK chapter of the Horror Writers' Association. His work has been optioned and adapted for the big and small screen, including for US network primetime television and as the feature film *Sacrifice* (which sold to Epic and stars *You're Next* and *Re-Animator*'s Barbara Crampton). His audio work includes the full-cast drama adaptation of *The Hellbound Heart* for Bafflegab, starring Tom Meeten (*The Ghoul*), Neve McIntosh (*Doctor Who*), and Alice Lowe (*Prevenge*), and the *Robin of Sherwood* adventure *The Red Lord* for Spiteful Puppet/ITV narrated by Ian Ogilvy (*Return of the Saint*). Paul's latest novels are *Lunar* (set to be turned into a feature film), the YA story *The Rainbow Man* (as P.B. Kane), the sequels to *RED* – *Blood RED* and *Deep RED* – the award-winning hit *Sherlock Holmes & the Servants of Hell*, *Before* (an Amazon Top 5 dark fantasy bestseller) and *Arcana*. He also writes thrillers for HQ/HarperCollins as P.L. Kane, the first of which – *Her Last Secret* and *Her Husband's Grave* – came out in 2020. Paul lives in Derbyshire, UK, with his wife Marie O'Regan and his family. Find out more at his site shadow-writer.co.uk which has featured Guest Writers such as Stephen King, Charlaine Harris, Robert Kirkman, Dean Koontz and Guillermo del Toro.

ACKNOWLEDGEMENTS

And now for something important – our chance to say thank you. Firstly to all the authors for their contributions, to Cat Camacho and the whole team at Titan Books for all their support, as always. Thanks to Jamie Cowen, and to our brood, without whom etc.